THE PERFECT LIE

THE PERFECT LIE

Karen Osman

First published in the United Kingdom in 2019 by Aria, an imprint of
Head of Zeus Ltd

Copyright © Karen Osman, 2019

A CIP catalogue record for this book is available from the British Library.

ISBN 9781786699206

Aria
c/o Head of Zeus
First Floor East
5–8 Hardwick Street
London EC1R 4RG

www.ariafiction.com

For Fahad, Zane and Ryan

Prologue

Even from this distance, she could see his fingernails bitten down to the quick and her body tensed instinctively, resisting the urge to run towards her son. It would only make things worse. Instead, she caught his eye and reassured him with a confident smile.

This will soon all be over, and everything will go back to normal.

Those had been her mother's words as they had all left the house that morning. She'd noticed her son's light brown hair had grown and it desperately needed cutting, but he'd resisted a haircut and instead combed it down with some gel. It was coarse hair, like her own, but unlike hers, it hadn't been subjected to various treatments. Had it only been six months ago that she'd laughingly squirted her son's stubborn tufts with water, threatening to tame his hair herself if he didn't do something about it? He'd giggled then, rewarding her with a glimpse back into his childhood when she used to tickle him as he sat on her lap for story time.

The memory assaulted her and her right hand involuntarily went to grasp her husband's, despite the gulf between the two of them. She could feel the tension emanate from him and she gently squeezed his fingers before releasing them and placing both of her hands together in prayer on her lap, reverting to her own childhood habit. She focused on her crossed thumbs, right over left, the usually long, manicured nails bare and jagged, and began the silent chant.

Everything will be all right. Everything will be all right. Everything will be all—

'All rise!'

She quickly got to her feet, her eyes urgently seeking her son's once more as the judge swept into the room, but all she could see was his taut back and the nape of his long neck as he looked at the ground. *Head up*, she wanted to cry out. *You've done nothing wrong!*

The judge indicated for the court to sit before the clerk spoke.

'Would the foreman of the jury please stand,' instructed the clerk.

Claire noticed the foreman was wearing a wedding band. Most likely he had kids himself. Surely he wouldn't let an innocent child be convicted for something he didn't do? She caught herself on the word *child*. He was almost eighteen. If found guilty, he would be sent to an adult prison along with the country's worst offenders.

'Have the jury reached verdicts upon which they are all agreed?' asked the clerk.

'Yes,' replied the foreman.

They couldn't take him away. Could they?

She felt her chest tighten.

Everything will be all right. Everything will be all right. Everything will be all right.

Her throat was closing and she coughed frantically.

Everything will be all right. Everything will be all right. Everything will be all right.

She was struggling to breathe and a silent primal scream rose in her throat.

Everything will be all right. Everything will be all right. Everything will be all right.

'In the matter of Aiker versus Carmichael, do you find the defendant guilty or not guilty?'

AUGUST 2017

I

Claire's husband strode through the front door and she observed him, trying to be discreet. It wasn't difficult. His blue eyes were locked on his mobile phone, entranced as his thumb moved quickly across the screen. Having found what he was looking for, the spell was broken as Chris raised the phone to his ear, his attention finally coming to rest on her. *Sorry*, he mouthed as he rolled his eyes and she smiled at him, keen to show patience and understanding. She hoped that this, along with the warm smell of the simmering beef casserole, would soothe his transition from stressed employee to loving husband and father. However, she suspected it would take another couple of hours for him to relax.

She felt a warm hand on her knee and turned towards her youngest son, Jamie, who held a toy train in his outstretched hand. She took it automatically, knowing what was required, and absent-mindedly choo-chooed the train along the arm of the sofa. Despite still thinking about Chris and his mood, her effort elicited a squeal of delight from their five-year-old son, and whilst it wasn't loud enough to drown out Chris's aggressive-sounding conversation, it was loud enough for Chris to shoot her a warning glance. She knew what that meant – keep Jamie quiet until he finished his phone call. Her husband's impatience and tiredness pervaded the air and Claire quickly placed a finger over her lips, whispering to Jamie to use their indoor voices.

As her son turned back to his trains, she sensed that tonight was not the right time to talk to Chris about her going back to work full-time. *But when then?* Maybe at the weekend when he might be a bit more relaxed? She quelled the flicker of impatience and silently counselled herself to bide her time – she only had one shot at this. Still, she was anxious. There were only a couple of weeks left of the summer holidays and she wanted to be full-time when Jamie started school. Plus, she had already confirmed with Julia.

That particular thought nestled uncomfortably. It was unlike her not to run something by Chris first, especially such a big change as this. She would *have* to talk to him tonight, and hope his mood improved.

Claire looked at her son, his attention now captivated by some crayons and a colouring book. She knew that both she and Jamie were ready. She had put Jamie in playschool for a few mornings a week and he'd loved it but since he'd stopped his afternoon nap at two-and-a-half years old, she'd struggled to keep him occupied during the long afternoons. He seemed to need a lot more stimulation than other children, certainly more than her first son, Joshua, who had been content to sit and play with his toys by himself for hours on end. But Joshua would be eighteen next year, and then next September, he would be off to university. If his exam results this year were anything to go by, he would have no problem getting into Cambridge to study law.

Claire smiled as she thought of him, her firstborn, her pride and joy. She didn't have favourites when it came to her sons – they were so different – but there was no doubt Joshua was a dream child. She'd rarely had a moment's worry over him – well, apart from the difficult few months they'd had the previous year, but that seemed to have all passed, thank goodness. He'd always done well in school and was well liked with a good circle of friends.

Her nightmares of him doing drugs or falling in with a bad crowd had come to nothing during his early teenage years and she felt confident that he now had enough common sense to make good choices. She didn't like to tempt fate by questioning her good fortune too much, but she secretly suspected it was perhaps because Joshua had had her all to himself for twelve years. When Jamie came along, Joshua had been old enough to help with the baby and, as a thirty-eight-year-old mother the second time round, Claire appreciated the help – especially as Jamie had been colicky. Her second son never seemed to settle easily, and his naps were sporadic to say the least.

Claire hadn't realised just how difficult it would be with a second child and she'd felt permanently tired for two years. But as Jamie got older, it became easier and he doted on his older brother, sometimes even preferring Joshua to her. Some of her happiest memories were watching Joshua entertain his baby brother and she believed it encouraged

Joshua to be gentle, and even more caring and loving than he already was.

Picking up her phone, she was about to scroll through some of her photos of her sons when she heard a loud crash coming from another room. Jamie jumped at the noise and Claire rose from the couch, or *sofa*, as her mother liked to call it, quickly going to investigate. Jamie trotted after her, a train in each hand as if ready to do battle with whatever had intruded on their playtime. She'd barely taken a few steps before she heard Chris shouting from his office and she stopped abruptly, Jamie bashing into the backs of her legs.

'Who left this bloody suitcase here? Claire!'

Shit, thought Claire, hurrying through to him. She had put the suitcase in his office, so he could lift it to the top shelf of the wardrobe. She would have done it herself, but she couldn't reach. She didn't think she'd left it where he could have tripped over it though.

Had she?

Stepping into the room, she saw the suitcase, along with a small table and lamp, all on their sides. He must have kicked the suitcase out of the way with such force it knocked over the table.

For God's sake.

'Sorry, love, are you okay? Did you trip?' she said now, careful to keep her tone neutral, conscious of Jamie standing in the doorway.

'No, I didn't, but what's it doing in my office?'

'I couldn't manage to lift it myself onto the top shelf of the wardrobe. Could you?' she asked. 'I'm not as tall as you,' she added.

As she'd hoped it would, his anger dissipated, the compliment a pacifying balm on his irritation.

'Sorry, love, bad day at the office again,' he admitted, righting the overturned furniture, and Claire felt herself relax slightly at the acknowledgement.

Chris lifted the suitcase and she saw the strong muscles in his back, his slim waist, and powerful legs. At school, Chris had always been the best-looking boy and even now at forty-three, his good looks had only intensified with age, as had her attraction to him. Chris easily slotted the empty suitcase onto the top shelf, and she came up behind him, wrapping her arms around his chest. His body felt tense; the strain of his job etched onto his muscles. Turning around to embrace her, he kissed her on the forehead before turning to Jamie.

'Come here, little man,' he said to his son, bending down, and Jamie propelled himself forward almost tripping over his feet to get to his father. Claire watched lovingly as the two of them hugged. Releasing his son, Chris stood up.

'I just need another hour to finish working on this proposal and then we can eat,' he told Claire. 'What's for dinner? It smells amazing.'

'Your favourite – beef casserole,' she replied with a smile. Taking Jamie by the hand, she quietly left Chris to his work and closed his office door behind her. Claire went back into the living room; thankful she'd successfully calmed him down. Who knew, perhaps with a glass of red wine over dinner, the conversation about her going back to work full-time might go down better than she'd expected. Claire led Jamie back to his trains and she sat down in the large armchair near his play area in the living room. Her phone beeped, and she picked it up and read a message from Joshua.

Staying at Mark's for dinner – won't be too late.

Claire put down her phone thoughtfully. With Jamie in bed, Joshua out for the evening, and Chris a bit more relaxed, tonight could be promising. Claire's approach to the topic would be simple; solution-oriented. She knew how her husband's mind worked; he would need to know that his life wouldn't be affected in any way and that he was still the main breadwinner. The former, she wasn't a hundred per cent sure of yet and the latter? Well, Claire knew she was very good at her job. She knew he was secretly proud of her, but she also knew he struggled when she did better than him, and not just financially.

Claire remembered years ago, when they were both taking their exams. Their A-level results had been the same – straight As – but when she'd got a first-class degree with honours from the University of Manchester and he'd got an upper second-class degree, it had brought out a side of him that she'd not really seen before. It had taken her weeks to work out what was bothering him. He'd been quiet and moody but every time she asked what was wrong, he had said it was nothing.

And then she'd gone off on her girls' holiday, a week in Portugal, flush with success and looking forward to some fun and sunshine. She'd hoped that a week apart would do them both good but when she came back, the situation between them was even worse. He snapped at her for the tiniest of things, constantly criticised her, and complained

8

about her leaving him for a week even though he'd said he didn't want to go on holiday after their exams.

It was only when Chris received a letter, offering him a position on the prestigious graduate management programme in a technology company, that she'd finally understood, mainly because his personality did a complete 180-degree turn, but also because he couldn't resist gloating.

'I may only have got a 2:1 but I still got the job!' he crowed, doing some ridiculous celebratory football dance.

'Congratulations!' Claire had said when she'd read the letter, giving him a huge hug. She was genuinely pleased for him. Over the following weeks, as he returned to his normal loving self, Claire felt herself relax around him again. They went out for dinner, drank champagne to celebrate, and they made plans to have a few days away together before Chris started work. He bought two new suits and did more research on his employer.

Claire was still waiting for responses to her applications and she hoped she would also be offered an opportunity in Manchester. She hadn't told Chris that she'd applied to one in London. She hadn't planned on applying outside of their home city but one of her law lecturers had encouraged her to do so and written a personal letter of recommendation. It was the best law graduate training programme in the country, so Claire had applied, reassured by the knowledge that only one in six hundred applicants got accepted.

So, when she *did* receive an acceptance letter for that particular course, she was shocked. But instead of celebrating, she told no one and instead she slipped the letter between her textbooks in her desk drawer and closed it firmly. A few days later, there was a flurry of letters on the doormat all addressed to her and she picked them up, quickly opening each one and scanning their contents.

While she hadn't been accepted for every single graduate programme she'd applied for, the three that she'd had her heart set on had all offered her a placement. She'd hoped for just one so she couldn't stop the smile spreading across her face as she hurried to her bedroom, clutching the letters and their envelopes, not yet ready to share her success.

2

Claire winced as she stood on a small piece of Lego, resisting the urge to shout at Jamie to clear up his bloody mess. It was her own fault – she should never have come in barefoot. Jamie's bedroom floor was covered in toys and she looked around in dismay.

Years ago, she'd given up the pretence of being easy-going about how much mess her children made. Why they couldn't just take out one toy, play with it, and put it back before taking out something else was beyond her. She'd always felt most comfortable in a clean and tidy house, most likely a hangover from growing up in her mother's home, which was always spotless – in retrospect, perhaps obsessively so. She could still remember her mum trailing after her, tissue in hand, ready to wipe, mop or dab.

It had been annoying, she remembered now, but the thought was still not enough to stop her from releasing a sigh of frustration at Jamie. But then she saw his little smiling face peeping out from his den and her irritation faded. That was motherhood right there – a revolving door of emotion. It was bedtime, just past seven o'clock according to the Gro Clock on the shelf.

'Hurry up, Mummy! The dinosaurs are waiting!'

'Waiting? Whatever for?' she asked in mock surprise. As if she didn't know.

'A story!'

'Well, we can't possibly keep them waiting! What story are we reading tonight?' she asked browsing through the bookshelf.

'*The Gruffalo*,' came the muffle of her son's voice. Claire guessed he'd gone back into his den to retrieve whatever treasures he wanted to take to bed with him. 'And the dinosaurs want the funny voices, like Daddy does.'

'Do they indeed? Well, what the dinosaurs want, they will get,' replied Claire, bending down to enter the den to try and entice him out and into his bed. She always failed though because he liked one story in his den and three in his bed. Jamie was very particular like that.

Five years.

Had it really been that long? She sat crossed-legged, the lurid plastic toys lined up in front of her and Jamie on her lap as she read out loud. At some stages, it had felt like forever, especially during the terrible twos. Jamie hadn't been the easiest child and Claire guiltily knew she would have preferred to be navigating the complex legal system on behalf of her most demanding client than trying to reason with a screaming toddler.

But she and Chris had both agreed that working as a criminal lawyer full-time and trying to look after a young child wouldn't work. Instead, she would take a year's maternity leave and work part-time as a professional support lawyer until Jamie turned five and went to school and then they'd review the situation. They'd done the same thing when Joshua was born but back then, she'd been so excited about having a baby, she would have given up work completely if Chris had asked her to. Looking back though, she was glad that she'd kept her hand in, even if she was only doing paperwork.

When Julia and herself had set up their own law firm in 2007, she'd been honest from the beginning about her desire to have another child and Julia had understood. Well, not the call of motherhood – Julia Stephens had always been clear in her preference to remain childless – but Julia had reassured Claire that they could work out a plan so that Claire could take maternity leave and then return with some flexibility. Indeed, Julia had even gone so far as to say that their own firm would be the perfect solution for a mother who still wanted to work.

And it would have worked well – it was just unfortunate that giving Joshua a sibling had taken longer than either Claire, Chris or Julia had anticipated. Claire knew her career had suffered but what was the alternative? You couldn't be at the beck and call of both a demanding judge and the needs of a baby.

Now, with Joshua soon off to uni and Jamie heading to school, she'd somehow managed to sell the idea of her going back to work full-time to Chris over a bottle of wine the night before. She had successfully leveraged the fact that one of their couple friends had just hired a nanny and apparently it had been life-changing, so they would hire a nanny too, to do the afternoon school run, and to watch

Jamie in the afternoons. Claire had been deliberate; she'd only broached the subject once the wine bottle was almost empty and as she watched him mulling it over, she knew that even if he didn't agree to her proposal, she would have to find a way to go back to work full-time somehow. Her brain physically ached for the hum of court. She missed having a purpose that was just hers, and hers alone. And when she won a case… well, there was simply nothing like it. And she used to win often. The adrenalin would keep her going for days.

Luckily, she'd timed it well with the wine and Chris had agreed, no doubt buoyed by the thought of the extra income from her salary. While he earned well, the pressure to succeed was constant and with the two of them working, perhaps he would be able to take it a little easier, thought Claire, as she finished reading the story to Jamie with her best impersonation of a Gruffalo. She knew how stressful it was relying on one salary especially with their high standard of living – their mortgage payments alone were eye-watering. But as Claire finished reading and closed the book, the little mouse safe in the wood eating his nut, she knew she was ready to take on more demanding and lucrative cases.

Claire was trying not to panic. She'd just finished the last of the six nanny interviews she'd set up for the day and not one of them was suitable, despite them all being brilliant on paper. She thought of Viktoriya who had a flawless

CV written in English but then could barely utter two understandable sentences. Or Rebecca, who spent most of the interview showing Claire her Instagram account and explaining how she had big dreams of becoming the next Kim Kardashian.

Why would I hand my child over to you?

Sighing, Claire went back to her laptop on the kitchen table and started a search in her inbox again. Maybe she'd missed someone? But as she started to reread the CVs, she knew she hadn't. She'd received a lot of rubbish and the interviews today were the best of a bad lot. She sighed, pushing the laptop away from her.

'You look like you need a strong cup of tea,' said Irene, her broad Yorkshire accent reminding Claire of childhood days out in the Dales. 'Shall I make you one?'

'Thank you, Irene, that would be lovely,' she replied as Jamie came storming through to the kitchen, a rocket in his hand, which was swooping precariously close to the biscuit tin.

'Mummy! Do you want to play rockets with me? I'm going to visit the moon!'

'I'd love to, Jamie,' replied Claire, swiftly moving the biscuit tin out of Jamie's path, 'but Mummy has a few things to do first. What are you going to do on the moon?'

'I'm going to play Snakes and Ladders,' announced Jamie.

'Oh, well that sounds like a lot fun. Why don't you go upstairs and put on your astronaut suit, then you'll be ready for your rocket trip.'

With relief, she saw his eyes light up and watched as he ran towards the stairs to go to his bedroom. A few more minutes of quiet while she had a cup of tea and then she would get back to her search. But just then the front door slammed, and she heard Joshua and his friends in the hallway followed by a loud crash. Claire and Irene looked at each other in alarm before rushing through to the hallway. A bunch of flowers was upended, water spilling all over the tiles from the gift box vase that Claire had bought the day before. Two of Joshua's friends were poised mid-wrestle, looking at the sodden mess.

'Sorry, Mrs Carmichael,' one of them said before extracting himself and starting to pick up the flowers, his wrestling partner following his lead.

'Sorry, Mum,' said Joshua, also bending down to help.

Irene and Claire watched in amusement as the two boys attempted to rearrange the flowers on the sideboard while another one took the tea towel Irene had handed him to mop up the water. Eventually, Claire stepped in.

'Why don't you go and get yourselves a snack from the kitchen and we'll finish up here,' she suggested. 'There's pizza in the fridge.'

They didn't need to be asked twice and Claire watched as they trooped past her before they charged into the kitchen. One of them had already put some music on and she could hear them slamming the fridge, opening cans of Coke, and no doubt smearing slices of bread with butter for sandwiches. After a few minutes, she heard them take their snacks and storm upstairs to Joshua's bedroom. After a final door slam, the music was turned up high and Claire breathed a sigh of relief. Finishing the flowers, Claire went to sit back down at her laptop while Irene cleaned up the kitchen.

'You don't know anyone do you, Irene, who might be looking for a job as a nanny?' she asked now as her weekly cleaner put the tea in front of her. She didn't know why she hadn't thought of asking her before. Irene had been born in Yorkshire and had moved to Castlefield on the outskirts of Manchester when she got married at eighteen. Now she was fifty-five years old, and knew pretty much everyone in the small town. She came in once a week to do the ironing and a little light cleaning. She was constantly sucking on Werther's Originals but there was no one who could get the creases in shirts as sharp as Irene. She was very much in demand in Castlefield and no doubt Claire would have to let Irene go if she managed to find a nanny. Irene pursed her lips in thought, the Werther's Original on hold for the moment.

'Well, there's Lillian's girl down at the bottom of Cressfield Lane. I know she's looking for something part-time.'

There weren't many run-down areas in Castlefield, but if there was one, it was Cressfield Lane. Still, if she hired a local girl, then language wouldn't be a problem.

'Interesting,' replied Claire. 'You wouldn't happen to have her phone number, would you?'

'Why don't I give her a call now and see when she's free?' suggested Irene.

'That would be great, thank you.'

She'd bought Irene a box of chocolates for introducing her to Lucy. As soon as Lucy had kneeled down to Jamie's level and asked him about his red car, she knew she was going to give her the job. They'd met in a coffee shop and as they'd sipped their drinks, Lucy had explained how she was currently studying part-time for her child-care diploma and would be able to work in the afternoons and early evenings. It was the perfect arrangement and while Lucy had no formal experience, she'd played a big role in raising her four brothers and sisters. After completing a reference check, Claire had invited Lucy to come to the house.

'Thank you for giving me this chance, Mrs Carmichael – I really appreciate it,' said Lucy.

'Please, call me Claire,' she replied trying not to notice the look of awe on Lucy's face as she took in her home. She supposed it might be considered grand, even for Castlefield. Despite the endless mess the boys created on a daily basis, wooden floors, plush white sofas, and glass chandeliers had been on Claire's wish list when she'd started decorating a few years ago. They'd just added the conservatory last year and as a result the kitchen had also expanded so it was large enough for an island and a dining table.

'And you're welcome,' she added now. 'It's a relief to know that I've found someone with so much experience!'

Lucy smiled and for a moment Claire wished she was young again – smooth skin and her whole life ahead of her.

'Joshua, do you have a minute? I just want to talk to you about something,' said Claire, peering into her son's bedroom and resisting the impulse to comment on the smell. 'Can I come in?'

Joshua nodded, his eyes never leaving the screen of his mobile phone, and Claire took the opportunity to discreetly open his bedroom window.

She sat on Joshua's bed and her son reluctantly put down his phone.

'What's up?' he asked now, putting his arms behind his head.

'Well, you know I'm planning to go back to work full-time when Jamie goes to school.'

'Yep.'

'Well, to do that I need to get someone to look after Jamie in the afternoons.'

Joshua nodded.

'I just wanted to check you're okay having someone else in the house. I've also asked her to keep an eye on you and make sure you're doing your homework and not just playing video games,' she added with a grin.

'Mum! Don't worry, I'm fine!'

'I know you are, I just wanted to check in, that's all.'

'So, have you found someone?'

'Yes, her name is Lucy. I think you'll really like her.'

Joshua nodded again, and she could see he was already losing interest in the topic.

She decided to change the subject. 'Are you ready to go back to sixth form?' Claire had worried that Joshua might get bored during the summer holidays but, if anything, the break had done him good. He'd gone for a week away on his first boys' holiday. Claire hadn't really wanted him to go but Chris had persuaded her. Said it was important to give him the freedom he needed and in the end she couldn't say no, not when all his mates were going as well. As Chris had predicted, Joshua had come back happy and relaxed and Claire felt nostalgic for the family holidays they used to take, desperately hoping that she would still have a few more to look forward to in the future.

'I s'pose,' replied Joshua feigning boredom, but Claire knew he secretly loved it even with the workload. 'I might go over to Mark's tonight,' continued Joshua picking his phone back up.

'Okay, love. What will you do for dinner?'

'We'll get something, Mum,' he replied, sitting up on his bed. Claire knew that probably meant a McDonald's meal and made a mental note to make him a sandwich before he left.

'Okay, well, I'll leave you to it. You're sure you're okay with me going back to work full-time?' she asked.

Joshua rolled his eyes. 'Mum, I'm fine!'

Claire made to stand up, somewhat reassured, but not before Joshua had the chance to grab in a brief hug. 'We'll miss you though,' he muffled into her shoulder and Claire felt her heart swell as he grinned at her before going back to his phone.

'I found a nanny!' whispered Claire down the phone, quietly shutting the bedroom door behind her. Chris had gone to bed early after a rough day in the office. His ability to fall asleep as soon as his head hit the pillow baffled Claire who had always found it difficult to switch off.

'Yes!' cried Julia, who'd heard all about the drama of trying to find someone suitable. 'I knew you would! That's great news!'

'It is, isn't it?' Claire said, still keeping her voice low.

'Why are you whispering?'

'Because Chris is sleeping.'

'Oh, okay. Speaking of Chris... is he... on board with it? You know, you coming back to work full-time?'

Claire frowned. It was unlike Julia to sound so tentative.

'Yes, of course, why wouldn't be?'

'No reason!' Julia quickly replied. 'You just mentioned it was a big change for him, that's all.'

Claire thought back to Chris's response when she'd told him she'd found a nanny. He'd seemed surprised that she managed to find someone so quickly.

'Yes, he's fine. Besides he's working so hard at the moment, he won't even notice I'm not here.'

'And Jamie?'

'The same – he's so excited about school and he's really enjoying having Lucy giving him so much attention and playing with him all the time.'

'Amazing – I'm so happy for you and I'm so pleased that you're coming back full-time! Can you believe it will be our ten-year anniversary as well? The business really needs you – we have so much on. Did Greg get you up to date on the recent developments on the Barker case?'

As Claire listened to the intricate details of one of their firm's most prestigious clients, she was reminded of when she and Julia had discussed setting up their own business all those years ago when they'd both worked in the corporate world at JWTS Solicitors.

'Come on, Clairey,' Julia had wheedled. 'You know it's the right thing to do!'

The fact that Julia was using the cute version of her name told her that she wasn't going to let the matter drop. Julia was not one for cuteness or nicknames.

'And you have to admit,' added Julia, building up her case, 'we would be amazing, wouldn't we?'

Claire picked up her glass of Sauvignon Blanc and looked out over the view. It was a beautiful day and they'd come out for lunch to celebrate a case Claire had won. It had almost cost her her sanity but she'd done it. Months of work for her and months of billing for JWTS Solicitors, which would no doubt make Matthew happy. She thought of her boss with his fat babyish face atop his man's body and involuntarily shuddered. He was a screamer and if something didn't go his way, he made sure the whole office knew about it.

Unfortunately, he was also a brilliant lawyer and despite numerous complaints, HR had failed in persuading the board to get rid of him. He'd turned the firm around in just two short years and JWTS now boasted an incredible portfolio of clients. But the pressure was immense, like a boiling pan of eggs, everyone waiting to see who would crack next. Luckily it hadn't been Claire or Julia, but since Claire had come back to work at JWTS after having Joshua five years previously, she knew it wouldn't be long before the stress would get too much. Children and a career in law just didn't work.

Of course, it was all there in writing – support for mothers in the workplace, later starting times, remote working and so on... but everyone knew how it worked. You got the crappy cases, your childless colleagues made your life hell, and you would never be made Partner. On numerous occasions, she'd been tempted to chuck it in altogether. What was the point in trying to do everything and enjoying nothing?

She should be celebrating her recent win but instead, she was sat here worried about the impact the last few months had had on her young son. There were too many missed bedtimes and school pick-ups. She'd missed sports day and the festive sing-along and although Chris had been able to make the sports day, her guilt that her son didn't have any parent there for the sing-along was like an open, festering wound. Every time she thought about it, she added a little more salt.

She looked at Julia – perhaps her idea was worth considering? Yes, it would be stressful to set up their own practice but at least she would have more flexibility. And no verbal abuse from fat-faced Matthew. Turning back to her friend now, she compromised.

'I'll think about it. Okay?'

'Promise?' wheedled Julia.

'I promise.'

'Amazing!' Everything was amazing with Julia.

'So,' Julia said, pulling some leaflets out of her bag. 'What do you think of this office space?'

'Office space! Julia! I said I would think about it and you've already been looking for offices?'

'I know, I know, but Claire, look!'

Claire caught sight of an image – a New York-style loft – huge windows with views looking over Manchester. Pulling it towards her, she peered over her sunglasses at Julia reproachfully before glancing at the leaflet. She couldn't help but be curious. 'I'm just looking, Julia – it doesn't mean I've agreed to this, okay?'

'Okay,' replied Julia, nonchalantly, hiding her smile behind her wine glass. But they both knew Julia had won. Together they would go into business and set up their own law firm, Stephens & Carmichael.

3

'This lamb is just perfect, Claire,' announced her mother and Claire looked up in surprise. It was unlike her mother to be so complimentary. She waited a moment before responding. There was usually something to follow. And sure enough.

'Did you cook it or did Lucy do it?'

Claire deliberately took her time to finish her mouthful of food.

'I cooked it,' she lied, looking her mum directly in the eye.

'Well, it tastes delicious,' said her father, clearly trying to make up for his wife's insinuation.

Claire took a gulp of wine and wished she hadn't invited them. She tried not to think how she could be curled up with Chris on the sofa reading or watching TV. She and Chris didn't get too many evenings together and she knew they'd get even less when she went back to work full-time.

'So, when do you go back?' her mum asked.

Honestly, it was like her mother could read her mind.

'Next week. I'll settle Jamie into school on Monday and then start properly on Tuesday.'

'Well, I suppose that's how it is today, isn't it? Working mums. Brings more problems than it solves in my opinion, but I'm sure you know what you're doing.'

Chris and Claire exchanged glances, both quietly hoping that Joshua would start a new topic of conversation. He could usually be relied on to charm his grandparents. But then Claire caught the faint glow of backlight from his mobile phone and knew he was secretly messaging under the table. Little bugger. Joshua knew how much she hated that.

'So, Joshua, are you ready to go back to sixth-form college?' Claire asked pointedly. 'Why don't you tell your grandparents about your new maths teacher?'

As Joshua began talking, in between shovelling huge forkfuls of food into his mouth, Claire and Chris both relaxed back in their chairs. Crisis averted. Once Patricia Sharpe – Claire's mum – got going on a subject there was no stopping her – not even her long-suffering husband who had given up even trying, years ago. As long as Claire's dad got his weekly football in, he'd learnt to be content. The time for change had long gone and they were both too old now.

The family were sat around Claire's dining table: her parents, Chris, herself, and Joshua. Jamie had already gone to bed. It was a monthly ritual that had started soon after Claire and Chris had got married. They had used to alternate – one month at Claire's, the next month at her parents', but when the kids came along, it had been easier for her parents to come to their daughter and son-in-law's home. But although the boys were older now, they'd never gone back to their previous arrangement, so each month Claire found herself cooking a three-course meal. She'd become proficient at it over the years although she didn't enjoy cooking. To her, it was just another task to be ticked off the never-ending domestic to-do list.

'Speaking of Lucy,' said her mother, interrupting her thoughts.

We weren't, thought Claire, *but go on, I know you won't be happy until you've said your piece.*

'Did you do reference checks on her?'

'Of course!' replied Claire. 'I was very thorough.' Out of the corner of her eye, she saw Joshua start with his phone again and she tried to find his leg under the table to nudge him.

'Well, that's good. We don't want our precious grandson left with just anyone now, do we, James?'

Claire's father avoided answering by pretending to be engrossed in his peas.

'Lucy's great, Mum,' replied Claire firmly. 'And she's still in the trial phase. She's only been with us a week but so far she's shown herself to be really good with Jamie.'

Claire wondered why she was even bothering to defend her decision.

'Well of course, I'm sure she's lovely. Where did you say she's from again, love?'

I didn't, but you've somehow found out and now you're going to make it an issue.

'She's local, Mum; Irene recommended her, remember?' But she knew it wasn't enough.

'Yes, but where exactly?' persisted her mum.

'Cressfield Lane.'

Damn it. Even Chris looked up at that one.

Her mum's face was aghast.

Oh, stop being so dramatic!

'Really, Claire? Do you think that's a good idea? You know what that area is like... drugs and all sorts. What if she brought them to the house?'

'Mum, she isn't a—'

'Chris, love, what do you think? Are you happy with this arrangement?'

Oh no you don't, Mother!

'Chris and I made this decision together, Mum,' stated Claire firmly before Chris had a chance to respond. 'He's on board with it.'

Claire and her mother both turned to Chris, his wife silently daring him to contradict her, his mother-in-law waiting for confirmation.

'It's all right, Patricia,' said Chris, his face breaking into the well-used smile he saved for his best clients. 'We checked her out thoroughly so no need to worry.' Claire watched her husband resume eating, hoping it was enough to close the matter.

'I have absolutely no doubt, Chris,' started her mother, refusing to be derailed.

Oh, for goodness' sake!

'But why take the chance?' she continued, speaking to Chris. 'I'd be more than happy to watch Jamie for you in the afternoons.'

Claire, now excluded from the conversation, seethed inside, but she knew if she wanted the best outcome, she would have to leave it to Chris to handle her.

'We know, Patricia, and it's lovely of you, but it's such a lot to ask. We couldn't possibly...' he protested, although not strongly enough for Claire's liking. Claire could practically see the numbers going through his head trying to weigh up how much money they'd save versus the potential pain of having his mother-in-law in the house when he got home. She could see the numbers were winning and Claire knew she had to do something quickly.

'What about your W.I., Mum? That's every Tuesday afternoon, and don't forget your weekly shop and afternoon tea with Moira on Fridays. Like Chris said, we couldn't possibly impose such a responsibility on you,' said Claire firmly.

Not to mention Lucy will do all the cleaning and cooking as well.

'Yes, I suppose you're right,' conceded Patricia. 'I am very busy these days. I honestly don't know what would happen to the W.I. if they didn't have me sorting everything out.'

Finally.

'But if you so much as get an inkling that Lucy is doing drugs, promise me, you'll call me.'

'We will, Mum,' replied Claire, relieved. Another battle fought and won.

'Oh my God,' complained Claire, removing her earrings as she sat at her dressing table. 'She never gives up, does she?'

Chris didn't need to ask who she was talking about it. He removed his shirt and tie, dumping them in the laundry basket. 'It was nice of your mum to offer to babysit though, wasn't it?'

'Honestly, Chris, you'd go nuts coming home to her here every day. And besides, who will do all the washing, cleaning, and cooking?'

'Is Lucy going to be doing all that as well?'

'Yep,' said Claire triumphantly. 'She's a great cook, isn't she?'

'Well, I wouldn't know,' said Chris coming up behind her and wrapping his arms around her. 'Unless that lamb wasn't produced by my wife's own sweet fair hands?' he joked, nuzzling into her neck.

Claire smiled. 'I guess you'll never know, will you?'

Claire pulled up the covers around her, luxuriating in the warmth. Turning on her left side, she slipped an arm around her sleeping husband's waist. She was tired, the evening having taken its toll, but despite the comforting presence of Chris, she couldn't sleep. Her mother had always been difficult, but she seemed to be getting worse. And when had her father become so passive?

Her mind raced backwards through her life – school, university, her first job, marrying Chris, the births of Joshua and Jamie – but nothing stuck out. Perhaps it was she who had changed? It was during such times that she wished she had a brother or sister to share her thoughts with. It was one of the reasons she'd been so adamant that she and Chris keep trying for a second baby – she didn't want Joshua to be an only child like she had been.

There had been some benefits though. You were at the centre of your parents' world. Which was fine when you were a child, but not so much when you were an adult.

And over the years, it seemed like the focus had become more and more intense, like being under a microscope and the dial just kept turning and turning. And what about her Dad? They had been so close – allies against the world. Now, the only thing that seemed to make him happy was his football.

Happiness. She'd never thought about it in relation to her parents before. Were they happy? She didn't know. She'd never asked them. She wondered what they would say, if she did. She knew she made them happy. Her dad always used to tell her that the day she was born was the best day of his life. Her dad had chosen the name Claire, although her mother had insisted on registering it with an I so it was spelt the French way.

What made people happy at that age, anyway? They were sixty-seven, not exactly ancient but not young any more either. They'd been married since they were twenty-two, having met at school. Her father had worked in retail. They'd lived in the same house, her father had worked for the same firm, and they'd been attending the same social club for as long as Claire could remember. But growing up, that was normal – what all her friends had as well. A mum, a dad, maybe a sibling or two; if you were lucky, a guinea pig, and if you were very lucky, a puppy. You went to school, Mum picked you up, Dad usually came home from work at five-thirty, bath at seven o'clock and into bed. Everyone did the same.

But she'd always had a feeling that there was something slightly different about her parents. Like the time they'd slept in separate beds for a few years. Mum said it was because of Dad's snoring. Dad said it was because of his snoring. At the time, she'd accepted that. But now she wondered if it was just another example of a broken marriage. There was certainly no physical affection between them; they didn't hold hands or even peck each other on the cheek. They didn't sit close – Dad had his chair and Mum had hers on different sides of the room, albeit both facing the television. But isn't that what all couples did? Over the years, she'd begun to wonder.

4

The crowd was three-deep, lining Castle Street for at least half a mile. They cheered loudly as Claire ran past them, flags waving, hands clapping, propelling her to the finish line. She could see it just ahead, the blue ribbon pulled taut, the digital clock luminous and truthful against the grey sky. With a last surge of adrenalin, Claire pumped her arms and legs as fast as she could, her desire to beat the clock propelling her forward. As her taut stomach touched the imaginary ribbon, she opened her arms, the relief instantaneous.

Breathing heavily, she ripped out her earphones, the fast beats of Calvin Harris's 'Summer' having done their job. Hands resting on her back, she walked in circles hoping it was still too early for anyone to have noticed her. As she took in the empty street, she brought herself back to her own reality – a bored housewife going out for a run.

Not for much longer.

Checking her fitness watch, she was amazed at the power of her imagination and the impact on her speed – she'd improved by three point five seconds. She'd always listened to music during her runs, but it was the first time she'd used visualisation. She'd come across the idea on a Ted Talk the night before. Chris thought she was addicted to Ted Talks – she consumed them eagerly, her brain soaking up the information. It didn't matter what the topic – her dedication to self-improvement bordered on the obsessive.

Sharing her new time on Facebook, Claire started the short walk back home. It was just after six in the morning and the last Friday of the summer holidays before school started the following Monday.

'Good run?' asked Chris, as he came into the kitchen and gave her cheek a kiss.

'Yep! I got a new personal best this morning. Twenty point four minutes.'

'Brilliant!'

She watched him buzz around the kitchen, grabbing a piece of toast and putting it between his teeth while helping himself to coffee and reading emails on his phone. She marvelled at his ability to be so alert within seconds of waking up. It had taken Claire almost thirty minutes just to get out of bed and put on her running gear.

'Going for a shower,' he told her now as he headed to the bathroom to get ready.

After taking a quick gulp of coffee, Claire started to prepare Jamie's breakfast. She put the bowl of cereal on the table, along with his milk, and went upstairs to put her ear to his door. She presumed he was still sleeping. She would leave Jamie for another fifteen minutes, she decided, while she finished her coffee. Joshua would probably sleep until at least nine a.m., but she liked to keep Jamie on a bit of a routine during the holidays, especially with school starting in a few days. Besides, she'd promised to take Jamie to Manchester today, so he could choose his new school bag and pencil case. They were planning to make a morning of it, go for lunch and maybe to the cinema.

She took her cup into the bedroom and stripped off her running clothes. After putting on a dressing gown, she got back into bed. She sank down into the pillows, the king-size-plus bed wrapping her in softness. No wonder it was so difficult to get up in the morning. She leant her head against the soft, velvet grey headboard, so different to the single bed she and Chris had shared in her dorm room at university. How had they even managed to sleep cramped together like that? She smiled remembering fun nights and drunken sex, the two of them wrapped in each other's arms, warm and comfortable in each other's company.

Her new friends at Manchester university had been surprised to learn that she already had a boyfriend and that she and Chris had deliberately chosen to attend the same university. Didn't she want to go out on the pull? Didn't she want the anticipation of not knowing who she would meet? But Claire wanted the complete opposite. She loved to dance and drink but the thought of kissing a random student in a nightclub did not appeal at all. At the time, it had only been a couple of years since *the incident* and she just couldn't…

She had never told any of her new friends at university what had happened. What was the point? It was over and done with and besides… she had Chris, who made her feel safe and protected.

And normal.

The fact that they'd managed to get into the same university after being together in their last year of sixth form was the cherry on the cake in Claire's opinion. And they had a plan. After graduation, she in law and Chris in business, they would get jobs and buy a house. They would get married in their mid-twenties, have baby number one at twenty-seven and number two at twenty-nine.

She knew Chris felt the same as she did, as they talked about it frequently. She also knew that his mates had egged him on to not settle down so early but when Chris was on his nights out, she never worried that he would succumb to the pressure. There was just one time when she went to his dorm room one morning around nine after one of his nights out and he wasn't there. She'd left his room, wondering where he was. Later, he said he'd got up early and gone to the gym and she'd believed him. And as the hormones of freshers' week settled down and the demands of the course kicked in, her friends started to envy the stability and consistency of her and Chris.

She watched her friends ricochet from one-night stands to potential relationships to depressing singledom at an alarming rate, all against a backdrop of alcohol-fuelled socials and parties. Over endless rounds of late-night toast and tea, she participated in countless hours helping her new friends analyse the number of drinks consumed, the attractiveness of boys snogged, and the likelihood of going to study in the library the next day. But towards the end of the first term, when Claire discovered she'd put on a stone *and* received a lower than average grade on an end-of-term paper, she knew that she had to sacrifice a few nights out. Claire had serious plans for her life and they didn't include being an overweight drinker.

Studying law had always been her dream and if she was honest with herself it wasn't because of any altruism on her part – it was mainly because she knew it was a high-paying career that would also allow her to use her brain. She'd seen what giving up work had done to her mother and it wasn't something she'd aspired to. Patricia Sharpe had pushed her husband constantly to apply himself for the next promotion, the next job and while he had always done well, it had never been good enough for her mother. It didn't help that her father was a cautious spender, even frugal. He always said it was better to keep as much as possible in savings – you just never knew what the future might bring – but it frustrated her mother who wanted everything that the neighbours had and more.

Claire watched as her mother needled and poked her husband for more housekeeping money, a new car, holidays abroad. But the more she pushed, the more closed off her father became. Maybe because he knew it came from a place that wasn't about enjoyment but more about competing. Either way, Claire had vowed that she would *never* be reliant on a man for money.

Just then, Chris came out of the shower, towel wrapped around his waist, dripping wet.

'Like what you see?' He grinned suggestively at her, doing a little shimmy towards the bed. It was impossible not to laugh.

'Chris! You're getting everything wet!' She giggled as he came and jumped on the bed, wrapping her in a damp hug.

'You're gorgeous, you know that?' he announced as he kissed her. 'Even in the mornings.' He winked. She swatted him away and watched him as he dried himself off and got dressed.

'Mummy!' The voice came from the room next door.

'Jamie's awake,' she said, as she got up from the bed.

'I'll get him; you finish your coffee and have a shower,' offered Chris, hurriedly pulling on his trousers. Claire sank back gratefully. Just a few more minutes and then she would get up and they would have a lovely morning in Manchester. She wondered if she could talk Joshua into joining them. It would be nice to spend some time with both of them. Plus, if Joshua came, she would get half an hour to look around the shops by herself while Joshua took Jamie to the arcades.

Maybe if she let him sleep in until nine, brought him some breakfast in bed, and promised him a look around the music shop – she knew he'd been eyeing a particular guitar that he was saving for. Well, with her new salary perhaps she could help out a little bit with that. Satisfied she had a plan, she gulped the last of her coffee and went to take a shower.

SEPTEMBER 2017

5

Claire slipped the white cape jacket over her silk shirt and black pencil skirt and looked at herself approvingly in the full-length mirror. Her sleek blonde bob – or lob, as her hairdresser had called it – framed her face and emphasised her eyes. She'd taken the time with her make-up, applying eyeshadow and lipstick as opposed to her usual quick flick of mascara and lip balm. All her running had kept her toned and she briefly admired her long shapely legs in the unfamiliar high heels. She felt like a different person. She looked like somebody in control of her life.

'Mummy!'

Well, not quite – there was still a little person at the centre of her world and she smiled as Jamie barged in to the bedroom, his rucksack too big for his little frame, but not his determination. His first day of school yesterday had gone well. She'd taken Lucy – who'd passed her nanny trial with flying colours – with her to pick Jamie up at half past three yesterday afternoon. Lucy had been with them for the last two weeks, getting to know the household routines in preparation for Claire to return to work. Lucy was efficient, easy-going, and the house sparkled. Claire's only regret was not hiring someone sooner.

Jamie had bounded out of the school gates straight into his mother's arms and as Claire buried her head in his shiny blonde hair, she'd had a moment's doubt at the thought of all the school pick-ups she would miss.

'Mummy!' he'd practically shouted. 'I made a robot!'

'A robot? How wonderful! Where is it?'

'Mrs Chiswick hung it on the wall in the classroom! She said it was the best robot she'd ever seen!'

'Of course she did!'

Taking his hand, Claire gave his school bag to Lucy.

'Say hello to Lucy,' instructed Claire.

'Hello, Lucy,' he parroted automatically.

'Hi, Jamie! How was your first day at school? Sounds like you had a good time!' replied Lucy, warmly.

'It was great. And I have a new friend – Luke. See? His mummy is over there.'

Claire looked over to see a beautifully dressed woman, holding her mobile phone in one hand and a school bag in the other, bending over a boy who she assumed was Luke. Just at that moment, the woman looked up and Claire gave a wave, keen to be friendly. The woman smiled and started walking towards them, her son tugging on her arm all the way.

'Hello,' greeted the woman, 'you must be Jamie's mum.'

'Hello! Yes, Claire,' she replied introducing herself, 'and this is Lucy.'

'Linda Alderton,' the woman said smiling, 'and you must be Jamie,' she continued, kneeling to Jamie's level. 'I've heard lots about you from Luke!'

Claire watched as her son smiled at his new friend's mum.

'I made a robot!' he announced again, pleased to be able to tell someone else.

Linda laughed and stood up. 'So, I hear. And a little birdie told me they're hung on the classroom wall!'

The two boys jumped around together, before breaking into a few robot moves.

'Well, it's lovely to meet you,' said Linda, turning back towards Claire. 'Perhaps we could arrange for the boys to get together after school? I work full-time, but I've taken today off...'

Claire felt a moment's pleasure about meeting another working mum on the first day. Not that she doubted her decision but still... she'd learnt from Joshua's time at primary school, the playground could be as harsh on the mothers as it was on the kids.

'I'm going back to work full-time tomorrow as well,' said Claire. 'A playdate sounds great.'

Linda looked up. 'You work? What do you do?'

'I'm a solicitor.'

'I'm in banking. Well, that's a relief – I thought I was the only bad mother round here!' Linda chuckled at her own joke, but Claire saw the thin layer of guilt beneath the beautiful clothes and expensively made-up face.

'Not at all!' Claire laughed, keen to put Linda at ease. 'Take my number and we'll arrange something for the boys. They seem to get on really well.'

43

Bored of their mothers' conversation, Jamie and Luke, under Lucy's watchful eye, had gone back inside the school gates and were inspecting something on the grass. Claire hoped it wasn't a worm. Jamie had gone through a phase of being obsessed by them, even putting one in his bed and saying goodnight to it before Claire had found it and removed it.

'They do, don't they,' replied Linda, following Claire's gaze. 'It's reassuring to know he's made a friend already.'

Claire nodded in agreement, searching in her bag for her mobile to exchange numbers, as they chatted.

'Right, I'd best get off,' announced Linda after a few minutes. 'Luke!'

Luke looked up and started running, Jamie and Lucy following behind.

'Nice meeting you, Claire, and I'll drop you a message,' called Linda.

'You too! Take care.'

As Linda had walked away, Claire could see her scrolling on her phone, her small son walking silently beside her.

Hopefully today – the second day of school – would go just as well. Claire would drop Jamie to school each morning on the way to her office and Lucy would pick him up so Claire could work a full day. She hoped to be back for bath time and dinner but she needed the flexibility of a nanny just in case. Chris also said he would make more of an effort to be back in the evenings, especially if he knew she was going to be late – and he would do the odd drop-off in the morning.

As Jamie stood in front of her now, smart in his freshly-pressed uniform ironed by Lucy, Claire picked up her bag ready for her own first day.

★

'Oooooh, someone looks smart!' Julia, who had been briefing Elaine, their receptionist, when Claire had arrived, looked up admiringly as Claire walked in.

Claire did a mock curtsy.

'Thanks! I thought I would treat myself to mark my return.' Claire grinned.

'Well, it looks great – I love that jacket,' said Julia walking over to embrace her. 'It's great to have you back. I'm just about to get on a call, but I've left a case file in your office. Perhaps we can have a chat about it later,' she added.

Curious, Claire looked at Julia questioningly as the two of them walked out of reception.

'It's on your desk – take a look,' Julia instructed, giving Claire a last hug before going into her own office.

Claire went through to her own private office, oblivious to the stylish monochrome décor. The file had been placed in the middle of her desk, its contents bulging. Putting her bag on the small table she quickly sat down, her fingers rifling through the file. Domestic violence? Murder? Theft? *Rape.*

The word jumped out at her, and Claire automatically recoiled. No wonder Julia had offered to have a chat with her – she rarely took such cases. Picking up the file, she went next door to Julia's office. Popping her head in, she saw Julia was on the phone finishing a conversation, but Julia waved her hand, indicating for her to come in. Claire sat down on the pale blue sofa opposite Julia's desk. A glass coffee table was beautifully decorated with fresh flowers, law periodicals, and a pitcher of water and glasses. Claire poured herself some water and sat back, the file on the sofa next to her.

'Did you mean this to come to me?' Claire asked, holding up the file, as soon as Julia had finished.

'Yes, that's the one,' replied Julia. 'Crown Prosecution Services said there wasn't enough evidence to prosecute so the client decided to go private. Apparently, our firm was recommended, and the client asked for you specifically.'

'They'd be better off with Alan or Greg,' countered Claire.

'I did suggest that,' replied Julia, 'but understandably she wanted a woman and I'm slammed at the moment. I'm sorry, Claire, I know it's not ideal but do you think perhaps it might be time to—'

'I'll call her and explain,' interrupted Claire, picking up the file and standing up. She'd started to leave but Julia spoke.

'Claire,' said Julia gently. 'If she's requested you, perhaps this might be a good opportunity to… you know, put the past behind you? Besides, it's a good piece of business—'

'I won't lose us the business,' replied Claire tersely ignoring the implication about her past. 'I'll just propose Chloe can take it on and Greg can assist.'

Julia nodded and let it go.

After walking back to her own office, Claire picked up the phone. The name on the file said Rose Aiker and she dialled the mobile number listed. It was answered immediately.

'Hello?'

'Hello, this is Claire Carmichael, from Stephens and Carmichael.' Claire could hear loud music playing in the background. 'Am I speaking with Rose Aiker?'

'Yep, it is. I've been waiting for your call.' Claire held the phone a few centimetres away from the receiver as Rose shouted down the phone, no doubt trying to hear herself above the music.

'Well, that's the reason I was calling,' continued Claire.

'What?' shouted Rose. 'Wait, let me turn this off.'

Suddenly the music stopped.

'I said, that's the reason I was calling,' repeated Claire. 'I would recommend you speak to one of my colleagues. We can of course arrange a female lawyer. Shall I get my assistant to make an appointment for you?'

Silence came down the line and for a minute, she wondered if Rose had hung up.

'Are you licensed to try this case?'

'Well, yes, of course, but—'

'Then I would like an appointment to see you,' replied Rose firmly.

Claire paused, Julia's warning about not losing the client coming back to her. 'Just give me a moment to check my diary.'

Perhaps during a meeting, Claire could be more persuasive. Confirming an appointment for the next day, Claire decided she would invite Chloe and Greg to the meeting as well. She would just have to explain that her colleagues had more experience in this particular field and Rose would have to see reason.

The rest of the day passed in a gratifying blur of meetings and phone calls. With the exception of a message from Lucy late afternoon and a call from Chris at lunchtime, she'd not had chance to think of her family, but as she sat with a cup of green tea reading over some documents, she wondered if she could leave in a few minutes and make it home in time for dinner.

She opened her laptop and scanned her diary. Her only appointment the following morning was Rose Aiker at eleven o'clock. She would go home and take Rose's file with her to read after Jamie had gone to bed. Chris wouldn't mind. He probably had his own work to do anyway and with no dinner to prepare or laundry to deal with, she would have plenty of time to review everything. Anyway, if she got her way, the case would be handed over to one of her team. Satisfied with her plan, Claire packed her bag and left the office, eager to see her sons.

6

Claire sat back, happy but exhausted in her chair at the office on Friday afternoon. One week done. She heaved a sigh of relief that nothing disastrous had gone wrong, either on the work or the home front. It had been the right decision. There had been a small part of her that had worried she would hate working full-time and missing out on seeing Jamie and Joshua in the afternoons and catching up with them about their day. And if she was honest, she did miss it, but it was a price worth paying in her opinion.

When she'd been working as a professional support lawyer, she'd ended up doing mainly predictable contract and administration work and her heart simply wasn't in it. And even though it had only been three mornings a week, she'd always been rushing. Rushing to drop Jamie off at playgroup, rushing through her job, rushing to pick him up and then rushing to make dinner, not to mention feeding Joshua and all his friends.

Now, she knew she had the whole day, five days a week to dedicate to her career and with Lucy watching Jamie and checking in on Joshua in the afternoons and doing all the domestic side of things, she felt much more relaxed. Even Chris had agreed they should have hired extra help sooner. If anyone appreciated a spotless house and home-cooked meal, it was Chris. He was slightly old-fashioned that way. Claire blamed his mother – she'd done everything for him growing up. What was great about Lucy was that she did the job well, but she also did it happily. She'd brought good energy into the house, thought Claire one evening when she'd come in late from work.

'Really?' Lucy had laughed when Claire had commented on it. 'Well, I suppose I'm just happy to be out of my own house! It's bedlam there!'

With so many brothers and sisters, Claire could only imagine what it was like for Lucy, and she wondered how Lucy's mum coped. It was challenging enough with two boys. The odds were stacked against you from the beginning as a working mum, not to mention the hormones, the guilt, the bitchiness of other women, the constant balancing act, and the blatant discrimination in most companies. Thank God, she and Julia had set up their own firm. She couldn't imagine how she would have coped otherwise. It would have been difficult to get back into a role like this at another firm after five years off.

Claire looked around her office now with a quiet sense of satisfaction. These were the same offices in the leaflet that Julia had put under her nose when she had first proposed the idea over lunch all those years ago. When they'd first moved in, the place was barren – a semi-derelict cave that would need some work, reflected in its attractive asking price. But the location! Claire had to admit Julia had chosen well. Located in St. Peter's Square, between Piccadilly and Deansgate, it had been a real find and it hadn't taken long for Claire to visualise how the office would look.

The two women had spent their weekends tidying, painting and redecorating, roping in as many family and friends as they could to help. With the exception of two private offices, which they would keep for themselves, and the meeting rooms, they had designed an open-plan layout giving enough space for approximately twenty associates and paralegals. Both Julia and Claire had furnished their offices with the best desks they could afford, conscious that clients would be visiting and that first impressions were everything. But apart from those, it was IKEA all the way.

Claire smiled fondly to herself – despite the exhaustion and stress, they had been great days. Every new client had been celebrated with a glass of champagne and as their reputation grew, so did their company. Despite the mix of male and female solicitors, their client base was mainly made up of women. They had started off small, then recruited to widen into commercial, corporate, and criminal law. In the last couple of years, they'd seen an increase in private prosecutions as well. They were one of the few female-led law firms in Manchester and it had taken time and hard work to compete with the big boys; but within a few years, they were doing well, and their accountant was happy. Even so it was a never-ending task to keep new business coming in and Claire was very much aware that Julia did most of the networking and wining and dining needed to sign new clients.

Claire looked at the clock – almost five. If she left now she could get back home for six. She saw the pile of case files on her desk, most of which needed to be read by Monday afternoon, including the Rose Aiker file. Rose had cancelled her last appointment. Claire had been disappointed – she'd been looking forward to getting that case off her to-do list. Elaine had told her Rose had rescheduled the appointment for the following Monday. Looking at the pile of files again, Claire decided she would work for another hour and be home by six thirty at the latest.

Claire's mobile phone rang, its sharp chirp startling her. She'd been engrossed in her reading. Picking it up, she saw it was almost seven.

Shit.

'Hey, where are you?' asked Chris.

'I've just left the office,' lied Claire, already shoving files into her bag, phone clamped between her shoulder and ear.

'What? I thought you'd be almost home by now. I'm just calling to say I'll be late.'

'Really? Why?'

'The Dubai account has gone pear-shaped and we need a plan by tomorrow.'

'Tomorrow's Saturday,' challenged Claire, although she knew it was a complete waste of time.

'Yep, but some companies in Dubai work on Saturday.'

'Chris, when we agreed that I would go back full-time, you reassured me you'd try and make more of an effort. What about the boys?'

'Claire, what do you want me to do? Besides, why are *you* late?'

'Never mind,' replied Claire, 'I'll head home now. What time will you be back?'

'No clue. I'll message you.'

Chris hung up and Claire threw the phone in her bag, anxious to get home to her sons. Did Chris really have to work on a Friday night? What if she had needed to work late? She didn't but that wasn't the point. What irritated her was that there was no discussion – he simply assumed she would be on hand to drop everything and be home for their sons. Closing her bag, Claire left the office, her earlier satisfaction replaced with annoyance.

Claire stretched out on the sofa, relieved to be out of her suit and high heels and in something more comfortable. The house was silent and for a few minutes, Claire appreciated the rare moment of quiet as she sipped a glass of rosé. She didn't usually drink on her own but after her first week at work, she felt the need to mark the milestone. Lucy had kept Jamie up a little later than usual being as it was the weekend, so Claire could put him to bed. Much to her relief, he'd fallen asleep happily with promises to go and see the dinosaur display in the shopping centre the next day. Chris was still at work and Joshua had gone out with his friends.

'Where are you going?' Claire had asked her eldest as casually as she could.

'To Mark's house, Mum. Video games.'

'Do you want me to pick you up later?'

'No, it's fine, I'll walk.'

'Okay, be back for eleven, okay?'

'I always am, Mum.' He winked at her now, indulgent of her daily reminder, and gave her a kiss on the cheek before leaving. Joshua had been friends with Mark for years and Claire thought Mark was a fairly good influence on him. There were several other lads they hung around with from school as well and they'd all gone through senior school together. She hoped it was just video games, but she suspected there would be booze as well. After everything they had been through last year with Joshua, she prayed he had enough sense not to go overboard.

At least he wasn't driving yet.

Claire knew that the minute he passed his test, she wouldn't be able to sleep a wink until he was safely back home. She felt a pang for his baby days when there was nothing more to worry about than whether he was hungry or needed his nappy changing. But as Chris was always reminding her, you had to let them grow up. It wasn't easy though.

Picking up her glass, she pushed the thoughts aside determined to make the most of a quiet Friday night alone. She might as well finish reading her files while Chris was out. She reluctantly picked up the Rose Aiker file. Knowing someone else in the company would handle it, she was half inclined to skip it, but the case pricked at her subconscious. *Rape.*

Taking a deep breath, she opened the file and began reading.

Case Number: TD / 08 / 67 / 3876

Incident: Rape

Reporting Officer: Constable Andrea Myers

Date of Report: Saturday 11 February 2016

At about 17:00hrs on Sunday 12 February 2016, I met with Ms Rose Aiker at her home address of 61A Sherbourne Road regarding an accusation of rape. Ms Aiker said she had gone out with a female friend in Manchester city centre and then to the opening party of Studio 65, a nightclub, at 23:45hrs. Ms Aiker admitted to drinking alcohol and taking drugs at the venue.

Ms Aiker informed me that at approximately 01:45hrs she left Studio 65 and went on to a party with a group of people. The party was held at 15 Crossway Avenue, approximately a twenty-minute walk from Studio 65. Ms Aiker spent approximately four hours at the party. During this time, Ms Aiker went upstairs to one of the bedrooms to lie down. When she entered there were two males, who she described as anything between eighteen and twenty-five years old. Ms Aiker told me the males wouldn't leave the room to let her lie down and she was unable to remember if anyone else came into the room. Her recollection of the event is as follows:

Section 4 of transcript 2 of case file TD / 08 / 67 / 3876

'They weren't gonna leave the bedroom were they, so I tried to push past them to find another bedroom, but they stopped me. I thought they were joking so we started having a bit of banter. It was dark in the

bedroom, but I could see their faces because there was a lamppost outside the house that was shining through the window. I don't think there was anyone else in the room although maybe somebody came in later. When I tried to leave again, they stopped me.

'At first, they kept trying to joke and chat and I played along for a bit, but then one of them held my arms and the other put something across my mouth. Then they put me on the bed and tried to make it out to be a game. When I resisted, the one holding my arms threw me on the floor and I tried to get up and run. I heard something, like a lock clicking and then I saw one of them pull down his trousers...' [Victim pauses for several minutes and is visibly distressed.]

'He got on top of me and pulled down my underwear... and... and then... he... forced me. I just kept trying to tell him to stop.'

'Did the other male do anything to you?'

'The first one said, "You wanna go, our kid?"'

'Apart from that did either of them speak?'

'No, I don't think so. I don't remember. I think one of them kept saying, "Hurry up!" He sounded a bit scared.'

'I'm sorry, Ms Aiker, can you describe what happened after that?'

'The first one got dressed. And then the other one...'
[Victim unable to continue and asks for a break. See
section 5, transcript 2 of case file TD / 08 / 67 / 3876]

Claire closed the file, heart pounding, trying to block
out the images, but they swooped in on her, insistent and
audacious, like vultures on a corpse. Rose, outnumbered,
lying there so petrified, wondering what would happen to
her, the dawning realisation that she might not get out alive.
Claire wondered what Rose was doing right now. Was she
at home wondering if she would ever feel safe enough to go
for a night out again?

Between the images, a memory pushed at her mind,
Claire lying on a couch, partially undressed, Paul's hands
over her, and the shame hit her with full force. She wouldn't
think about that now. It was just one more reason to hand
this case over to someone else and as quickly as possible.
Rose had done the right thing, called the police, made a
statement, and subjected herself to a physical exam. It was
a strong case and one that could be won. Just not by Claire.

OCTOBER 2017

7

'Jamie! Shoes on! NOW!'

How many times...?

'Can you help me, Mummy?'

Claire sent a silent plea for patience. Taking a deep breath, she put down her bag and travel mug and leant over to help her son.

'Okay, love, but we have to be quick. We're late!' she urged, pulling the Velcro across his shoe. Picking up her things, she grabbed her car keys and opened the front door ready to go. It was then she noticed Jamie didn't have his school bag.

'Jamie, your school bag – where is it?' asked Claire.

'I don't know, Mummy.'

'Well, is it in your room?'

'Maybe...'

'Jamie, come on – you're a big boy now – you need to have your things ready! Look, here it is.'

Relieved, Claire pulled the Paw Patrol themed bag out from behind the stool in the hallway. It must have fallen down the back.

'Come on then, let's go,' she cajoled.

With Jamie trailing behind, she unlocked the car, dumped the bags on the front seat and put her travel coffee mug in the cup holder. Then she opened the back door and helped Jamie get in. After slamming the door, she got into the driver's seat, looking at her son in the rear-view mirror.

'Put your seat belt on, Jamie, please.'

As she saw Jamie pull the belt across him, she started up the engine.

'Can you manage?' she asked him, carefully reversing the car.

'Yes, Mummy.'

'Okay, good job, Jamie.'

She was rushing. Claire had woken up just twenty minutes before they were supposed to leave after a late night working at home. Chris had also been late, but he'd been up early, and she was annoyed that he had left it so late to wake her. He was out the door as soon as he'd handed her her coffee. At least he'd dropped Joshua off, she supposed, but still – would it have killed him to drop Jamie off too?

Putting the car into drive mode, she accelerated quickly. Checking her rear-view mirror, she could see the belt across Jamie's chest and tried to relax. At least he'd managed to do one thing by himself this morning. It was only ten minutes to the school so they'd only be a few minutes late. Then, once she'd dropped him off, she would call the office and let them know she'd be late for her first appointment. It wasn't ideal. Her mind was whirring with her to-do list. Yesterday, Lucy had asked her where the receipt was for Chris's dry-cleaning. Claire would need to find it and get it collected that afternoon otherwise Chris wouldn't have any shirts to wear, but she had a horrible feeling she'd actually thrown the receipt out. *Thank God it was Friday.*

The initial euphoria she'd felt about going back to work was slowly dwindling as the long hours started to take their toll. Come on, Claire urged herself, it's only been a month. She just needed a few more early nights, that's all. And she would talk to Chris. He was acting like she was still part-time rather than working full-time. He needed to help out a bit more and pull his weight. She would talk to him this weekend, she decided.

She was so distracted she didn't see the woman with her pram walking across the pedestrian crossing. Claire slammed on the brakes hard to avoid hitting her and Claire's head snapped forward. The bags on the front seat flew, hitting the dashboard before landing on the floor, their contents spilling out. But it was the thump against her back that made her stomach slide.

'Jamie!' she screamed.

Releasing her seat belt, she got out of the car and yanked open the back door. Jamie was crouched in the footwell. She reached for him and held him close, examining him all over, oblivious to the impatient drivers behind her tooting their horns.

'Oh, Jamie, I'm so sorry, are you okay?'

'I'm sorry, Mummy, I didn't put my seat belt on properly.'

'Oh, it's okay, my love, it was my fault, I should have checked.'

Claire kissed her son on his face and gently put him back in his car seat and fastened the seat belt. Giving him another once-over, she got back in the car, shaking. She was just about to drive away when someone knocked on her window. The woman with the pram. Thank God she hadn't hit her. She looked furious.

'It's a fucking crossing, you dumb bitch,' she shouted without even waiting for Claire to wind down the window.

Sorry, sorry, Claire mouthed. Putting the car in gear, Claire slowly drove away, hoping Jamie couldn't hear the torrent of abuse that followed her.

'Time for lunch?' asked Julia, placing a take-away bag on her desk. Claire looked up from her laptop in surprise. She hadn't heard Julia come in. Since she'd got into the office, she'd worked non-stop. She'd gone straight into her first meeting and it hadn't gone well. The client was pissed off to be kept waiting and he wasn't shy in voicing his displeasure. At just five foot four, Harry Benner had a temper as short as his stature and since they'd started representing his firm, he'd done nothing but complain. Her lateness had only given him more ammunition.

Julia unpacked the bag of food and handed her a sandwich, chicken with no mayonnaise. Claire took it gratefully. She was starving.

'So, what's the situation with the Rose Aiker case?' asked Julia sitting opposite her and opening a packet of crisps.

Even the client's name made Claire's stomach lurch. Putting down the sandwich, she finished swallowing.

'Well, I met Rose three weeks ago but since then Greg and Chloe have been working with her. You want me to get Greg and Chloe in to give you an update?' replied Claire reaching for the phone.

'Well, here's the thing, Rose just called me and she's still insisting on you being part of the representation.'

Claire removed her hand from the phone and sat back in her chair. The silence between them lengthened.

Finally, Julia leant over and took Claire's hand. 'I know it's difficult but *he* has cast a shadow over your life for so long, maybe it's time to let it go.'

Claire nodded numbly realising the truth of Julia's words.

'And you know, by *not* taking on this case, in a way, it's like *he's* winning. And that's not the Claire I know. The Claire *I* know is someone who would *never* let anyone get the better of her. Every case you take on you fight to the bitter end for your client. You have a fierce reputation – everyone knows that.'

Claire let her friend's words settle over her.

'Besides, why do you think I asked you to go into business with me? You think I would ever want to come up in court against you?' joked Julia. The atmosphere lightened, and Claire felt the corners of her mouth form a small smile.

'All I'm saying,' continued Julia, 'is perhaps it's time to use your past to the benefit of others and bring the Aiker perpetrator to justice. If anyone has the passion and the skill, it's you, Claire.'

'You're right, I know,' conceded Claire, 'of course you are.' She squeezed her friend's hand before letting go. 'It's just…'

Just what? She couldn't explain it to Julia. To anybody.

'I know,' said Julia, soothingly. But she didn't. Not really. They both sat quietly for a few seconds, waiting for the other to make the first move. Julia went first.

'Look, I know it's difficult to work on a rape case, especially with what happened,' she said delicately. 'So how about this. We keep Chloe and Greg on the case and you just sit in on meetings – be the face of the thing.'

Julia paused. 'I know it's not ideal, Claire, and I would do it if I could, you know I would, but what with trying to maintain my own clients and working on bringing in new business...'

'I know,' interrupted Claire, 'you've got loads on.'

It was true, and Claire felt the guilt acutely. Julia never hesitated to do what needed to be done when it came to business.

'But perhaps this as an opportunity to right a few wrongs. A healthy way for you to heal, so to speak,' concluded Julia.

Claire pulled herself up straight. Her past was affecting her career and it needed to stop. 'You're right,' agreed Claire. 'It's time to move on.'

Julia came around the desk to give her a hug. Claire leant back into it.

She only had to be the face of the case.

Julia released her and stood up, straightening her navy, wool pencil skirt. The matter was settled.

'Right, best get back to it. I've got Stanham & Stanham coming in this afternoon for a session, so I'll be tied up most of the afternoon. You?'

'Benner came in this morning...'

'Ahhh, how was that?' asked Julia. Not waiting for a response, she raised a knowing eyebrow. 'Just think of all those billable hours,' she added with a wink.

Getting up, Julia walked to the door while Claire cleared away the remains of lunch and put them in the bin. She watched as Julia paused at the door, one hand on the door handle. 'Have you ever heard from him?' Julia asked not turning around.

'Who?' replied Claire, although she knew exactly who Julia was referring to and she was probably the only person in the world brave enough to ask about him.

'Paul.'

'No. Never.'

Julia nodded and quietly left the room.

8

'When we agreed about you going back to work full-time, you told me you'd only be late *occasionally*,' called Chris from the living room.

At least let me get one foot in the bloody door.

She dropped her bag and threw her keys in the bowl on the dresser in the hallway. She could hear the pump of music, no doubt from Joshua's bedroom, and she closed her eyes against it. Why hadn't Chris told him to turn it down? Had Chris even bothered to check Joshua had done his homework?

She took off her coat and, when she saw the already overcrowded coat hooks, was tempted to let it fall where she stood. Instead, she shoved it in. Hadn't she just cleared the hall out last week? She couldn't remember. It was eight o'clock in the evening and she was exhausted. All she wanted to do was get into bed and sleep for the whole weekend. She glanced at the stairs. How easy it would be just to tiptoe up, peek in on a sleeping Jamie and a video-playing Joshua and climb into bed.

'Claire?'

No chance.

Plastering a smile on her face, she walked through to the living room where she saw Chris in his running gear.

'Hi!' *Bright and breezy. Easy.*

'Did you hear me?' asked Chris, not even bothering to look up from his laptop.

'I did,' she replied soothingly. 'And I'm sorry. It's been a devil of a week.' She went over to him and stood behind his chair, resting her hands on his shoulders, and leant over to kiss his cheek.

'How was your day?' she asked, leaving one hand on his shoulder.

'Awful – Dubai have pulled out. Grant threw an absolute fit.'

No wonder he's in such a bad mood.

'Oh, Chris, I'm so sorry. Is it very bad?'

'Bad enough,' replied Chris. 'I've been at these numbers since Jamie went to bed – whichever way we slice it, we're not making budget this month.'

'But you've done so well the rest of the year,' encouraged Claire.

'Grant doesn't see it like that,' complained Chris. 'It's not enough for him to hit our targets – he wants to beat them to a pulp.'

'Well look, it's Friday night; there's nothing you can do about it now. Why don't we have a glass of wine and relax for a bit?' suggested Claire.

'You go ahead – I was planning on going out for a run,' said Chris putting his laptop to one side and getting up from the chair.

He walked into the hallway and she could hear him getting his trainers out from the shoe cabinet. Following him out of the living room, she watched him plug his earphones into his mobile.

'Hope it helps,' she said as he opened the front door.

Chris didn't reply, simply nodded, and as he shut the door behind him, she tried not to mind that he hadn't bothered to ask her about her day.

The next morning, Claire woke up alone. Glancing at the clock, she saw it was almost eight. After telling Joshua to turn his music down and checking he'd done his homework, she'd done some more work herself before going to bed last night. Feeling slightly disorientated, she rose out of bed and grabbed her dressing gown. As she descended the stairs, she could hear Chris and the boys in the living room. She needed coffee.

Going into the kitchen, she was dismayed to see the state of it. They had clearly been making pancakes, the creamy batter a trail of splodges on the worktop. The large mixing bowl had been left abandoned with just a small pond of mixture in the bottom. A bottle of syrup stood without its cap, the sides of the bottle smeared with its contents. A half-full carton of strawberries lay to one side while a frying pan sat on the cooker waiting to be cleaned.

The dining table was no better and the sight of the mess made Claire want to turn around and head straight back upstairs. Instead, she went to the coffee machine, inserted a coffee pod and watched as the machine gurgled and spat, trying to ignore the din that came from the living room. Picking up the cup, she inhaled gratefully. After a few moments, she felt calmer and followed the noise.

Walking into the living room, she saw Chris on all fours, Jamie straddling his back wearing a Superman cape. Joshua sat in the armchair with his phone, trying his best to not look interested, although Claire could tell he was desperate to get down on the floor with them as well. It was the way his eyes followed them, trying not to laugh as Chris made ridiculous neighing noises.

Oh, but he was such a good dad!

Chris could be a difficult man, but you couldn't fault his parenting when he did get involved. She knew Joshua could easily be off with his own friends, doing his own thing, but Chris was so much fun and so energetic with them. The very fact that Joshua was not locked away in his bedroom on one of his devices or sleeping was a testament in itself.

'Morning.' Claire smiled, sitting down on the couch, placing her coffee cup on the coffee table in front of her.

'Mummy! Daddy's a horsey!' shouted Jamie. On cue, Chris did one last buckaroo, sending Jamie into fits of laughter as he clung on to his father's neck.

'Superman! Come on! We have to save Mummy!' Chris galloped – as best as he could with a five-year-old on his back – over to Claire and deposited a sliding Jamie onto her lap.

'Mummy! I've come to save you!' cried her son as Chris got to his feet and flopped down next to her.

'Jamie, when did you get so big?' said Chris, rubbing his own back.

When indeed. The days were long, but the years were short.

Her mother's words came to her now and she held her youngest son as if he was a baby. She kissed him and released him, his limbs eager to be moving again.

'Come on, Joshua – you're the horsey now,' demanded Jamie and in an instant Joshua was off the chair scooping Jamie up in his arms and flying him around.

'Superman!' cried Joshua and Jamie copied his brother's cry, delighted. Joshua ran out with Jamie tucked under his arm, no doubt to their den where they could play video games.

'Thanks for getting up with Jamie,' said Claire now, once the room had gone quiet. 'It was nice to have a little bit of lie-in.'

'I miss them,' said Chris, simply. 'I thought I'd take them to the park this morning, being as the weather is so nice. Kick a football around.'

'They'll enjoy that.'

Claire felt the luxury of a free morning stretched ahead of her.

'You look tired. I hope you're going to get a bit of rest rather than doing work,' said Chris, looking at her pointedly. 'I meant what I said last night – all these late nights – they're starting to take a toll.'

On you or me?

'You're right,' said Claire instead hoping he would let the matter drop. 'I might go back to bed for an hour.'

'What's keeping you so busy?' asked Chris.

'We just have a lot of cases on at the moment. And with Donald away, we're also carrying his work as well.' Donald was one of the senior partners but his wife had fallen ill unexpectedly. 'I don't know how long he'll be off for. We're hoping to get an update on Monday from him. It's a tricky one – we don't want to push him with Vera being so ill.'

'No, of course not,' replied Chris. 'What cases are you working on?'

'A big fraud case,' answered Claire, feeling pleased he'd asked. 'A couple of thefts as well but I'm also overseeing some of Donald's work and then there's the rape case...'

'Rape?' queried Chris.

Claire immediately wanted to kick herself.

'Yes, but I'm just helping out on that one – not leading it,' replied Claire. 'Anyway—'

Chris looked at her, eyebrows raised in surprise.

'Rape? Are you kidding, Claire? After everything you went through?'

'I know, I know. I declined it at first but then Julia...' She trailed off, immediately regretting bringing her into the conversation. While always polite to each other, Chris and Julia had never really hit it off as she'd hoped.

'Julia what?' asked Chris, eyes narrowing.

'Nothing. Like I said, I'm just the face of it – nothing more than that. Chloe is handling it mainly and I'm just there to support,' replied Claire firmly. She needed another cup of coffee.

'Claire, are you sure that's such a good idea?'

'It's fine. I'm fine,' said Claire, getting up. 'Now I'm going to tackle the kitchen and get some toast. Do you want anything?'

Chris didn't reply but she could feel his eyes boring into her back and knew she should never have mentioned the Rose Aiker case.

9

'Hi! Come in, come in,' greeted Linda, opening the front door wide. Even though it was a weekend, Linda was again beautifully made-up. Luke came charging down the hallway.

'Jaaaammiiiieeeee,' he shouted, clearly thrilled to see his friend on a Sunday morning outside of school. Luke was wearing a pirate outfit, the eye patch skewed on his face. Linda smiled. 'He's been excited all morning.'

Claire grinned as the two boys ran off. 'I hope they don't destroy your house! It's beautiful by the way,' she complimented, looking around.

'Thank you! Yes, we're very happy here. Don't worry, the playroom's in the back and there's loads of toys – they'll be happy for hours. Well, twenty minutes at least!' Linda laughed.

'Thanks for inviting us over,' said Claire as she followed Linda into the kitchen.

'It's a pleasure. Ian works away a lot so it's nice to have the company. I hope I haven't interrupted any family time.'

Claire thought of Chris at the dining table, hunched over his laptop and Joshua, still asleep when she left.

'No, not at all,' said Claire. 'Oh, this looks lovely,' she added catching sight of the dining table. 'Croissants, fruit salad, pancakes... Where do you find the time?'

'Well, weekdays are so busy – trust me – it's literally a bowl of cereal shoved down Luke's throat, so I do try and make a bit of an effort on the weekends,' replied Linda.

'Well, it looks great.'

'Thanks – sit down and I'll get you some coffee,' said Linda, before walking through to what Claire guessed was the playroom.

'Boys! Are you hungry?' Linda's question was answered by a thunder of footsteps as the boys ran into the kitchen. Claire hoped Jamie wasn't going to be difficult about the food. He could be a fussy eater when he felt like it.

'Jamie,' coaxed Claire. 'Come and look at this spread! There's even pancakes!'

Jamie peered cautiously over the table before tentatively raising a hand to touch the food. Claire knew it could go either way. He would either eat everything or refuse to even sit at the table.

'Why don't you come and sit next to me and then you can see everything?' added Claire temptingly. She picked up a strawberry and popped it in her mouth, looking anywhere except at her son in order to give the impression that she really didn't care either way whether he sat down or not. Out of the corner of her eye, she saw Jamie clamber up on to the chair and Claire silently congratulated herself.

'Boys, would you like some orange juice?' asked Linda.

'Yes please, Mummy,' replied Luke.

'Jamie, would you like some juice as well?' prodded Claire.
'Yes, please,' he said.

Claire was impressed. She had been working on getting Jamie to say please and thank you since what seemed like forever.

'Right then,' said Linda, bringing the drinks, including Claire's coffee, and sitting at the table. 'I think we're all set. Tuck in, everyone.'

Everyone started eating, even Jamie, and after a few mouthfuls Claire could see why. The food was delicious.

'So, how have your first few weeks back at work been?' asked Linda.

'It's been great,' said Claire, automatically. She paused. 'For the most part anyway – you know how it is!'

'I do indeed,' replied Linda ruefully. 'It's exhausting sometimes, isn't it, trying to be everything to everybody.' Linda leant in conspiratorially, keeping her voice low so the boys couldn't hear although they were so engrossed with their sword fight using their forks that Claire doubted they were paying any attention. 'And you know what, I'm actually glad sometimes that Ian does work away so much.'

Claire tried to keep her face expressionless and nodded noncommittally, but the surprise must have shown on her face.

'Oh, not because I don't love him, or anything like that,' backtracked Linda. 'Just because I'm so exhausted in the evenings, I don't have anything left to give. It's quite nice to just do what I want in the evenings.'

Claire thought about the night before, Jamie refusing to go to bed, Joshua egging him on, and Chris's eyes locked on the TV studiously ignoring them, forcing Claire to intervene.

It had been almost ten o'clock when she managed to get a minute to herself.

'I can only imagine. I barely have time for myself these days and when I do, I'm too shattered to do anything!'

'Exactly,' replied Linda. 'And I only have one child! You have an older son as well, don't you?'

Claire nodded. She must have mentioned Joshua when they'd first met in the playground.

'How old is he?' asked Linda.

'Seventeen. He'll be taking his A-level exams next year.'

'You do have a lot on. Is it stressful with the exams coming up?'

'Oh, he's fine,' replied Claire. 'Joshua is one of those kids who sort of sails through life, very easy-going, nothing is too much trouble.'

Claire wondered if it sounded like she was boasting, so she quickly added, 'Although we did have a rough few months with him last year. Plus, he sleeps all the time!'

Linda laughed. 'You know, I'm actually looking forward to Luke's teenage years – I might be able to get a bit of a lie-in then!'

Claire chuckled too, warming to her new friend. It was nice to meet someone who understood what it was like to be a full-time working mum and it was great that she lived so close – just a ten-minute walk away. Claire adored Julia – they'd been best friends since they'd met at JWTS; she was her one constant, but their lifestyles were very different. Julia was single, having gotten divorced a few years ago. It had been a difficult time for her friend but looking back, it had been the making of her. Perhaps the constraints of marriage just didn't suit some people.

Julia lived life to the full. She put so much of her energy into their business and was a massive part of its success – much more than Claire if she was being honest with herself. Julia also had an extensive social life and knew anyone and everyone in Manchester. She networked regularly, bringing in much of the business and was the face of the firm from a PR perspective. Claire knew she was lucky to have such a dynamic business partner and while she adored her family, she did feel the occasional blast of envy at Julia's carefree lifestyle. She wondered if Julia felt the same envy when she came over to Claire's house for a meal, especially during times like Christmas. Somehow, she didn't think so.

'So, what exactly do you do for the bank?' asked Claire. The boys, bored of their sword fight, were starting to fidget.

'Mummy, can I get down?' interrupted Jamie.

'Have you finished your breakfast?'

'Yes.'

Claire looked at his plate and was surprised to see it empty. 'Well done for eating everything up! Can you say thank you to Linda for making you such a delicious breakfast?'

'Thank you,' replied Jamie automatically, already getting down from the chair.

'Just a minute, Jamie, let's wait for Luke to finish as well,' replied Claire.

Seeing Luke still chewing his food, she hoped Jamie would be patient. Turning back to Linda, she was relieved to see Jamie start helping himself to some more strawberries.

'I'm VP for the investment banking division,' replied Linda. 'Our head office is in Manchester.'

Claire felt slightly taken aback and then chided herself. She had automatically stereotyped Linda the morning they'd met at the school, thinking that she worked in the bank itself, perhaps as a cashier or a floor manager.

'Wow, that sounds exciting – and stressful,' replied Claire, impressed.

'Mummy, can me and Jamie go and play?' asked Luke.

'Yes, just take your plate and put it in the sink and off you go,' said his mother.

Claire watched as Luke carried his own plate and put it in the kitchen. She was forever clearing up plates and cups from Joshua's room and he was seventeen! Jamie jumped down from the chair as well and although he didn't take his plate to the kitchen sink, he did take his cup and Claire gave him a wink of gratitude.

'It is a bit stressful,' replied Linda, watching the boys run off, 'but I love it. I took a year off when Luke was born but apart from that I've always worked. I can't imagine doing anything else – as much I love being a mum, I think I would struggle to do it full-time.'

Linda paused, taking a sip of coffee. 'You know that's the first time I've ever admitted that out loud.'

'What?'

'That I wouldn't like to be a full-time mother.'

'It's strange isn't it, how we are supposed to be programmed to just love motherhood,' acknowledged Claire. 'Even though I only went back to work part-time after each of my sons was born, I still felt so judged, you know? Even by my own family!'

What was she doing? She never talked about this stuff.

Linda looked Claire straight in the eye. 'Well, fuck 'em!'

The expletive was such a shock coming out of Linda's mouth that Claire began to laugh.

'Fuck 'em all! You know what one mother said to me at the school gates the other day?' said Linda. 'She said, "Oh, Linda, how nice to see you! If you can spare a minute away from your mobile, I'd love a quick word." What the...?!'

'Let me guess – that was Tate's mum. Tall, thin, always in her gym gear?'

'Yep, that's the one. Know her?'

'Only in so far as she seems to be the queen of the school gates,' said Claire. 'I do my utmost to avoid her at drop-off. A quick "hi" and I'm done.'

'I should have guessed. She tried to rope me into helping out on the PTA. I told her I'd think about it.' Linda rolled her eyes.

'I've done quite a lot over the years, what with Joshua going to the same school and even after he left. But when Jamie started, I told myself no more.'

'I don't blame you – it's the last thing I need, but I do feel I should do it especially as we're quite new to the area.'

'Oh really? Where were you before Castlefield?'

'Well, we lived in central Manchester, but it wasn't ideal with a small child. We had to make the move to the suburbs at some point!'

'Do you like it?'

'I do but sometimes I find it all a bit provincial. I miss the anonymity of the city. How about you?'

'I've pretty much lived here all my life,' said Claire. 'I went to university in Manchester and Chris and I lived in the city for a while, but then we had kids, and you know, like you, we decided to move a bit further out and commute in.'

'So, you must know everyone around here, then?' asked Linda.

'Most people,' acknowledged Claire. 'It's a nice town although everyone does like to know everyone's business.'

I would know all about that.

'Really? Like who?' asked Linda, clearly curious.

'Oh, you know, you'll see them at the school gates. Sheena – have you met her yet? She's Annabelle's mum – be careful what you say to her because she loves a good gossip. And Tamara will always try and rope you into having her twins over to your house but never inviting your child – at one point, I was pretty much her permanent babysitter!'

Linda laughed. 'Thanks for the warning! To be honest, I haven't had time to meet anyone. Luke's nanny Lena picks him up and drops him off most days.'

'Yes, I think I've seen her a few times – she looks nice.'

'She's brilliant,' said Linda. 'I honestly don't know what I'd do without her during the week!'

'Well, she can handle the school gate mums then!' Claire laughed.

'Yeah, Lena doesn't take crap from anyone – especially Luke! I give her full credit for Luke's behaviour and manners.'

'You've both done a great job,' said Claire, feeling, for the first time, Linda needed some reassurance. 'He's a lovely little boy. Jamie talks about him all the time.'

'Thanks – and likewise. It's not easy is it, this parenting thing.'

'No, it's not and the worst thing is nobody warns you!'

'Well, cheers to us,' said Linda, raising her coffee cup in a mock toast.

'Absolutely,' joined Claire.

It was several hours later when Claire left Linda's. Breakfast had turned into lunch and the two women had chatted pretty much non-stop. Claire usually disliked playdates. Women forced to make conversation when the only thing they had in common was their offspring.

But Linda seemed different. She was proud of her career ambition and yes, Claire could see that her new friend felt guilty occasionally but ultimately, Linda knew that being a working mum was the right decision for her. Unlike Claire, there was no doubt in Linda's mind and Claire could see it sent a confident message to her son. It still amazed Claire just how much young children picked up in terms of their parents' feelings. She knew Jamie could sense immediately if she was stressed or feeling impatient. She'd also seen him play up occasionally if he saw her going to work and he knew exactly how to manipulate her. It worked every time.

As she walked home hand in hand with Jamie, Claire vowed to be more confident in her decision to go back to work, both with her children and her family. Chris hadn't stuck to his promise of trying to be home earlier or helping out a bit more. And while Lucy was there to do it all, she would have preferred if Chris had made more of an effort. It was important for the boys to have their father around more. If anything, he seemed to be working later and travelling even more since she went back to work. Probably because he knew Lucy was there, thought Claire.

As Jamie chatted beside her, she made a mental note to message Linda the details of the next night out she had planned with Julia and her friends, most of whom were from her university days. While many had moved away, there were still a few who lived in and around Manchester. Each month, there were anything between six and ten of them who went out for an evening of drinks in town. Occasionally, if the mood was high, a few of them might go out to a nightclub, but as the years had passed by, they were now more likely to go to a quiet wine bar where they could talk rather than a pub with live music like they used to.

Claire was glad that she'd kept up with them all. It was mainly Julia who had encouraged her to attend regularly, especially when the boys had been very small and all she'd wanted to do was curl up in bed. They were fun nights out and Claire looked forward to them. As Linda was new to the area and they'd got on so well, it felt right to invite her, and she'd even offered for Luke to sleepover and Chris would babysit so that Linda could have a lie-in the next day. Yes, as soon as she got home, she would send Linda a thank you message along with the details of the get-together the following week.

10

'So, how's Dad?' asked Claire, desperate to change the subject. It was Sunday afternoon and Chris had taken the boys out to the park. She was supposed to be doing some work, but the phone had rung.

'He's fine, love, you know your father. But I have to say, he's also very worried about this whole situation, Claire, as am I.'

Claire hoped her sigh wasn't audible down the phone. They'd been at it for almost twenty minutes now and no amount of reassurance seemed to soothe her mother's anxiety about her working on a rape case.

'The fact that Chris told me shows just how worried he is about this, Claire.'

Chris told you?

Claire felt the anger surge through her. 'We don't want you to have another turn, that's all,' continued her mother.

Claire closed her eyes at her mother's antiquated language. *Another turn? It's called a nervous breakdown, Mother!*

'I know, I know,' pacified Claire, 'but I promise you I'm barely involved in it.'

'Well, that's what Chris said,' acknowledged her mother, 'but you know he already thinks you're overdoing it at the office.'

Damn Chris for dragging her mother into this.

'Why? What else did he say?' quizzed Claire.

'Nothing, nothing, love, just that you'd had a few late nights, that's all.'

'And what about all *his* late nights?' countered Claire, no longer able to restrain herself. She knew she sounded like a petulant child, but she didn't care. Neither her mother nor Chris had truly supported her going back to her career full-time. Of course, they'd made all the right noises, said all the right things and so on, but deep down she knew what they really thought.

'He's just worried, that's all. He didn't mention any details of the case, just that it might bring back some difficult memories and he wanted me to be aware of it so I could support you if need be.'

More like give me a hard time about it.

'How thoughtful of him,' murmured Claire but the sarcasm was lost on her mother.

'Is it worth arranging another appointment with... you know who?'

Oh for goodness' sake!

'You mean my therapist, Mum,' replied Claire pointedly, willing her to say it.

'Yes, yes,' she replied hurriedly. 'Anyway, will you make an appointment while this case is ongoing? It would put my mind at ease. And your father's,' she added after a fraction of a second.

Smart move bringing Dad into it.

'It really isn't necessary, Mum, but being as everyone is so concerned about me working on this case, I'll make an appointment.'

'Thank you, dear, I'll sleep better for it.'

Well as long as you're all right...

Claire heard the front door slam. Chris, Jamie and Joshua were back. She'd been seething since she'd got off the phone from her mother and not even her work could distract her.

'Hi!' greeted Claire as she watched them troop into the living room. 'Joshua, can you take Jamie to wash his hands?'

'Nooooo,' cried Jamie immediately.

'Come on, little man, you're filthy!' said Joshua. He chased Jamie up the stairs making it into a game.

'Chris! What the hell have you been saying to my mother!' hissed Claire once the boys were out of earshot.

'Nothing!' he quickly responded. He looked at her, eyes wide, innocent, and for a moment he reminded her of Jamie when he'd snuck a chocolate biscuit.

'Really? Because she's been on the phone to me and because of your *concern* is now wanting me to see Dr Kingston again. So, thanks for that.'

'She called me to see how Lucy was getting on,' admitted Chris. 'I may have mentioned this case you're working on.' The fact that he had the decency to look somewhat ashamed mollified Claire's anger. But then he turned. 'Can you blame me, though? I can't believe you're not taking this seriously, Claire. It's going to trigger some horrible memories and what happens if you have another breakdown? Then what?'

He was pacing, his agitation visible.

'Shush! I don't want the boys to hear!'

'Why did you take the case on, then?' His voice was lowered but hardened. 'Isn't it enough that we have to deal with you going back to work?'

Finally – we get to the real problem.

'What do you mean, *we* have to *deal* with it,' retorted Claire. '*You* don't have to deal with anything! As usual, it's all me – I'm the one who now works full-time and deals with everything at home!'

'You're joking!' Chris laughed, sarcastically. 'Lucy does everything!'

'Who do you think tells Lucy what to do?' Claire's voice was escalating now but she didn't care. She was fed up of being the one to think of everything. To do everything. During the weekends when Lucy was off, who was the one cleaning and washing? She was. Of course, Chris would never think to clean up after himself. Chris was happy for her to go back to work just as long as it fit in with his life. Well, she was tired of fitting in. They stared at each other, both shocked at Claire's raised voice and for moment, amongst her anger, she felt a pinprick of anxiety. But then she didn't care any more.

'Your meal – which *I've* made for you – is in the oven – you can serve yourself and the boys. I'm going for a lie-down.' She turned on her heels and marched upstairs and only when she was alone in the bedroom with the door firmly closed did she let the tears flow.

★

Claire woke an hour later, disorientated. It was only when she felt Chris's lips on her forehead that she remembered their argument. In the dim evening light, she saw her husband's outline. He sat down on the bed and she inched her body back slightly to make room for him.

'I'm sorry, I'm an idiot,' he started. 'I shouldn't have told your mother. She called me, I was in the middle of something, I wasn't thinking...' He trailed off.

Claire pulled herself up. Chris handed her the cup.

'Here, I made you some tea,' he said needlessly.

'Thanks,' murmured Claire, forcing herself awake.

'Do you forgive me?' said Chris and for the second time she was reminded of a little boy with his hand caught in the cookie jar. Sipping her tea, she didn't reply straight away. She looked at Chris and saw, like always, that he believed he simply had to apologise, and everything would be forgotten. Things would just go back to the way they were. Claire knew that if they were going to work as a family, Chris needed to support her career now as much as she'd supported his.

'Will you help me a bit more in going back to work?' she asked now.

'I do—'

'Don't just pay it lip service,' she interrupted. 'But really support me – like no more complaining if I'm late. Like working together to look after the boys. You can't just be a weekend parent any more, Chris.'

'I know, I know. I'm sorry I've been so difficult. It's just taking me a while to get used to it. Lucy's great and everything but...'

'But what?' asked Claire.

'Well, I like to come home and see you, not Lucy,' he replied.

Claire felt herself thawing. 'I know,' she said, softly. 'But it won't be late nights forever – just while I get my feet back under the table, okay?'

'Okay,' agreed Chris. 'But will you please consider dropping this rape case? I'm really worried about it, you know. I just don't want you to have another breakdown like last time.'

'I know, and I appreciate that. But I've agreed to it now. My involvement is so minimal though, so you really don't need to worry.'

'You sure?'

'I'm sure,' replied Claire.

Chris nodded and took the cup from her. He put his arms around her and her body responded, relieved that they'd sorted things out. He released her and lay down next to her on the bed, intertwining his fingers in hers.

'Where are the boys?' she asked.

'Downstairs watching TV.'

'I thought the house seemed quiet. Did you have a nice time?'

'Yes, we did. We had a right laugh. It's great to see Joshua back to his normal self again…'

Claire thought back to the period last year, which she now referred to as Joshua's *going off the rails* phase.

'Yeah me too – I wouldn't want to go through that again,' said Claire. 'I'm still trying to keep a close eye on him though, as is Lucy, especially with his A levels coming up.'

'Yeah, good idea,' said Chris. 'I guess it's going to be quite a stressful year for him.'

'What time is it? Why don't we all go to the cinema tonight,' suggested Claire, 'instead of our usual film night at home? Next Saturday, remember I'll be out with the girls so I won't be able to do join you then. And don't forget Luke is doing a sleepover that night as well.'

'Luke?' asked Chris.

'Yes, remember? I told you about him. Jamie's friend at school. His mum is Linda, also a working mum so I asked her to join us for our girls' night out. Her husband works away a lot so I told her she could drop Luke off at our house and sleep over, so she doesn't need to get a babysitter and she can have a bit of a lie-in the morning after.'

'Okay, no problem,' said Chris. 'It'll keep Jamie occupied for a bit anyway.'

'So, shall I check the film timings for tonight?' asked Claire getting out of bed.

'Hey, where are you going?' replied Chris, reaching for her.

'I think I've spent enough time in bed today!'

'Never! It's too late for the cinema now anyway. The boys are already watching a film downstairs, which means...' said Chris and as he pulled her towards him, Claire sank into his arms, their lips meeting, their argument forgotten.

I I

'Your eleven o'clock is here, Claire,' announced Elaine down the phone.

Claire checked her watch. Fifteen minutes early.

'Thanks, Elaine – can you let Greg and Chloe know? And show Rose through to the meeting room at eleven.'

'Will do.'

Claire had been reading a message from Linda, which she'd sent the day before about their night out the previous Saturday.

> Thanks so much for inviting me! It's great having a social life again ☺ It was nice to meet your husband, albeit briefly, and please tell Joshua thank you for babysitting!

Unfortunately, Claire hadn't enjoyed the night out as much as Linda because at the last minute, Chris had roped Joshua into babysitting for the two boys while Chris went out. Claire had tried to tell herself it wasn't a big deal and she knew rationally that it wasn't. It was just the fact that Chris had committed to doing something and then done a U-turn so he could meet his colleague Andy for a drink.

'He's going through a rough time, Claire, and I said I'd meet up with him for swift pint,' Chris had explained. 'Joshua will keep an eye over everything for a few hours, won't you, mate?'

Claire had then had to tell Linda about the change in plan, that it would be Joshua not Chris looking after the boys. Linda had been fine with it but still. She'd had to let it pass, but later that evening as she'd stood in the wine bar with Linda and Julia and the rest of her friends, she'd felt irritated.

Turning her attention back to her upcoming meeting, Claire picked up the Rose Aiker file. She'd reread it earlier that morning when she'd come into the office. Chris, true to his word, had agreed to drop Jamie off at school three mornings a week, which meant she could get into the office earlier on those days. Despite not being a morning person, she liked to get a head start on the day. Waking up was tough, but once she was out of bed and in the shower, it was all downhill from there.

There was something so secretly satisfying about being the only one in the office. The quiet – if you took a moment to appreciate it – was bliss and she liked to pick up a coffee from the local deli downstairs on her way up. Yes, she could make one in the office, but she liked a little reward for getting in so early. Take-away coffee in hand, she'd finished reading the updated Aiker file at her desk first thing and somehow the professional environment of her office had helped Claire focus on the job at hand rather than her memories.

Besides, it was years ago and Paul is long gone.

She felt confident and in control. At such moments, Claire could believe that her past hadn't actually happened, that it had affected someone else or it was a story she'd read in the newspaper. In fact, months could go by and she wouldn't even think about him. But occasionally something would remind her – usually something small, like seeing a group of high-school boys walking home or something on TV – and she'd be back there, in that musty drama room, him on top of her. As she pulled the file towards her ready to go to the meeting room, a page fell out and she picked it up. She glanced over it again, like a child picking a scab.

Section 5, transcript 2 of case file TD / 08 / 67 / 3876

'Can you tell me what the other man did, Rose?'

'I'm not sure...'

'I know it must be difficult. But anything you can share now can help us find these men and stop them doing it to anyone else. Can you help us, Rose?'

'Okay, I'll try.'

'Well done, Rose, you're doing really well. Take a deep breath first...'

[Muffled crying]

'It was still darkish although I remember there was a torch – I think it was a torch from a phone and it was shining on me.'

'On you?'

'Yes, on my face. And after... after the man... then on my body.'

'What happened after the first man, Rose? Can you tell me?'

'His mate came and lay on top of me then. He was heavier than the first one and he'd removed his cap.'

'Did you manage to see his face? Do you think you could identify him?'

'Yes.'

'Did he rape you, Rose?'

'Yes.' [Victim is crying.]

'What happened after that?'

'Then I heard...' [Victim is still crying.]

'It's okay, Rose, take your time, you're doing really well.'

'I heard one of them say, "How much time do we have? We should go." And then someone else replied, "Don't be stupid, we just got here." I think one of them lit a cigarette then – I could smell smoke. I was still lying on the floor and I tried to sit up but one of them told me not to move. I felt sick and dizzy, so I lay back down. I don't know how long I lay there, maybe half an hour. During that time, they didn't talk very much, just sort of stood around. Maybe one of them went out for a bit. I heard the door open and close. But then one of them said, "Right, I'm going again."'

'And what did you do?'

'I prayed.'

Rose Aiker was standing at the window, stock still, looking at the view when Claire saw her through the glass door of the meeting room. Manchester was not at its best. The late October sky threatened rain and the grimy buildings of the city were a dirty red against the grey clouds. Before pushing the door open, Claire took a moment to scrutinise Rose's profile. It had been almost a month since Claire had met her for the first time and again Claire was struck by the nineteen-year-old beauty. Long almost-black hair hung around her shoulders, but it was her face that enticed a second look with beautiful blue eyes, high cheekbones, and a generous mouth. Curvaceous and dark, she was pretty. Very pretty.

Rose looked up expectantly when she heard Claire enter the room.

'Rose, hello, nice to see you again,' said Claire politely holding out her hand.

'Finally,' replied Rose, her large blue eyes never leaving Claire's face.

'I understand you talked to Julia again to request my representation despite advice at our initial meeting,' replied Claire. *May as well get to the bottom of this.*

Rose paused before answering. 'Yes, I did.'

'May I ask why?' asked Claire, although she knew the answer, but there was always hope.

'As I said, you came recommended,' replied Rose mysteriously, not giving anything away.

'By whom?' replied Claire.

'A friend. They said they thought you might be able to understand more.'

'Shall we sit down?' replied Claire, indicating towards the table and chairs. Without waiting for a response, Claire sat and busied herself with the file. 'Greg and Chloe won't be a moment.'

Wherever she went, this nightmare would follow her. It was hardly a secret though – Charlotte had made sure of that when she told the rest of the girls and then the whole school knew. And then everyone's parents knew along with most of Castlefield.

Breathe.

After a few moments, Claire felt calmer and she looked up at Rose who was now sat opposite her.

'Well, as it's already been mentioned several times, I don't usually handle such cases but here's what we're going to do: Greg and Chloe will represent you, but I will be here to help with your testimony.'

'Will you be in court with me?' asked Rose.

'Yes.'

'Will you be in the meetings here with me?'

'Yes.'

'Okay,' replied Rose, seeming satisfied. She smiled then and Claire saw something in the young girl's eyes. Bravery? Yes, but there was something else.

Just at that moment, Greg and Chloe came in, Chloe in front, all warm and friendly. Her primary job was to focus on Rose, make sure she was prepped and ready for what would be, Claire knew, a horrendous ordeal ahead of her. It was one of the reasons so many victims didn't want to go to trial. Having to relive the experience, come face to face with their attacker, and often all for nothing – less than a third of young men prosecuted for rape were convicted.

'Right, Rose, nice to see you again. We've already done a lot of good work but there's still more to do. Are you ready to begin?' asked Chloe, after all the greetings were made and she had settled herself next to Rose. Greg had taken a seat opposite.

'So, in today's session,' continued Chloe, 'we'll continue with all the work we have done so far. You're doing great, Rose, but it is going to get harder. Both Greg and I have tried similar cases before so I need you to keep that in mind as we move through this. I know at times, it's going to be very difficult and there might be days where you wonder how you will keep going. But any time you feel like that Rose, let us know and we'll do everything we can to help, okay?'

Rose glanced at Claire before nodding again, and Claire wondered if the young girl sat before her really knew what lay ahead of her. Perhaps she thought that after her ordeal the worst was over? But as Claire listened to the proceedings, it was hard to stop her own memories and as the case unfolded, Claire was reminded of her own past.

SEPTEMBER 1989

12

Her mum had left it on her bed, the large GO SPORT carrier bag concealing its contents. Claire had pounced on it, desperate to see what was hidden beneath the layers of tissue and plastic and as she caught a glimpse of grey and mint green, she couldn't help but let out a shriek of delight.

'I thought you might like it,' said her mum, coming into the bedroom.

Claire ran towards her, her arms outstretched for a hug in a rare display of affection.

'How did you find it?' she asked in disbelief. 'Not even Charlotte has this bag and she has everything!'

'I have my ways.' Her mum smiled and at that moment, Claire thought she had the best mum in the world.

'I have to pack it!' she cried excitedly, her hands pulling the bag out. She looked at it for a few moments, admiring the gold zips in the shape of the HEAD logo. With its detachable side pocket and lock and key, it was the only thing she'd wanted for her final year at school. The girls would be so jealous!

Opening the main compartment, she carefully placed her new pencil case and gym kit inside. Holding the strap, she slipped it over her shoulder and admired herself in the mirror. If this didn't seal the deal to get into the Queen Bees, the exclusive secret club run by popular Charlotte Jarvis, she didn't know what would. Well, she would find out soon enough. Tomorrow was the first day of school after the summer holidays and she couldn't wait to show off her new bag.

Claire applied her Body Shop lip balm in the girls' bathroom. Kiwi-fruit-flavoured. Gross. She hated it but all the girls had it, so she did too. She had about five minutes before the bell went and she smiled to herself with satisfaction. What a great first day back it had been so far. She'd been right about her new school bag – the girls had crowded around her admiring it and demanding to know where she had bought it. She'd been as mysterious as her mother the day before and it had worked like a charm.

'You're an absolute shoo-in now,' whispered Anne, her best friend. Anne Nicholl had been inducted into the Queen Bees last term just before school had broken up for the summer and while she'd been pleased for her friend, she'd had to work hard to supress the jealousy that it hadn't been her.

But today was her day. Claire was sure of it. Just one more class to go and then she would be inducted. That morning, as the girls had marvelled over her new purchase,

Charlotte had entered the cloak room followed by what Claire silently nicknamed her faithful three – Tiffany, Louise, and Vivian. The group surrounding Claire had parted to let Charlotte through. The two girls had eyed each other before Charlotte spoke.

'Hey, Claire… how was your summer? Been shopping I see?' Charlotte eyed the bag appreciatively before turning slightly and Claire saw Charlotte carrying a lilac and white version of the sports bag. But then with glee Claire had noticed it didn't have the detachable section like hers did.

'It was good thanks, how about you?' Claire answered hoping her own larger version wouldn't work against her before adding, 'Loving the colour of your bag.'

'We're like twin sisters,' replied Charlotte, acknowledging the compliment with a smile and Claire had felt relief at the approval.

'Let's meet in the drama room after school,' Charlotte had said before turning to the rest of the group. 'I think we're ready for a new member!'

Claire's heart had soared – she was in!

And now as she combed her long blonde hair and adjusted her navy-blue skirt, so it was just the right length, she knew she was going to be the best Queen Bee member Charlotte had ever seen.

'Open your books to page fifteen and we'll start from there. Right, who would like to read the part of Helena?' asked Mrs Matthews, her long beads jostling around her neck as she walked around the classroom. Normally, Claire would jump at the chance. Not only did she look the part of the main character, Helena, from *A Midsummer's Night Dream* with her tall figure and long blonde hair, but she was a good reader too – clear and confident. English was one of her favourite subjects, but today the lesson dragged, and Claire found herself daydreaming, her mind too preoccupied with her Queen Bee induction after school.

Charlotte had been the one to set up the Queen Bees the year before in their fourth year of senior school and at the time Claire hadn't thought much of it. It had started with a few whisperings between Charlotte and her Faithful Three and then they'd invited Emma and Janet and then Rachel and Nicola and before she knew it, the group of fifteen girls, who had all grown up together in Castlefield and had promised to never let anything come between them, was divided in two. And the Queen Bees were clearly having more fun.

They had gate-crashed the sixth-form social and had spent the evening drinking and dancing. It was even rumoured that Charlotte had snogged Stuart Cooper. Another time, the Queen Bees had gone on a shopping trip to Manchester and then watched The Stone Roses in concert. There were private gatherings at Charlotte's house and secret letters passed in class. They even all had the same charm bracelets – flashes of secret silver that were hidden under the sleeves of their school jumpers.

As the club grew by invitation only, every girl wanted to join and not just from their class either. The stories about the Queen Bees had spread to the rest of their year group and there was even a rumour that Charlotte had a waiting list. And then Anne had been invited to join and Claire, who had been happy enough with her best friend and studies, knew that she would do anything to be a part of the Queen Bees.

Claire checked her watch: 3.55 p.m. She'd been here since half past three and was starting to wonder if she was in the right classroom. Drama room three. It was more of a storeroom than anything else, tucked away at the end of the corridor. But then she heard a burst of laugher from the corridor and quickly picked up her Just Seventeen magazine and started to flick through it.

'Claire, hi! You made it! You ready?' Claire looked at Charlotte as she got down from the desk she'd been perched on. With her permed blonde hair and slightly oily skin, Charlotte wasn't the prettiest girl in their year but there was an aura about her, a confidence that attracted boys and girls alike.

'Yep! Can't wait!'

'Good – us neither!' Charlotte smiled at the group of girls around her and suddenly Claire felt uneasy. She tried to catch Anne's eye, but her best friend was watching Charlotte.

'Tiffany, close the door, would you? We don't want anyone to hear us,' ordered Charlotte. 'Helen, Emma, start putting the chairs in a semi-circle.'

The girls moved to do their jobs and Claire envied the way Charlotte dominated the room.

Claire felt a thrill go through her – she'd waited a long time for this and she couldn't wait to wear her bracelet.

As the girls began to sit down, Claire felt uncertain. What was she supposed to do? Charlotte remained standing at the open end of the semi-circle and indicated for Claire to stand opposite her. Suddenly, the hum of activity stopped, and the room went quiet.

'Claire Sharpe, are you ready to become a member of the Queen Bees?' asked Charlotte, her face solemn.

'Yes,' replied Claire.

'Are you willing to follow the Queen Bee rules and obey all orders as directed by the Queen Bee guidelines?'

'Yes,' replied Claire. She was tempted to ask what the rules and orders would be but thought better of it. She could always ask Anne later.

'Are you ready to accept your final challenge in order to secure your place as a Queen Bee?'

Claire paused. *What challenge? Anne had never said anything about a challenge when she'd got inducted.*

Charlotte's eyebrows went up a fraction, impatient for her answer.

'Wh-what challenge?' asked Claire.

'The Queen Bees only accept yes or no answers,' announced Charlotte.

Of course, she knew that – Anne had told her that in advance. But why hadn't she mentioned anything about a challenge?

'Again – are you ready to accept your final challenge in order to secure your place as a Queen Bee?'

'Yes,' replied Claire firmly. Surely, it couldn't be that bad.

'Very good.' Charlotte turned to pick up a plastic bowl that Vivian held out to her, which contained several folded-up pieces of paper. 'Anne, as Claire's nominator, could you please pick her a challenge from the bowl?'

The room was silent in anticipation as Anne swirled her hand in the bowl, and Claire watched as her fingers clutched a piece of paper and handed it to Charlotte's outstretched hand. She read it, before grinning, and put it in her shirt pocket.

'So,' announced Charlotte to the group. The girls looked up at her, expectant. 'The challenge is this: you have to ask, and go on a date with…'

Charlotte paused dramatically, the tension in the room palpable.

'…PAUL JONES!'

There was a brief moment of silence before the room exploded into laughter. Charlotte indulged them for a minute before holding up her hand for silence.

'You have a week to ask him and go out with him…' More sniggers. 'Annnnnddddd,' drawled Charlotte, 'you have to kiss!'

The girls shrieked so loudly Claire felt herself smiling in response.

Go out with the school swot? Well, that wasn't too bad. She would ask Paul to go to the pictures with her, one kiss in the dark and that would be that. Sorted. She would ask him tomorrow.

'And then… welcome to the Queen Bees, my friend!' finished Charlotte. The room was in uproar as everyone cheered and clapped, the light bouncing off their silver bracelets, and Claire felt herself get pulled into the energy of their group.

13

Paul kicked the stone moodily against the wall of his house thinking about his first day back at school. It had been even worse than he'd imagined. The stench of burning polyester still hung in his nostrils and Paul felt the charred residue of shame. He'd been in chemistry class when it had happened, Mr Simmons the teacher having left the room to get some more supplies.

Paul was just about to lift the test tube into the flame of a Bunsen burner when he saw the flash of school uniform move and grab him from behind. It was Dillon, one of Gavin's gang, who held him by the arms while Kev had yanked Paul's school tie and put it in the flame of the Bunsen burner, forcing Paul's face close to the open flare. He could see the electric-blue nucleus of the fire and the heat pressed horrifyingly on his eyeballs. Just before he'd squeezed his eyes shut, he watched as the burner curled the tie, a black mark spreading across the material towards him.

As Paul felt his skin start to singe, a sharp whistle signalling Mr Simmons' arrival flew across the room and Kev released him quickly, boomeranging Paul upright. He saw Barry, who must have been guarding the classroom door, Kev and Dillon run back to their workbench. Mr Simmons returned to a classroom full of studious bent heads, none the wiser. Paul had sat down on his stool, shaking. What would have happened if Simmons hadn't come back when he had? Paul felt fear crawl in his throat. None of his classmates had intervened.

Cowards.

Paul felt rage replace shame and he kicked the stone even harder, imagining it was Gavin's head. He was usually safe in the classroom as Gavin and his gang normally hassled him during the breaks or after school. It hadn't always been like this, though. There was a time when Paul had loved senior school, especially the first couple of years. But in the third year, everything changed. One minute he was everyone's mate and the next he was an outsider. It had started when the classes had been streamed into tiers based on ability. Paul had been placed in the top tier for all subjects while his friend Gavin had been placed in the lowest tier – tier three. At first, it had just been a few jibes.

Teacher's pet.

Swot.

He'd ignored it. Everyone had to put up with a bit of teasing at school. But then it started to turn nasty as Gavin and a few of his new mates from tier three had ganged up on him, kicking his shins as they passed in the corridors or following him into the bathroom during break time and emptying his rucksack all over the floor. His tier-one classmates were just happy they weren't targets and as they disassociated themselves from him, it wasn't long before Paul found himself pretty much alone.

He had one friend though: Brian Robbins who he'd met in his maths class the year before they'd been streamed into tiers. They'd been partnered together for one of the problem-solving sessions and discovered they both had a love of BMX biking. Paul had been surprised when Brian had invited him to bike with him the following Saturday morning in the woods on the outskirts of Castlefield and since then Paul and Brian met up most Saturdays in the same spot, just the two of them.

Paul couldn't imagine his life without those sessions to look forward to, especially as he and Brian only had one class together. Brian had football practice most days after school and he always seemed to have a ball in his hands. It was usually a small bouncy ball or a tennis ball that he would fling from hand to hand, almost like a tic. Tempted as Paul was to join the football team, so he didn't have to walk home alone after school, he knew he didn't have a coordinated bone in his body and would probably just invite even more ridicule. So, most afternoons, he would run home from school to the safety of his bedroom. His mum would bring him in a hot chocolate and he would immerse himself in his homework.

He knew he was intelligent – he'd been told often enough by his parents and teachers. Legend had it that when he was just a year old, he'd mastered his letters and numbers and from then on, his mother had told him every day he was a child prodigy. Paul had always loved books and read widely; it didn't matter what subject – all the subjects at school came easily to him and he was one of those rare students who actually enjoyed studying. Things made sense in the textbooks – the information was either right or wrong; there was no grey area.

But it was science that he really loved – especially biology. His dream of becoming a doctor had been resolute since he'd broken his arm last year. He'd sat in absolute agony in the hospital waiting room before being x-rayed. A nurse had taken him through to the ward and as he'd sat on the bed, his mother trying to hold his hand as if he was a three-year-old, he'd watched as the team of nurses fluttered around the ward, brisk and efficient.

He'd never been in hospital before and Paul counted five nurses in total, immediately identifying the Ward Sister. She was wearing a navy-blue uniform, unlike the others who all wore pale blue. To Paul, most of them just looked like ordinary women but there was one nurse who was very pretty. She reminded him of Cindy Crawford and Paul hoped she would be the one to deal with him. When Cindy came over to Paul's bed, all smiles and reassurances, he lay back on the pillow enjoying the attention, his throbbing arm forgotten.

But a few moments later, he felt a charge in the air and Paul opened his eyes a fraction. A man was walking towards him, his white coat and stethoscope causing Cindy to stand to attention.

'Right then, what do we have here?'

'Good morning, Doctor,' trilled Cindy. 'Possibly a broken arm. I've brought you the x-ray.'

She placed it in the light box and Paul saw the foggy outline of his forearm, the bone broken in two.

'Hmmm.' The doctor took a step closer to the light box and Cindy waited quietly by his side. Everyone was silent – even his mother, who had not stopped wittering since he'd fallen from his bike, her panic reminding him of the desperate chirps of a trapped bird.

As they all waited for the doctor to speak, he knew in that moment he wanted to be a doctor. Not because he was selfless. Not because he wanted to help people or heal children. No. He wanted to become a doctor because there was no other profession that commanded such respect and admiration. And why shouldn't he have that too. He had the brains to become a doctor and he enjoyed science. All he had to do was get through high school and one day – even if it took decades – when Gavin lay in a hospital bed, helpless and alone suffering from cancer or another hideous disease – Paul would stand over his bed in his white coat and stethoscope and both of them would know that it was Paul who now held the power.

14

At first, Claire thought Paul was going to say no to her invitation and she panicked – *that* would be even more embarrassing than having to go out with him. She could just imagine the taunts from the girls.

Claire couldn't even get swotty Paul to go out with her!

How humiliating. It was true that she hadn't actually been out with a boy before – not just the two of them anyway, like, on a proper date. She had kissed a few boys though. Her first kiss had been with John Griffith.

It was last year when she'd still been wearing her braces. There had been a party at someone's house and they'd sat in a circle playing spin the bottle. When she'd spun it and it had landed on him, he'd grinned at her, the cheers of his mates egging him on. John wasn't the best-looking boy, but he certainly wasn't the ugliest. Despite the illicit swigs of cider, she could feel her palms sweating. Surreptitiously wiping them on her jeans, she'd got up on her knees, edging her way to the centre of the circle to meet him. There was a moment of silence as they stared at each other, the ring of teenagers disappearing as they contemplated the performance ahead.

Suddenly, John had leaned in, crushing his lips firmly against her own. Instinctively, she had clamped her lips together against the persistent probe of his tongue. She felt slightly repelled, but she knew she had to satisfy the whoops and cheers, so she tentatively opened her mouth, letting him explore before pulling quickly away. Sometimes when she saw John now, he would wiggle his tongue at her, reminding Claire of a snake.

She'd found Paul in the library, engrossed in his work, sitting at a table near the librarian's desk. She was in the same classes as Paul for most subjects except French. She was in the second tier for that, the only blip on her tier-one status. She didn't care though – she hated French. All the words seemed to run together making it difficult to understand anything. Not even the school trip to Calais in the first year of senior school had warmed her to the subject. She knew Paul was one of the few students in the top tier across the board and she was secretly impressed, although she knew he got grief for it.

Pausing behind a shelf of science books, she had a few moments to watch him unseen. His strawberry blonde hair was cut close at the back and longer on top, occasionally obstructing his view of his work and he brushed it aside almost constantly. His glasses were too big for his face and his pale, slightly acned skin was saved by the bluest eyes Claire had ever seen.

He'd looked up then and she thought she saw a glimpse of fear. It was quickly replaced by curiosity when he saw it was her. As she watched the librarian leave her desk and begin returning books to their shelves, Claire approached. She didn't ask if she could join him, she simply sat opposite him and it was this assumption that she could see had made him nervous. It was the way he glanced over her shoulder to see if there was anyone else behind her, but Paul needn't have worried, the library was empty. It was the reason why she'd chosen to ask him out during the lunch break. Claire decided to get it over with as quickly as possible.

'So, I was wondering if you wanted to go to the cinema with me on Friday night? A few of us are going...'

They weren't but having discussed it endlessly with Anne the night before on the phone, Claire thought it might make him more comfortable if it was a casual invitation. She also would have made it sooner than Friday, but she knew her mother would start asking questions if she went out on a school night.

Claire waited for a response but instead he just stared at her. She decided to continue.

'I'm not sure what's playing yet, but I can let you know. It usually starts at seven thirty.'

Still no response. She watched his eyes flicker to the left and right. Claire was starting to get annoyed. No wonder the lads gave him a hard time – he couldn't even answer a simple question.

'So...?' prompted Claire.

'Errr, yes, sure,' replied Paul. As he answered, he picked up his pen and began flicking it between his fingers.

'Great!' said Claire, relieved. 'Shall I meet you outside the cinema at quarter past seven?'

Paul nodded, seemingly incapable of verbalising anything else, but a flush had started rising up his neck.

Well, she'd asked him now.

All that was left to do was go on the date, kiss him and then on Monday, she would be in the Queen Bees. She was starting to get up from the chair to leave when something in Paul's notebook caught her eye.

'You managed to work it out!' she exclaimed, her astonishment making her temporarily forget she was in a hurry to leave. 'I struggled with that question for ages and I'm still not sure my answer's right.'

Surprised, Paul looked down at his work.

'You mean question seven?'

Claire nodded.

'Yes, it's a bit of trick question,' said Paul, 'but once you work out the first part of the sum, the rest follows.'

'You got sixty-seven? I'm pretty sure that's not the answer I have.'

Claire sat back down, rifling through her bag to find her maths book, all thoughts of her Queen Bee challenge forgotten. Pushing her bag to one side, she took his pencil and started to rework the sum, oblivious to Paul watching her.

After a few minutes, she looked up. 'What?'

'Nothing!'

'No – there's something. What is it? Do I have pen on my face?'

'No!'

'Well, what is it then?'

'Nothing!'

Sighing, Claire turned back to the sum. 'How did you get sixty-seven?' she finally asked in dismay.

Paul leant towards her, turning her notebook so he could read her work. Claire could smell him, a boyish mix of shower gel and deodorant. And something sweet, like liquorice or jelly babies.

'Here,' said Paul, tapping the paper. 'You've missed the multiplication bit.'

'Multiplication? With what?'

'You need to multiply it by four.'

Claire frowned. 'Four? Not six?'

'No, four, otherwise it won't work.'

Claire pulled the notebook back towards her and reworked the sum. After a few minutes, she looked up triumphantly. 'Got it! You're brilliant!'

Their eyes met across the table, each lost in their admiration of each other although for completely different reasons.

Suddenly, a door opened, and several loud voices ruptured the quietness of the library. The intimacy was broken, and Claire quickly got up from her seat, stuffing her work back into her bag.

'Thanks a lot.'

'No problem,' replied Paul and Claire noticed he was watching the loud group of lads who had come into the library.

'Right, well, I'll see you Friday outside the cinema,' she concluded and quickly turned on her heel, without waiting for his response.

15

There had to be a catch, thought Paul, hoisting his rucksack on his shoulders, ready to leave the chemistry lab. Why would blonde, beautiful Claire Sharpe ask him to go to the cinema? Had Gavin and his mates put her up to it? Was she planning to stand him up? Or worse, would she lure him there and then they would jump out at him and beat him up?

He didn't know Claire very well but what he did know of her didn't really fit such a trick. If it was Charlotte or one of the other hoity-toity bitches, he could definitely imagine something like that happening. But Claire was different. She was popular but quiet. She didn't have to try as hard as everybody else.

Paul tried to think. It was the last class of the day and he was debating whether he should leg it home or wait for half an hour and start his homework in the relative safety of the lab. Mr Simmons had finished the class a few minutes late and Paul was nervous. He decided to wait until he was sure

Gavin and his gang were well ahead of him on the route home.

Satisfied he'd made the right decision, he pretended to do up his shoelace until the rest of the class had disappeared before taking out his books and going over the homework. But he couldn't concentrate. He thought of Claire's long blonde hair pulled into a high ponytail, revealing her beautiful face. He'd seen her in classes for years, but it was the first time she'd actually talked to him and seeing her up close was fascinating. Unlike some girls, she didn't seem to wear any make-up and her skin was clear, almost translucent. Her eyes were as blue as his. He'd noticed her small ears, pierced with studs in the shape of stars and underneath her shirt collar, he had caught a glimpse of a thin silver chain. He had turned away then, not wanting to be caught staring but he knew she'd caught him anyway.

Paul adjusted his position on the stool and attempted to refocus on his homework, trying not to think about how she'd made him feel. But it was no use. He recalled how happy she'd looked when she managed to work out the maths question; he'd wanted to kiss her then, just so he could feel her smile. Perhaps she really did want to go out with him, thought Paul, remembering how she'd told him he was brilliant. Apart from a touch of acne, he knew he wasn't the ugliest in his year.

He tried to remember if he'd ever seen Claire hanging around with Gavin or his friends. He couldn't be sure, but he didn't think so. Paul closed his textbook knowing he wouldn't get any more work done. He thought of Claire and the sliver of silver chain around her bare neck and knew with certainty that not even the thought of a beating from Gavin would stop him meeting her on Friday.

'Is that you, pet?'

Crap.

Even though Paul had closed the front door as quietly as he could, his mum had still managed to catch him.

'Yeah,' he shouted back. 'I'm going to do my homework.'

But before he got a chance to put his foot on the stairs, his mum appeared in the hallway, her hair a halo of frizz around her plump face.

'Wait! I made some cake – would you like some?'

It was impossible to ignore the desperation and Paul hated himself in that moment. He looked at his mum, her face eager, her fingers playing with the pocket of her apron. He was about to say no but he found himself pausing. Maybe it was his conversation with Claire or the fact that he'd escaped a beating on his way home from school that day, or simply because the smell of baking was so good.

'Chocolate?' he asked.

'Yep!' His mum's smile was instant, and he felt an odd mix of guilt and pity. He knew he'd become distant at home. Just a few weeks ago, he'd heard his mother trying to seek reassurance from his dad whether it was normal for a teenage boy to be so sullen and quiet.

'We used to have such a good relationship,' fretted his mum. 'Now I don't even know what's going on with him. I'm worried it's more than just teenage hormones, Bill.'

Paul hadn't stayed around to listen to his father's response. He had crept back up the stairs then, not wanting to be caught eavesdropping. His mum was right though – he had been close to his mother, telling her anything and everything. At thirteen, he'd still used to hold her hand. She had been his best friend and she always said he could talk to her but how could he tell her that the boy he grew up with – Gavin, whose parents were friends with his own – had turned half the class against him? If he told her, she would start talking to Gavin's parents, to the school and that would just make everything worse.

As Paul followed his mother into the kitchen, he noticed a can of Coke waiting for him along with a large slice of chocolate cake. He was never allowed Coke and as he sat down he saw his mum had her 'we're going to talk everything through' face on. He was beginning to regret not going straight up to his bedroom.

His mum smiled and poured the Coke into a glass while he dug into the cake, shovelling it in as quickly as possible.

'It feels like ages, Paul, since we had a catch-up!' she started, sitting opposite him. 'How's school?'

'Fine.'

'What's your new timetable like?'

'It's okay.'

'Mr Calvert for biology, isn't it? What's he like?'

'He's okay.'

'Does he give you lots of homework?'

'It's fine – manageable.'

'Of course it is, pet.'

There was a pause in the conversation and Paul slurped his drink, relishing the sweet fizz of the unexpected treat. He knew his brief responses were frustrating for his mother, but he also knew that if he started opening up to her he might never stop.

She tried again. 'How's Gavin? You never seem to mention him these days.'

Paul felt his stomach drop at the sound of his name.

'Well, we're not in the same classes any more so I don't see him that often.'

'That's a shame – shall I call Susan and see if she and Gavin want to come over?'

'Mum! I'm too old for playdates!'

'I know, I just thought it might be nice to catch up – I haven't seen Susan for ages and Gavin – well, I'm not sure I'd recognise him! Do you remember when the two of you were learning to ride your bikes?'

She laughed, a high unnatural sound and Paul knew he had to get out of there.

'Just don't, Mum. Just don't call anyone, okay?'

She looked up at the tone of his voice as he stood and the expression on her face all but broke him.

'I've got homework. Thanks for the cake.'

And with that, he fled.

16

Claire rubbed at the lipstick with a tissue in disgust, leaving her lips stained. What was she doing? She hardly ever wore make-up. Why was she making so much effort for him anyway? Claire stared at herself in the mirror. With her long blonde hair, blue eyes and a forehead she'd always thought too big, she looked the same as she always did. So why did she feel different? Was it the thought of having to kiss him?

Since the Queen Bees had given her the challenge, she'd been so relieved that it wasn't anything too horrible (she'd eventually found out that Anne had had to storm into the staffroom and scream *fire*, getting detention for a week, for her challenge). Claire hadn't really thought about the impact of her own actions. But when she remembered the look on Paul's face when she approached him in the library, she was conscious of the fact that she was *using* somebody, and it wasn't a pleasant feeling. She knew her parents would be horrified if they found out.

Oh, for goodness' sake, thought Claire crossly. It's one trip to the cinema not a marriage proposal. Paul would be fine. Afterwards, she would just tell him that while she liked him, she didn't have time for a boyfriend while preparing for her exams. Unexpectedly, Claire thought of Paul's hands as he pointed out the method in her textbook, his long fingers caressing the page.

Don't be stupid. He's the class nobody.

Impatiently, she rubbed off the rest of the lipstick and smoothed her lips with her kiwi lip balm. She debated whether to crimp her hair. She decided just to brush it, leaving it loose around her shoulders before slipping on her denim jacket. She had told her dad she would walk to the cinema and she would call him from the phone box for a lift after the film. The thought cheered Claire that in just a few hours, this stupid dare would be over and she would back to her normal life, but this time with the prestige of being in the Queen Bees. And it was then that Claire realised it wasn't having to kiss him that bothered her, it was the deceit.

The walk into town was cool but despite this, she could feel the sweat under her armpits and she was glad she'd brought her denim jacket to put over her top to hide the damp patches. She'd tried shoving tissues under her arms, but they had moved around. She had been going to wear her black lace top but had changed at the last minute because it felt too dressy for the cinema. She shoved her hands in her pockets, trying to think about anything but the upcoming evening, but as she turned the corner and saw the cinema ahead, her palms started to sweat. Would he be waiting for her? Would he even turn up? She thought of the last glance they'd shared before she'd left the library and knew instinctively that he would. As she drew closer to the building though, she couldn't see him.

Damn. There was no way she was going to get there first.

She checked her watch. She was a few minutes early. She would walk to the nearby shop and pick up some chewing gum. Confident that she wasn't about to be stood up, she turned left, away from the cinema and towards the crossing at the traffic lights. As she waited for pedestrian signal to turn green, she heard a familiar burst of laughter. Turning, she watched in dismay as she saw Charlotte, Tiffany, Louise, and Vivian walking in the direction of the cinema linking arms. There was another girl with them as well.

Was that…? No, it couldn't be.

Claire squinted. The fifth girl was on the far side but she knew it was Anne by her bouncy walk. It always made her hair jump up on her shoulders. Claire felt the dampness under her armpits again. She should have known the challenge wouldn't be so easy. What were they planning to do?

'Claire!'

Charlotte had seen her and was gesturing for her to come over.

Shit.

Claire turned away from the crossing and went to meet them. Before she was even within a few feet of them, they were whistling and catcalling and Claire knew that the evening with Paul was not something she was going to be able to do without an audience.

'Hi! What are you doing here?' Claire tried to sound casual.

'Hello! You didn't think we'd let you come on your own, did you? Swotty, snotty Paul on a date – this we have to see!' Vivian smirked, her pineapple ponytail swinging. Claire noticed that Anne at least had the decency to look embarrassed.

'Don't worry,' added Charlotte, linking arms with Claire and leading her towards the cinema. 'We'll sit right at the back, so we don't disturb you two – right, girls?' The others started making kissing noises and Claire noticed even Anne joined in.

Cow.

Reluctantly, Claire felt herself being pulled along. Would Paul be waiting for her by now? All of sudden, she wasn't sure which was worse: him not turning up or him turning up and the two of them having to endure popcorn thrown at their heads all night. But as they rounded the corner, she could see him waiting, dressed in black jeans and a Guns N' Roses T-shirt. Claire thought of her own Guns N' Roses T-shirt at home and wondered if he liked INXS as well.

'Oooh, Paul scrubs up rather well for a weirdo, doesn't he?' announced Tiffany. The others giggled, and Claire pretended to laugh.

'Right,' said Charlotte, all business. 'For every challenge, at least one founding member of the Queen Bees has to be there to make sure it happens – and Anne's here because we invited her,' she added, answering Claire's silent question. 'You have to kiss him for at least five seconds. You ready?'

Claire nodded seriously as if accepting a state mission.

'And remember,' said Charlotte, 'we'll be watching!'

Claire walked away to the sniggers of the girls and for the first time wondered if she really did want to be a Queen Bee after all.

'Hi!' said Claire casually, conscious of the watchful eyes of the girls on her. She combed her hair away from her face with her left hand and shoved her hand back in her pocket.

'Hello,' replied Paul. He grinned, his relief that she had turned up evident and Claire felt her stomach contract with guilt and something else she couldn't identify. She met his eyes briefly, the blaze of blue at odds with the black rock T-shirt, before she saw him glance away looking over her shoulder at her friends.

'Yeah, sorry about that,' said Claire with a shrug.

'Shall we go in?' he asked, clearly as keen to escape them as she was. They climbed the stairs and queued without speaking, listening to the loud screeches of female laughter echoing in the stairwell behind them, both silently urging the cashier to hurry up. When it was their turn, Paul waved away Claire's purse as he paid for both of them and asked her if she wanted any popcorn. She said no but he bought her some anyway.

Why did he have to be so nice?

Claire felt herself relax a little as they entered the theatre. It was dark and quiet, a cave where she could imagine this was a proper first date and not some cruel challenge. They would sit next to each other in the red velvet seats, talking about music and school while waiting for the film to start. Every so often their hands would touch as they shared the box of popcorn and then the film would start and Paul would gently take her hand in his and she wouldn't sweat at all.

'Claaaaaaaire! Mwah, mwah!'

The heckle interrupted her daydream, the catcall altering her name to sound ugly and harsh. She resisted the urge to look around and instead sneaked a glance at Paul, his face staring intently at the screen.

Claire discreetly looked at her watch. The last hour and a half had been horrid. She hadn't been able to concentrate on the film at all, distracted by the whispers and giggles of the girls sat a few rows behind her. Now, thank God, the film was almost over. But if she didn't kiss him soon, she would miss her chance. How on earth was she going to do this?

She shifted in her seat using her hands on the arms of the chair to lift herself. As she moved, he glanced over at her, moving his own arm to make way for hers. She smiled at him encouragingly and hoped he would take her hand. He didn't. She had no choice – she would have to make the first move. Staring at the screen, she wiped her damp palm on her jeans before tentatively reaching over, praying he wouldn't reject her. As her fingers clasped around his, she sensed him looking at her in surprise, but he didn't shrug her off and she felt his own hand close around hers.

Claire tried to regulate her breathing. His hand was warm and dry and for a moment, she allowed herself to continue her real-date fantasy. But then on screen, as Daniel prepared for his final fight as the Karate Kid, she knew she only had minutes left to kiss him.

She couldn't do it.
She had to do it.
But she couldn't.

But then what about the Queen Bees? School would be a nightmare if she didn't do it. Just yesterday, Anne had told what happened to Mandy when she'd failed her challenge of opening the glass cage of tarantulas at the zoo and putting her hand inside to get one out – they'd called her a scaredy-cat for weeks and then every time she opened her bag or her locker, there was a plastic spider in there. Then one time, they'd put a real spider in her locker and Mandy had screamed and cried hysterically until one of the teachers had come to see what all the commotion was about. Of course, Mandy wasn't daft enough to tell tales, but it certainly explained why Charlotte and the rest of the Queen Bees had ostracised Mandy and she was always the last one to be picked for teams and partner work.

Claire closed her eyes.

She had to do it.

It was five seconds of her life.

She would lean over, put her lips on his and count to five.

Now.

Do it now!

Her thoughts were racing, and she could feel the sweat down her back. Her right hand, held by Paul, was also starting to get clammy again. Gently she removed her hand from his, and the movement made Paul turn to face her.

Do it!

She leant in, her face tilting to the right. His face was so close to hers she could see the confusion in his eyes. But then he seemed to understand and their lips met in the darkness. She counted to five but she didn't pull away and after that, her mind stilled, and as the lights came up, she barely heard the hoots and cheers from the back row.

'Oh my God, that was like something out of *Dirty Dancing*!'

She'd not even been home ten minutes before Anne was on the phone.

'What. A. Kiss! And way longer than five seconds! I can't believe it! Charlotte didn't say very much but I could tell she was impressed,' said Anne. 'Oh my God! You're so in! I'm so happy!'

Claire held the phone away from her ear slightly, but she couldn't help grinning. Anne was right. She was in! On Monday, they would induct her or whatever it was they called it in the secret ceremony and finally, she would get her bracelet.

17

Paul woke up in bed, his penis hard, his Superman duvet cover twisted around him. Glancing at the clock, he saw it was still dark outside. When was the last time he'd woken up before nine on a weekend? He couldn't remember. But this morning was different. Today, he'd woken up knowing that he had kissed a girl. And not just any girl.

Throughout his early teens, he'd imagined what his first kiss would be like and wondered when it would happen. *If* it would happen. But not even his most erotic dreams had prepared him for something like this. It was better than getting a Game Boy for his birthday. Better than being able to do a stand-up wheelie on his bike. And much, much better than the top-shelf magazines that he kept well hidden under his bed.

Paul lay for a few moments, his eyes getting used to the darkness, thinking about Claire. He'd been prepared for her not to turn up at the cinema the night before and so when she'd walked towards him, he'd pretended not to see her, his eyes determinedly fixed on the pub across the road, only turning as she got nearer. Her very presence had floored him. He could smell her perfume and he'd wanted to reach out and touch her hair, feel the soft blonde strands between his fingers and before he could stop himself, he imagined grabbing a handful, tugging it, so her head tilted back to meet his.

Her shy greeting had interrupted his thoughts and he forced himself to concentrate on opening the cinema door for her, deliberately letting it slam shut on the catcalls of her friends behind them.

What the hell had they turned up for? Claire had said there would be some others, he supposed. But still. Charlotte? He knew Charlotte of course – everybody did. He just didn't get why everyone seemed so into her. To him, she was vapid. Of all the people to become Miss Popular at the school, he certainly wouldn't have put his money on her. She didn't even know the Periodic Table after weeks of studying.

In the first year of high school, Charlotte and Paul had been paired up by Mrs Chelmhurst to work on their chemistry projects. Without a doubt, it had been the most painful six weeks of Paul's life. Charlotte knew absolutely nothing about chemistry and had no interest in learning anything. He had a feeling that Mrs Chelmhurst had done it deliberately; when he'd tried to explain to her that he wanted to work with someone else, she hadn't even bothered to listen to him.

In the end, he'd completed the project by himself. Of course, they had got an A, because he'd done all the work and then Charlotte had sat there preening, not even bothering to thank him, just looking at herself in a stupid sparkly mirror that she carried everywhere with her. Some people had it so easy. He'd wanted to push her then, off the stool and onto her skinny arse. He wanted to watch the mirror smash into a thousand pieces, to watch her stupid, ignorant face look up at him – to finally acknowledge him.

Paul sunk lower under the covers and thought about Claire again. Thank God it had been dark in the cinema otherwise it would have been very embarrassing. After they'd kissed, he could only stare into her eyes, oblivious to even Charlotte and her witches. He remembered the look on Claire's face.

Desire.

As the lights came up, he'd quickly pulled his jacket over his lap. But then Claire's attention had been caught by Charlotte and he wanted to shut them down. To obliterate them. Anything just to have that moment back with Claire. He thought about her, the softness of her lips, the gentle probing of his tongue, and he reached under the covers.

'You seem different,' said Brian, a few hours later. They'd ridden their bikes down to the woods as usual where they'd set up what they grandly referred to as an army assault course, but that wasn't really much more than a series of ramps to practise their stunts on. For over an hour, they'd gone up and down the makeshift slopes, trying to get higher and higher with every attempt but then Brian had turned his front wheel too far, landing awkwardly, so they were sitting on a log taking a break, their bikes abandoned at their feet.

'Do I?' said Paul. 'You mean because I was able to do the rear peg wheelie three times in a row and you couldn't even do one?'

Brian looked up and grinned from his hunched position on the end of the log where he was using a small branch to make circles in the soft ground.

'No, you prick. I don't know – I can't put my finger on it.' Brian continued prodding the ground, the stick jabbing. Paul waited, wanting to be asked, but he couldn't help himself.

'Last night I went out with Claire,' blurted Paul proudly. 'She asked me out at school last week.'

Brian looked up in surprise.

'What? Don't look so shocked!' said Paul.

'You little shit. And you didn't tell me!' But Brian was impressed, Paul could tell.

'Yeah well. I didn't see you yesterday,' replied Paul, trying not to sound resentful about Brian playing football every day after school. But he couldn't help it – Gavin might be less inclined to hassle him on the way home if Brian was with him.

'Annnnnnnd... we snogged,' announced Paul, not wanting to mention it was Claire who had kissed him as he hadn't had the balls to make the first move. 'In the cinema. In the dark. It was fucking fantastic,' finished Paul.

'Whoa, hang on a minute. What do you mean you snogged?' asked Brian.

'I mean – we kissed! Have you never seen anyone kiss before?'

'Well—'

'Leant right in, her mouth on mine – tongue and everything. She was loving it,' he added, unable to stop himself boasting. 'She would have done more I reckon if

Charlotte and her mates weren't behind us screaming their heads off.'

'Charlotte was there?' asked Brian, his eyes suddenly narrowing.

'Yeah, with her witches.'

'Really? You know…' Brian tailed off as if he was about to say something but then changed his mind. Instead he said, 'Good for you, mate.'

But Paul barely noticed. 'So, what do you think? Shall I call her?' He felt his bravado slipping away. He knew somehow he had to see her again and soon. But how?

'Nah…' replied Brian. 'You'll see her in school on Monday, won't you?'

'Yeah but then everyone will be around,' said Paul.

'Trust me, mate,' assured Brian. 'You don't want to call her. You don't want to seem too keen, you know?'

'I suppose so,' said Paul although he was disappointed. He'd looked forward to discussing the details of the phone call with Brian.

'How do you know, anyway?' asked Paul doubting his friend's advice.

'Duh! Simon,' shot back Brian.

Paul conceded immediately. Simon was Brian's older brother, in his last year at sixth form. He'd been with sexy Nicole for the last six months.

'Okay, Monday then. But then what? Do I go up to her, do you think?'

'No,' said Brian quickly.

'Really? Then what?'

'Where did you first meet her? I mean, where did she ask you out?'

'In the library,' replied Paul.

'Then go to the library and wait. See if she comes again,' said Brian decidedly.

'You reckon? It seems a bit, you know, hit and miss. How will she I know I'm there?'

'Really?' Brian looked at his friend. 'You're always in the library, you moron.' He punched his friend lightly on the arm.

Paul laughed. 'I suppose so. Okay, I'll give it a week. But if she doesn't come then we need another plan. In the meantime, ask Simon.'

Brian nodded, the matter closed.

Paul let himself in through the back door quietly, wanting nothing more than to go up to his bedroom, lie on his bed and think about Claire.

'Paul – is that you?'

For fuck's sake.

'Yep – was just with Brian,' he shouted over his shoulder already halfway up the stairs. He could see his bedroom door at the top of the landing just a few metres away. He was almost there, his hand reaching for the door when he heard his mother at the foot of the stairs.

'Paul?'

He froze. 'Yes?'

'Can you turn around please?'

Reluctantly, Paul turned to face his mother, her gaze scanning him from top to toe and he knew she was trying to ascertain what he'd been up to.

'I was worried,' she said eventually. 'Why didn't you say you were going out? You're never up this early and I'd made breakfast for you.'

'Sorry, Mum,' he replied. His fingers tapped the door handle, desperate to be out from under her scrutiny.

'So, where have you been?'

'I told you already,' he said impatiently, 'out with Brian. We rode our bikes through the woods. Like we do every Saturday.'

At the sarcasm, his father appeared, a stern figure, who even on the weekend dressed as if he was going to the office.

'Don't speak to your mother like that,' he ordered, coming up behind her.

Fuck you.

'Like what?' Paul retorted. It was a risk. He saw his mother's left eye twitch with anxiety as she discreetly signed a warning by touching her left earlobe.

'It's all right, Bill,' she soothed.

'No, it's not all right, Maureen, he's been moody and difficult for months now,' snapped Bill, working himself up. 'What's he got to be moody about? The boy doesn't want for anything. His whole future ahead of him.'

Paul and his mum locked eyes, sensing the danger.

Not today, Dad, do not do this today.

'Come on, Bill, why don't we go and have a cup of tea and a scone. It's only eleven. Let Paul get on with his homework.' Maureen trailed off, starting to move away from the bottom of the stairs. But the tenseness of her shoulders showed Paul that she was already regretting quizzing her son with Bill in the house.

'You don't help matters, Maureen, spoiling him the way you do. He has to learn,' stormed Bill and Paul held his breath already anticipating his father climbing the staircase towards him; but to his relief, he saw him follow his mother into the kitchen and he knew Maureen would make him a hot chocolate later when his dad had calmed down by way of an apology.

He was free.

For now.

He didn't hesitate. Opening his bedroom door, he closed it behind him and lay on his bed letting his mind take him to the night before, but try as he might, his father's face twisted in anger kept inserting itself, his mind like a faulty slide projector.

18

'Will you stop going on, woman! You never, ever stop!'

'Why didn't you tell me about this trip last week – what else are you hiding, James?'

Claire heard her father let out a sigh of frustration.

'For God's sake! Will you just—'

Claire put her Walkman headphones over her ears and turned up the volume to maximum. Like Paul, Claire was also lying on her bed, but she wasn't thinking about him. She was just wishing her parents would shut the hell up. She remembered the first time she'd heard her parents arguing. She must have been about four years old. Her dad had put her to bed, read her a story, and then he'd gone downstairs. She was just about to fall asleep when she heard the shouting. She lay there listening, too terrified to sleep.

Over the years, it had followed a similar pattern. She didn't really understand what her dad did for a living, just that he worked in retail and travelled a lot for business

– at least once a month. She looked forward to when he was away, not because she wanted him out of the house but because during that time, there was no arguing. It was a trade-off though because in the lead-up to her father's trips, the tension intensified. While Claire missed him, he usually came back with a present for her, especially when she was younger. They were small things, no doubt picked up hastily from the airport – a thimble with a dolphin on it, a cuddly toy, a puppet, a pen with a sparkly pom-pom on the end.

As she got older, she started asking questions about the places he'd been to and from then on, he usually bought her a travel guide. She had loads of them lined up alphabetically on her bookshelf and she knew she could open any one of them and see the mark her father had made on the map showing exactly where he'd been on that particular trip. She remembered him telling her that one day she could travel wherever she wanted to. What started off as an easy gift idea had turned into her dad's way of encouraging her to explore the world.

But over time, it became clear to both of them that she was a home bird and very content to stay in the welcoming confines of Manchester and its suburbs. She'd been on many holidays abroad with her parents – Spain, Greece and even Florida one time – and she enjoyed them, mainly because her parents didn't seem to argue as much, but she was always happy to come home.

She wondered idly if Paul had been abroad. Shame seeped through her at the thought of him. Would he find out he'd been part of a Queen Bee challenge? Probably. What a shit thing to do to someone. Claire let the blast of the Guns N'

Roses lyrics obliterate her guilt. The worst part of it all was that he was actually really nice. Most boys her age were complete idiots, but Paul seemed different – and that kiss! She hadn't expected it to feel so...

Intense.

Urgent.

After John Griffith, Claire had kissed other boys at various parties. There was Cameron with his braces and saliva, Rich who had licked her teeth, and Tony – probably the best of a bad bunch, with his eager tongue. But Paul – kissing him reminded her of diving into a swimming pool – that blissful, almost euphoric moment when her body penetrated the water and became something else. And while Claire had been absolutely petrified of making the first move, she recalled how powerful she had felt afterwards.

But she knew she never would have done it had it not been for the Queen Bee club. Claire held up her wrist, imagining the little charms of the bracelet, the glint of silver against the cuff of her school shirt. All the girls who wore the bracelet kept their sleeves slightly higher above the wrist to make sure it could be seen. And you could bet your life on it, Claire would be doing the same.

'Your father is travelling tomorrow, Claire,' informed her mother at the dining table later that day when they were sitting down for lunch. 'Why he's travelling on a Sunday, I have no idea – maybe you can get it out of him.'

Claire looked at her dad. He looked fed up.

'I already told you, Pat, the conference starts Monday, eight o'clock.'

'It doesn't take a whole day to get to London, James.'

'It does on a Sunday. Look, we've been over this. Why don't we just enjoy our lunch?' replied James picking up his spoon. He indicated to their daughter, but the gesture was lost on his wife.

'Well,' continued Patricia, 'I had planned to cook a nice Sunday roast followed by a family walk around the park, but there doesn't seem much point now.'

Her mum had always been big on family outings. Growing up there'd rarely been a weekend when they hadn't done something. Parks, museums, picnics if the weather was fine. As Claire had got older, she'd been less inclined to go on them, but her mother insisted at least once or twice a month. Claire used to love them but these days they felt forced and she wondered why her mum still clung to the ritual. She suspected it was because it was something to talk about with her friends and neighbours.

'What will I do with the chicken? It's such as waste,' continued her mother.

No wonder Dad travels so much.

'Don't worry, Mum,' interrupted Claire, easily slipping into her role as peacemaker. 'Tomorrow, cook the chicken – we can still enjoy the roast and go for a walk just the two of us? Or…' said Claire, hoping to break the tension, 'we can watch *Bullseye*. You wouldn't be able to do that if Dad was here.'

To her relief, both her parents chuckled. It was a long-standing joke about Patricia Sharpe's secret addiction to the dart game show.

For a few minutes, there was only the sound of cutlery and Claire felt her shoulders relax. Just today and tomorrow to get through and then it would be Monday and her new school life would begin! When Anne had joined the Queen Bees, there had been occasions when Claire had stayed at home while Anne went out to secret meetings and parties. They had always done everything together and Claire had felt excluded and hurt. Anne had always called her straight after and while she was secretive about what happened there, her excitement was palpable down the phone and Claire burned with jealousy. She understood why Anne had to be so cagey though – there was only one thing worse than not being in the Queen Bees and that was being thrown out of the Queen Bees.

Everyone knew that's what had happened to Jennifer O'Reilly, although she told everyone that she got fed up with all the stupid rules and being told what to do. Either way, it was social suicide and she now hung around with some random girls from the year below. Claire had always been in the popular group. Not a leader as such but definitely an important member – there'd been about ten to fifteen of them and they did so much together. It was only when Charlotte had set up the Queen Bees that the group had become fragmented.

And now Charlotte was very much the leader. Claire thought of her; yes, she was pretty, but it was something more than that. She had a confidence about her that made her stand out and she always seemed to be one step ahead of everyone else.

Claire remembered Rachel coming into school one morning proudly showing off her brand-new Walkman. But it wasn't the normal black or grey one like most people had. It was yellow! Apparently, Rachel's dad had gone to America on business and had picked it up there. And then Charlotte had seen it, had flicked her bag open, and taken out her own – a stunning red Walkman, with its own strap that went over the shoulder. You could wear it cross-body, like a bag. Everyone had gasped and crowed over it, desperate to try it on and, just like that, Rachel had been forgotten.

And then there was the time Charlotte had organised and starred in the school uniform fashion show to model the trousers that girls were now allowed to wear. From then on, all the girls had worn trousers instead of skirts and Charlotte had shown everyone different ways to wear them. To Claire, they were just simple, navy-blue trousers but Charlotte had somehow managed to make them look like they deserved to be on the cover of *Vogue*. You could wear them turned up with cute ankle socks; you could wear them with the waistband turned down to create a low-rise jean effect or you could sew on tiny little sequins down the seam of the pocket. Never had a pair of trousers caused so much of a stir and it was then that Charlotte seemed to rise from the gaggle to someone just slightly superior.

A few weeks after the fashion show, Charlotte ran for head girl and won the number of votes by a large margin, despite being under a C average. Somehow the lack of grades only made the feat even more impressive. And then Charlotte had come up with the idea of the Queen Bees. She'd announced it one morning break time to the cluster of girls around her and when it was clear something exciting was going on, Anne and Claire had joined the fringe, curious.

'...and it's going to be called the Queen Bees. But not just anyone can get in. First, they have to be invited and then go through a secret initiation.'

Squeals of delight had erupted, and the girls had turned to each other clamouring with questions. What kind of secret initiation? What happens when you get into the Queen Bees? The bell had rung then, signalling the start of the next class and Charlotte had breezed off down the corridor, her troop following behind.

'Could be fun,' Anne had said as they walked to their classroom.

Claire had shrugged her shoulders noncommittally. 'Could be.'

But privately, she felt a flicker of doubt, a hint of hesitation about the whole thing. It was the fact that some people would get in and some people wouldn't. She hated competing because she hated not winning. Take the school cross-country run, for example, where it was easy to see who came first and who came last. It was ironic because she actually enjoyed running, just not in a race. This Queen Bee club had a similar feel – it was all in public and everyone knew who would be in and who would be out.

As she sat down next to Anne in class and began taking her books out of her bag, she felt the panic of wanting to get into the Queen Bees just so she wasn't publicly humiliated about being excluded. At that moment, she'd hated Charlotte for setting up the stupid club. But now that she had passed the challenge and was about to be inducted, she forgot all those feelings. Like all the other girls who had passed the test, she couldn't wait to show off her new membership. As she finished her soup, she wondered what would happen on Monday. The initiation process had always been a carefully guarded secret and Anne hadn't even hinted about what she could expect.

Claire's thoughts were interrupted by her mother clearing the dishes and automatically Claire got up to help. Her mother, who had been mostly silent for the remainder of lunch, had obviously gone into martyr mode, but it was better than the alternative. After clearing the table, Claire asked to be excused. She was due to meet Anne in town at two o'clock. Her mother simply nodded, while her father offered her a lift.

'Thanks, Dad,' she said. The weather looked pretty miserable. While it wasn't raining the cloudy sky looked threatening.

'Do you need anything from town, Mum?' she asked, before heading to the sanctuary of her bedroom.

'No, thank you,' replied her mother primly. 'Will you be back for tea?'

'Yes, I'll be back no later than six.'

Her mother nodded.

'Leave in ten?' she asked her dad now who was settling down the newspaper.

'Ready when you are.'

After hurrying upstairs, she sat down at her vanity and applied some lip gloss. She also put on some clear mascara, the only type her mother would allow, and squirted Charlie Red perfume on her wrists. She went to her money box and took out some change, slipping it into her jeans pocket. When she went back downstairs, her dad saw her and stood up, picking up the car keys from the table.

'See you later, Mum,' she called from the hallway.

'Bye,' came the reply. Her mother must be in the small front room. She noticed her dad didn't say anything but opened the front door and walked to the car. Claire hoped while she was out her parents would sort it out otherwise her mum would be difficult while her father was away. It was only a ten-minute drive from their house into Castlefield.

'Where do you want me to drop you?'

'At the library, please.'

Her dad nodded approvingly. If only he knew that she and Anne would spend several hours gossiping rather than reading.

'I'll miss you tomorrow, Claire Bear. Sorry about having to leave so early.'

'That's okay, Dad.' She felt like she should tell him she was too old for such a babyish nickname, but she secretly loved it so she didn't. 'What's the conference?'

'Emerging Destinations for Retailers,' he said grandly with a wink. 'Four days of networking, events and information sessions.'

'Sounds fun,' replied Claire.

Her dad laughed, a nice sound that filled the car. 'Well, let's see. I'd rather be home with you but that's life. What's your plan this week?'

Claire thought about telling him about her initiation ceremony on Monday into the Queen Bees. Even though it was one of the most exhilarating things she'd ever done in high school – even more exciting than winning the Young Writers award or being selected as the President for the debate team – she had a sudden premonition that he might not understand. She knew he certainly wouldn't approve of the challenge she'd just completed. Her mother, on the other hand, would certainly approve of the Queen Bees.

'Not much – you know – schoolwork, homework.'

'Well, you have your GCSE exams coming up in June.'

'Yep.' Claire felt dread at the mere mention of her exams. Her teachers had predicted mainly straight As on the basis of the mock exams and she worked hard enough but there was always the anxiety that she might fail. Her father must have sensed her worry because he leaned over and patted her on the knee.

'You'll be fine. You work hard and your mock results were fantastic.'

She looked over at him gratefully. 'Thanks, Dad.'

'You need me to help you with anything? Test you?'

The offer made Claire feel guilty about letting her dad assume she was going to the library to study. She decided on the spot to check out a few textbooks and bring them home and do some reading that evening.

'No, I'm fine, thanks, maybe closer to the time though.'

'Anytime.'

The library came into sight and her dad slowed down the car. She could already see Anne waiting inside the foyer.

'Thanks!' she said jumping out of the car.

'Hey, Claire Bear!' he called. She turned around, one hand already on the door handle ready to slam it shut. 'You need a lift home?'

'I don't think so, but I'll call you. I think Anne mentioned her mum coming to pick us up.'

'Okay, well, call me from the payphone if you need picking up. Have you got some change for the phone box?' Claire watched him scrabble in his pocket.

'I do, Dad,' she replied eager to get into the library.

'Well, here's another ten pence just in case.'

She took it, shut the door, waved to him and ran up the steps. At the top, she saw her dad drive off and she opened the door to join Anne.

'Monday!' said Anne triumphantly, bouncing on her feet with excitement. Claire could tell she was relieved that Claire was finally in the Queen Bees. Now that they would both be members, they could talk about everything to their heart's content. She knew Anne didn't like keeping secrets and there were times when both girls were uncomfortably aware of the divide in their friendship over the summer. At the back of her mind, she wondered if Charlotte had deliberately done it that way but she quickly dismissed the thought. It was an exclusive club only for those who truly deserved to be in it. It was for winners. And finally, Claire was a winner.

19

Paul had ridden his bike to school on Monday morning. He knew it was a risk, but today, he was too happy to care. He'd spent most of his weekend daydreaming about Claire and in his mind, he pictured them together, boyfriend and girlfriend. What would Gavin make of that, he wondered gleefully. Paul going out with one of the *popular* girls. And not just popular but beautiful as well. He was obsessed with her hair, the long, golden waves making her look angelic and it got him hard just thinking about it. Gavin might even stop giving him a tough time – they could go back to being mates, just like before. They'd grown up in the same street for the first eleven years of their lives – it was only when Gavin's dad had lost his job and they'd had to move to a rougher estate that things had gone sour between them. That and the streaming of the classes by ability.

As Paul double-locked his bike up and hoped no one would damage or steal it, he envisioned his new life. He and Claire would do *everything* together – study, do their A-level exams, apply to the same university, and graduate with honours, he as a doctor, and she... well, he didn't know what her plans were, but she was intelligent and he would ask her what she wanted to be next time he saw her.

Gavin and he would be good friends again and Gavin would actually come to him and ask for advice on how to get a girlfriend. Brian would joke about being his best man at his wedding and Paul would shrug it off as if it was the last thing on his mind but really, he knew Brian would be his best man for sure.

Claire would call him every day after school and at weekends they would meet and study in the library together and kiss and hold each other and then she would say to him, *Paul, you're the one. You're the one I want to be with*. And he would look deep into her eyes and hold her and although she hadn't said specifically, he would know exactly what she had meant, that he wanted him to take her and he would whisper back to her, *Soon, I promise you, very soon*.

Suddenly, Paul felt a sharp pain in the back of his head and heard a hoot of laughter as his neck catapulted forward and he heard the bounce of a rugby ball as it rolled away from him, like a discarded peanut shell in a bar.

'Oi, Paul – watch where you're going, you twat!' While the laughter from the group of boys drowned out the voice, he knew it was Gavin. He reached behind his head, feeling his scalp, and walked quickly away, his head down to try to deflect any more attention. But while his body may have given the impression he had given up, he had only one thought about Gavin. *Just you wait.*

★

'Excellent work, Paul, as always,' said Mrs O'Leary.

'Excellent work, cocksucker, as always,' snickered a voice behind him imitating Mrs O'Leary as she walked away out of earshot. Paul didn't dare look behind him, but he knew it was one of Gavin's gang again. He'd always been relatively safe in the top-tier classes as Gavin and his mates were in the middle or lower sets but clearly Gavin had found a few more people to make his life hell in the classroom as well as outside of it.

Paul sat in his chair looking resolutely ahead as if the physics paper in front of him held no interest at all. Five minutes to the bell and he was going to make sure he was the first one out of the door. He would leg it to his bike, hop on, and get home as quickly as possible. Paul felt his heart rate speed up in anticipation. He discreetly put his books and the paper in his school bag, leaving only a pen and a slip of paper on the desk to write down the homework. But Mrs O'Leary was determined to take her time, stopping at every student to give verbal feedback on the paper.

Come on, come on, Paul said silently to himself. He glanced at the clock. Three twenty-nine. One minute to go. There were two papers left in Mrs O'Leary's hand. If she spent ten seconds with each student, then she had forty seconds to tell them the homework. But Paul knew from past experience that she wasn't going to let them out on time and at that moment he wanted to punch Mrs O'Leary in the face so hard. He imagined the feel of his knuckle as it connected with her squishy jowl, her body ricocheting back, eyes wide with shock, that he, Paul – her top student – could exert such violence. But she *always* did this, raged Paul silently, just kept them back a few minutes past the bell. When she finally let the class go, Paul raced out to the bike rack, but he already knew what he would find. His bike had gone.

Bastards.

His dad was going to kill him.

Paul let himself into his house, praying that his mother wouldn't be in. It had taken him over an hour to get home, leaning over his damaged bike, his ribs bruised. It was rare she wasn't there when he got home from school, but it happened occasionally. He'd hidden the bike in the garden shed under some tarpaulin and hoped his father wouldn't find it until he'd had a chance to fix it.

As he closed and locked the back door quietly behind him, he listened. Silence. His wounds and pride could bleed in private. After racing to the school bike rack and finding his bike gone, he'd searched the nearby bushes, hoping he could at least find it and get it fixed without his dad finding out. But it wasn't there. He'd then spent almost half an hour searching the rest of the school grounds before finally walking to the end of the school field, which led to a patch of woods. Although the school field was gated to prevent kids going into the dense woodland, the students did it all the time during school break times, mainly to secretly smoke or drink. Occasionally a teacher would get their arse into gear and do their rounds as far as the woods but most of the time, they couldn't be bothered.

Paul approached the woods cautiously. Slipping through the rungs of the flimsy fence, he picked up a nearby stick and started prodding the undergrowth, in the hope that his bike had been dumped. Fifteen minutes in and still nothing. He looked around him in despair. It would take him hours to search the woods and he still wasn't even sure it was here. But just then, he'd heard a twig snap and he whirled around. Gavin and three of his gang stood there, grinning like apes, the mangled bike between them.

'Looking for this piece of shit, mate?' shouted Gavin. The others laughed and one of them, thick-set and with his blonde hair gelled up in a Mohican, kicked the back of the wheel as if for emphasis.

'What're you willing to do to get it back, eh?' added Gavin, and in that moment, Paul wondered how they'd ever been friends. Gavin, who at eight years old had helped Paul up when he'd fallen off his bike. Gavin at six years old, who had given him his last Opal Fruit even though he never shared his Opal Fruits with anyone. Gavin at ten years old, who he'd played Scalextric with for hours, just so Paul could escape his dad. Where had that boy gone?

'Give it back,' Paul demanded, hoping he didn't sound as scared as he felt.

'Awww, poor baby, he's lost his bikey-wikey,' taunted Mohican. Paul stood his ground trying to anticipate Gavin's next move.

'Like I said, what're you willing to do to get it back?' reiterated Gavin. Paul thought of his dad and the beating he would get if he found out he'd lost his bike. The answer to Gavin's question was, unfortunately, anything.

'What do you want?' asked Paul.

'Now we're talking. Because if you hadn't entered into negotiation, we would have been forced to beat the crap out of you,' Mohican declared.

Who the hell was he?

Mohican's accent was different – it was stronger, rougher. In a split second of horror, he realised that Mohican was Danny Lewis, the boy everyone had been talking about over the last few weeks. Danny had joined from an inner-city school in Manchester and apparently, he'd been suspended for throwing a student down the stairs and then burning him with a cigarette. He'd managed to inflict eight burns before he got caught.

Paul felt the intertwined snakes of fear and anger slither through him.

'To save you a beating and to get your bike back, how about you do our homework for the next month?' suggested Gavin. He could have been suggesting a game of football, his tone was so relaxed.

'What, all of you?' asked Paul, incredulous.

'Make it two months,' interjected Mohican. 'Or do you prefer having the shit kicked out of you?'

'No, no, I'll do the homework. As long as I get my bike back,' added Paul desperately.

'Yeah, yeah, don't wet yourself,' said Gavin. Paul could tell he was losing interest, but Mohican had a strange look in his eye.

Paul agreed to do the four lots of homework and Mohican dropped the bike on the ground as if making to leave. As the group of boys walked past him, Paul had let his tense shoulders droop in relief. But he'd let his guard down too soon. A searing pain hit the back of his legs and Paul crumpled to the ground, trying to breathe. But he didn't have time before he was kicked in the gut, three times in a row. They ran then, leaving Paul with his face smeared in earth. Through a muddy cobweb of leaves and soil, he could see his bike and it was only then that he let himself sob softly.

Several hours later, when his parents had gone to bed, Paul had slipped out to the shed to fix his bike, but he was disappointed to find that it would need a new tyre and some of the gears were no longer working. He could live without the gears – his dad would never find out – but the tyre was a problem. He would have to persuade his mum to drive him into town and get the bike fixed and then there would be questions. Maybe he could ask his mum one Friday night, while his dad was out at the pub. Tell her he'd fallen from the bike and the wheel had bent. He'd have to play it down though otherwise his mum might stop him from riding it, saying it was too dangerous, and that was the last thing he needed.

Leaving the shed, he was satisfied he had a plan but instead of going back inside, he slowly sat down on the back doorstep nursing his sore ribs with one hand. He imagined Claire gently running her hands over them, her face filled with concern. The air was cool against his bruises and as he looked up at the night sky, he could see a million stars, their luminance emphasised against the inky night sky.

He sighed and picked up a stone, wondering how he would survive the next year of school and two more years of sixth form. Would Gavin go on to sixth form? He hoped not. The thought cheered him. But Gavin would still be in Castlefield. Would he continue to torment him? He turned the stone around in his hands before throwing it on to the garden. His thoughts churned, and he continued the pattern, picking up a stone, throwing it, picking up a stone, throwing it.

Out of the dark night though, came a squawk and Paul realised he'd accidently hit something. He could see an outline of what looked like a bird jumping and hopping and he got up from the step for a closer look. It looked like its wing had broken. Paul went back to his seat on the doorstep and continued hurling stones until it no longer squawked.

20

Claire could barely concentrate. It was the last class of the day and the second time she'd been brought up by Mrs Lyther for not listening. She discreetly checked the clock for the hundredth time. Twenty past two. Only ten minutes to go. The Queen Bee initiation ceremony had been postponed to today, Tuesday, because Charlotte had had a *thing* the day before. No one knew what that *thing* was although rumours were that she had an older boyfriend who she saw in secret, so her parents didn't find out. Claire and Anne had been disappointed. But Tuesday, three thirty p.m. was almost in sight.

If Mrs Lyther would just get on with it instead of droning on about kings and queens. Who cares?

Finally, the bell rang, and Claire grabbed Anne's hand as they rushed out of the history classroom. They turned to each other, their faces mirroring each other's elation.

'This is it!' squeaked Anne. 'Come on!'

Claire followed her friend down the various corridors to the music and drama department. The ceremony, explained

Anne grandly, was to be held in drama room three, the unofficial headquarters of the Queen Bees, mainly because it was used more as a storage room than a classroom. As they approached the room, Claire was already reaching out one hand for the door handle, but Anne pulled her back.

'Let me,' she said. As Anne opened the door and peeked into the room, Anne became a headless body and Claire hopped from foot to foot wondering what she was saying.

'Two minutes and then we can go in,' reported Anne, pulling back and closing the door. 'You nervous?'

Claire looked at Anne in surprise. It had never occurred to her to feel nervous – all she felt was excited.

'Should I be?' she asked.

'No, no, of course not,' reassured her friend, but Claire thought she saw a brief uneasiness cross her face. The two of them waited impatiently, not speaking. A few minutes later, the door opened and a hand, holding a black piece of material, shot out. Anne took it and the door slammed shut.

'What's that for?' asked Claire.

Anne didn't answer. Instead, she gently turned Claire around and placed the material over her eyes.

'Anne?' called Claire, although she knew it was pointless.

She could feel Anne pull the blindfold tighter around the back of her head. Why didn't she respond? Was Anne not allowed to talk even now? Suddenly, she felt Anne's little finger reach for her own, intertwining the two pinkies. They hadn't done that since they were children. Claire heard the door open again and Anne guided her slowly into the room, before shutting it behind her. She sensed Anne's presence next to her had disappeared and she could hear the giggles of the other girls as Claire instinctively put her hands out, like a sleepwalking mummy.

And then the jabs came.

Little prods in her side, her stomach, and her bottom. She whirled around in whichever direction the digs came from, always too late to grab the offending hand. Quickly, Claire was so dizzy she almost fell. She was tempted to snatch the bandana from her eyes, but she knew if she did that, they might not initiate her. Just then, a quiet fell over the room and she had a sense that people were gesturing. Were they planning to leave her here overnight and lock the door? But then the room filled with low rhythmic chanting. It sounded like it was coming from a stereo rather than the girls themselves and, despite her fear, she suppressed a chuckle at the ridiculousness of it all.

'Claire Sharpe,' came Charlotte's voice over the chanting. 'Do you swear your complete loyalty to the Queen Bees, to keep all club information to yourself, and complete this secret initiation challenge? If so, say "I do."'

Another challenge?

'I do,' replied Claire, keen not to have been caught hesitating.

'Queen Bees, do you accept Claire Sharpe as our new member of the Queen Bees and swear to trust and protect her at all times?'

'We do,' the room chorused in unison.

'Queen Bees, are you ready to subject Claire Sharpe to her final challenge?' Charlotte's voice was rising and Claire felt a shift in energy in the room around her.

'Yes,' screamed the girls.

'Ready, steady, go!' cried Charlotte.

Claire tensed her shoulders, curled her hands into fists and braced herself. But the impact never came. Instead, she felt a light fluttering around her, like streamers at a party.

What on earth was happening?

'Don't forget her legs,' cried one girl.

Vivian?

And just then she felt a paper material across the back of her legs.

Were they tying her up?

But it felt too flimsy to hold her down. Managing to sneak a feel with her right hand, she guessed it was toilet paper. They were covering her from head to toe in toilet paper and Claire relaxed slightly.

Suddenly, the room was still again. There was another whisper of giggles and she felt disorientated. Someone was removing her blindfold and she wiggled her head, desperate for it to be off. As she blinked, the first thing she saw were the masks. They veiled each girl, transforming them into a jeering, eerie clan. Each mask was a different colour but there was one that was strikingly distinctive, and she knew it was Charlotte's. It was deceptively simple – a black brocade eye mask enhanced with crystals around the cut-out eyes. What made it magnificent was the surrounding black netting, punctuated with diamond studs, feathers, and lace.

Just then, one girl, her mask slightly skewed to one side, stepped up in front of her, holding a banana in one hand and a silver foil packet in the other. She'd seen a condom before, she wasn't that naïve, and she knew then what they were going to make her do.

'The challenge, should you accept it,' announced the girl, Claire guessed it was Vivian, 'is to put the condom on the banana.'

Vivian grinned, ripping the condom packet open, as the girls whooped and cheered before Vivian added, 'With your mouth.'

The clamour in the room surged tenfold and Claire hoped nobody would hear them and investigate. She'd never been in any sort of trouble before and even the thought of it brought her out in a cold sweat. Claire glanced around the room at the group and then at Vivian's outstretched hand, the lubricated plastic reminding her of a washed-up jelly fish. Quickly, she leant down and took the condom between her teeth.

Claire lay on her bed, fingering the silver charm bracelet that was now finally hers. After she had completed the absurd banana challenge, the girls had lifted her high in the air, cheering for their new member and Claire had felt so much pride she hadn't stopped smiling since. The Queen Bees met once or twice a week in drama room three and had secret pow-wows. The next one was on Thursday and Claire couldn't wait to attend as a member. There was a party on Friday night and on Saturday afternoon, the girls were planning a shopping trip to Manchester. Finally, she belonged.

She tried not to think about Paul and how she had used him, but he had been on her mind more times than she liked to admit. Her guilt was the only thing that punctuated her happiness about being in the Queen Bees. But what could she do? She felt especially bad because she knew he was already targeted by some of the other lads.

But there was something else she realised with a jolt; she actually *wanted* to see him again. Paul hadn't been at all what she'd expected. She'd expected a boring, skinny boy who simply muttered but the reality had been quite different. Before the film had begun, they'd talked and laughed a little, ignoring the commotion of Charlotte and the girls behind them. And that was what had impressed her the most – he really didn't seem to care about them; his attention was firmly focused on her. If she was honest with herself, she was slightly surprised he hadn't called her. Maybe she'd got it wrong? Maybe he didn't like her as she thought he did?

The shrill ring of the phone interrupted her thoughts and for a minute she was sure it was him, convinced she had psychic abilities. But then her mum shouted up the stairs.

'Claire – it's Charlotte on the phone.'

Claire flew from her bed and ran to the top of the landing. Charlotte had never called her. Had she changed her mind about letting her into the Queen Bees?

'Will you take it upstairs?' her mum asked.

'Yes,' replied Claire over her shoulder as she hurried to her parents' bedroom where there was a second phone.

'Hello?' Claire heard the click of the phone as her mother replaced the receiver downstairs and then Charlotte's voice came down the line.

'Claire? It's Charlotte.'

'Hi!' Claire said over-enthusiastically. She sounded like an American cheerleader, for God's sake.

'I normally call new members just to say welcome to the Queen Bees!' enthused Charlotte. 'How did you find the initiation ceremony? Not too bad, huh?'

'Well, I'm glad it's over,' giggled Claire in a flush of confidence. 'So, are there different initiation challenges for each girl then?'

'Oh yes, we have a whole list and then they get put into a bowl and the newest member picks out the challenge,' replied Charlotte.

'Wow! Where do you get all your ideas from?'

'My brother – he's at Newcastle Uni – they make them do absolutely horrendous things though like drink each other's piss – it's disgusting.'

'Gross,' agreed Claire, wishing that she had an older brother.

'There is the goldfish challenge in our bowl though so it's lucky you didn't get that one!' Charlotte laughed. 'Basically, there's a goldfish in a pint glass and you have to drink it!'

Claire thanked her lucky stars she didn't get that challenge because if she did she was pretty certain she would have failed.

'You did well on both the challenges,' said Charlotte. 'To be honest, I thought you would fail at the first hurdle with Paul.'

'It was okay, but I'm glad it's over. What a bore he was!' lied Claire.

'Isn't he, just? He'd be all right if he just made an effort but he mopes around all day long with his head in a book!' complained Charlotte. 'Anyway, I'll see you Friday night? Don't forget your bottle. See ya!'

And before Claire could even ask what bottle Charlotte had hung up. She stared at the phone and then quickly replaced the receiver before picking it up again to dial Anne.

Anne picked up on the first ring because she had a phone in her room, but for once Claire wasn't envious, she was just grateful Anne had picked up so quickly.

'Charlotte told me to bring a bottle on Friday – does she mean like a bottle of cider or something?'

'Claire?'

'Yes, yes, it's me,' replied Claire trying not to sound impatient. 'Well?'

'Well, what?' asked Anne.

'Does she mean a bottle of booze? And if yes, where on earth am I going to get that?' repeated Claire.

'Yes, she means a bottle of booze,' sighed Anne. 'Everyone has to bring a bottle to Charlotte's parties.'

Was it her imagination or did Anne sound a bit fed up?

'You okay?' Claire asked her friend now.

'Yes, I'm fine – just trying to work out the French homework. Have you done it yet?'

'What? Oh no, not yet,' admitted Claire.

'Wow, that's not like you,' said Anne. 'Look don't worry about the bottle. Just steal it from your dad's drinks cabinet – that's what I do.'

'My dad doesn't have a drinks cabinet,' complained Claire. 'He only drinks wine.'

'Well, a bottle of wine will do,' concluded Anne. 'Just take one – he won't notice.'

Claire wasn't so sure. And besides, she didn't like the idea of stealing from her parents. Perhaps she could just ask them for one? But then they'd tell her she was too young to be taking bottles of wine to parties.

'Look don't worry about it. Try and sneak one from your dad but if you don't manage it, I'll bring an extra one just in case, okay?'

'Thanks, Anne,' said Claire, relieved. She knew her friend would help her somehow.

'But,' continued Anne, 'after that you'll have to work out a way to get booze yourself. Charlotte wouldn't like it otherwise.'

Claire wondered silently how Charlotte would even know.

'Perhaps you can get a fake ID?' suggested Anne. But even she sounded doubtful. Claire was one of the youngest-looking girls in their year.

'Hmmm, you think?'

'No, you're right. Maybe not,' agreed Anne. 'Hey, what about Paul? He could easily get some ID.'

Claire's stomach contracted at the thought of him. 'Don't worry, I'll work something out.'

'Okay, see you tomorrow in form room?'

'Yep, see you tomorrow.'

Claire replaced the receiver and was about to go back to her bedroom when she decided to have a look in the dining room. There was a side cabinet that held plates and cutlery and other tableware. It also had a cupboard where all the wine was kept. Opening the door, she counted six bottles of wine. Her parents didn't drink that often – would they notice if one went missing? Probably not. She closed the cupboard and went back upstairs to her room. She *would* take one on Friday – show Anne and the girls she could get her hands on booze just like the rest of them. Besides, she didn't want Anne running to Charlotte. And as Claire lay back down on her bed, she realised what she'd just thought about her own best friend. Anne wouldn't do that to her.

The next day Claire waved Anne off and then walked in the direction of the school library. She and Anne had lunch together most days but today Anne had a dentist appointment and her mother had come to pick her up to take her. Claire was planning to do the homework they'd been set that morning, so she wouldn't need to do it at home.

Well, that's what she told herself. It was Thursday. Five days since her date with Paul and two days since she'd got into the Queen Bees. Unexpectedly, Paul had played on her mind and she was hoping to see him. As she entered the library, she appreciated the sense of quiet, the bedlam of the corridors a whole world away. She walked into the room and saw him. And then he looked up. And Claire knew then that she liked him.

Crap.

21

Paul was feeling very pleased with himself. Not only had he managed to convince his mum to take him into town for a new wheel for his bike, but Claire had also come to the library a grand total of four times.

'She must really like you,' said Brian when they'd met up one Saturday to ride their bikes through the woods. Brian, his bike abandoned at his feet after several rounds of the assault course, was throwing a small ball in the air and catching it over and over again while he was talking. But Paul could see the envy in his friend's eyes. It was nice to be envied. Usually, it was the other way around with Paul envying Brian's life. Brian wasn't the best-looking or the most intelligent – he was in the middle set for every subject – but he was easy-going and funny and everyone just liked him: boys, girls, teachers. He had a quick wit and a quick smile and Paul was beginning to learn it was a powerful combination to help you sail through life.

Paul had once tried it for a day and had failed miserably. He wasn't quick enough with the funny remarks. Besides, Paul thought he looked like a baboon when he smiled and when one teacher asked him if he was okay after he'd grinned like a fool for most of the lesson, he realised he was wasting his time. But Brian also had another weapon to navigate through school – sport. He was on the rugby and football teams and most afternoons were spent practising. Brian was tall for his age anyway, but he was also strong, and his physique had prevented many a beating.

But what was really unusual about Brian was that he didn't belong to any group at school. He could hang around with his sporty friends as easily as he could hang with the nerds and he flitted around at break times, bouncing around with his ever-present ball, to whoever took his fancy at the time. Somehow it made Brian even more of an enigma and even more popular. That wasn't to say he wasn't a target – he'd also been called a sport-nut, Dumbo (on account of his rather large ears), a numpty and all the rest, but Brian always assumed it was in jest and played up to it, usually making everyone laugh in the process. Paul wondered if Brian had met Mohican yet and asked him as much.

'Danny Lewis?' asked Brian, as they sat on a log, their bikes beside them. 'Yeah, he's on the rugby team. Ferocious guy,' he added, almost in awe. 'Glad he's on our team and we don't have to play against him!' Brian laughed, and Paul wondered how he and his friend could have such different experiences of the same boy.

'So,' started Brian, slipping the ball into his pocket, and Paul knew he was going to come back to Claire. 'Have you asked her out yet?'

'No,' replied Paul, despondently. It had been on his mind as well. He'd had several opportunities in the library but every time he'd bottled it.

'Why not? She's come to the library – what – twice now to sit with you?'

'Four times,' corrected Paul immediately.

'Whoa! And you haven't asked her?'

'I know, I know. I just didn't know how to… where to…'

'Listen,' said Brian. 'It doesn't have to be anything fancy – just take her to the cinema again. That's what my brother always does. He says it's the best place if you want to, you know…' Brian had trailed off and looked embarrassed his fingers automatically reaching for his ball as he started throwing it between his two palms.

'What?' asked Paul.

'Well, you know, cop a feel,' mumbled Brian.

Paul imagined his hand sliding up Claire's top, the darkness of the cinema shrouding them as his fingers gradually felt the curve of her breast. He couldn't breathe just thinking about it, so what would the real thing be like?

Paul stood up resolutely and looked at Brian. 'I'm going to do it. I'm going to ask her the next time she comes into the library.'

His friend looked up with his trademark grin and optimism. 'Go for it. She'll say yes, for sure.'

It was Wednesday the following week and Paul was sat in the school library unable to concentrate. Now that he'd made the decision to ask her, Claire seemed to have disappeared. She hadn't been in the library all week. He'd spent Monday doing his own homework and then Tuesday doing Mohican and his gang's homework. It had kept him distracted enough and luckily Mohican, Gavin and their mates were all in the same class, so it was a case of repeating the work but just changing a few of the answers so they weren't all the same. As Paul was going through the questions, he thought how easy the work was. How were they going to pass their exams if they were still only doing stuff from the fourth year?

Idiots. Well, when he was a doctor, he would show them.

He imagined himself in his white coat striding down the halls of Manchester Royal Infirmary issuing directives, the nurses scurrying to do his bidding, the patients and their families looking at him as if he was God. He had it all planned out. After medical training, he would move through the ranks to be a consultant. A Mr.

He wasn't a hundred per cent sure which area he wanted to specialise in but he knew it had to be surgical. He was fascinated and regularly imagined his first slice into a human body. His hand, encased in a surgical glove, would be completely still, poised to cut. The whole theatre would be silently on standby for anything he might need for the anesthetised patient in front of him. He imagined the tapered blade slitting into velvety flesh and tissue, followed by cutting and probing, removing and stitching.

When Gavin and his mates were really giving him a hard time, this was the little corner of his brain he escaped to. But now the daydream was even better, because he knew Claire would be by his side. Just then the library door opened, and Paul looked up expectantly, but it was only one of the first-year students dropping a book into the returned items box before slipping back out of the door. Paul returned to his work convinced Claire wasn't going to appear today so when he felt someone's presence in the room, he was surprised to see Claire standing in front of his table.

'Can I join you?' She smiled.

Oh God, that smile.

He moved his things aside to let her sit down next to him. Glancing quickly at the librarian's desk, he realised she had gone out for lunch. They were alone and now would be the chance to ask her.

Why couldn't he speak for God's sake? Say something, anything!

'It's nice to see you,' he muttered.

Is that the best you can do?

'It's nice to see you too,' said Claire, opening her books. 'What are you working on?'

Immediately, Paul started explaining in great detail a project he was working on for chemistry. He was so caught up in what he was saying, he didn't realise she was trying not to laugh.

'What?' he asked now, his face colouring.

'Nothing, nothing. It's just you're so brainy!' she said, and Paul swelled with pride. Many people had told him the same thing over the years, but it was different coming from her – special.

'Why are you laughing then?' he asked, suspicious.

'Stop scowling.' Claire laughed and she leaned over, placing her finger on the centre of his forehead as if to wipe away the frown lines.

Was she flirting with him?

He thought she might be. Her touch had been electric, and he couldn't help himself. As her hand came down from his face, he caught her by the wrist. For a few moments, they sat there, looking at each other, her wrist in his hand. And slowly, as the magnetic force grew between them, they leaned in to each other, their lips meeting.

Paul shut his bedroom door behind him, finally alone. The events of the afternoon raced through his brain, flooding his body with adrenalin. Claire. The kiss. Asking her out. Her agreeing. Their whispered conversations and secret glances after the librarian had come back from her lunch break. They'd spent an hour together in the school library and it was the best hour of Paul's life. They'd agreed to meet in the same place after school the next day and she'd agreed to go to the cinema with him on Saturday night.

Apart from that, they'd sat, secretly holding hands under the table, Paul reading his textbook, and Claire writing up her notes. She was left-handed Paul noticed, her writing a beautiful cursive script that he'd never managed to master. He could feel their hands grow clammy under the table but still, she didn't move her hand away and Paul hardly dared to breathe as he concentrated very hard on the book in front of him. It was only when another student came into the library that Claire pulled away and let her long blonde hair fall like a curtain between them.

But to Paul, the secrecy only added to the excitement and soon he promised himself, he would pluck up the courage to ask her to be his girlfriend. Should he run it by Brian first though? Was he moving too quickly? Wouldn't Brian advise him to be a little more elusive? But he knew Claire liked him and he knew how much he liked her. He wanted to be with her every minute and those long hours at home were torture. But less than twenty-four hours to go until he was back in the school library with her and then just two days until their night in the cinema. It seemed like a lifetime away and as Paul flopped on his bed, his schoolwork forgotten, he closed his eyes and imagined being close to her in the darkness of the theatre.

22

The water swirled around Claire, the chlorine-laced ripples shrouding her senses. She swam two or three times a week at the local pool and had been on the school swim team for the last few years. She'd always enjoyed swimming, but it was only in the last year or so that she'd begun to appreciate its numbing effects. In the pool, Claire wasn't preoccupied with thoughts of her parents and their constant bickering, or the stress of her upcoming GCSE exams. When she was swimming, she didn't think about Charlotte and the Queen Bees and why it was so important for Claire to be a part of it. Nor did she think about Paul, her guilt and desire wrestling for prominence. For a few hours each week, as her limbs propelled her forward, her mind was like a beautiful desolate countryside – alive but blissfully uninhabited.

She pushed herself out of the pool, droplets streaming off her body, relishing the exhilaration from the fifty lengths.

'Thirty-nine minutes, twenty,' shouted her coach, throwing her a towel.

Claire dried her face, smiling into the towel.

'Well done. Get dressed. See you outside,' ordered Coach Timmons, already focused on the remaining swimmers.

Coach Timmons, or Timmy as he was known behind his back, always talked in staccato. She knew some of her team members didn't always appreciate his approach, but Claire found it as refreshing as the water itself. If you were good, he told you, if you were bad, he told you. There was no ambiguity, no hidden meanings – everything was clear.

She hurried through to the changing rooms, happy that she'd beaten her personal best. She was even happier when, twenty minutes later in the pool foyer, Timmy read out the names of those participating in the next swimming competition and included hers. Swinging her bag on her shoulder she went outside to see if her mother had arrived to pick her up. Seeing the blue car, her mother at the wheel, she climbed gratefully inside, the heater on full blast.

'Hello, love,' said her mother, as she put the car in gear and took off. 'How was it?'

'It was good – thirty-nine minutes, twenty seconds and I'm competing in the next round.'

'Well done, love, that's amazing news. Your dad will be pleased.'

'Thanks, Mum.' Claire sank back into the seat and watched the descending darkness of twilight. It was late October and barely five o'clock in the afternoon.

'I wanted to ask you what you wanted to do for your sixteenth birthday,' said her mum, her eyes focused on the road. 'I can't believe it's only a couple of weeks away – sixteen! It feels like only yesterday when I brought you home from the hospital. Do you want to have a party at home?'

'No thanks, Mum, I'll have a night out with Anne and everyone.'

'Really? Are you sure? In my day, we always had a party at—'

'Honestly, Mum, it's fine.' Claire shuddered at the thought of the Queen Bees all coming to her house and her parents chaperoning them as if she was eight years old.

'Well, if you're sure. Shall I book a meal out then, just the three of us? Or do you want to ask Anne to come as well?'

'Sounds good, Mum,' replied Claire, relieved to have it sorted. 'Don't forget I'm going out tonight to Charlotte's sleepover party.' This would be the third time Claire had gone to Charlotte's house since she she'd joined the Queen Bees and once she'd solved the problem of getting her hands on alcohol, she'd started to look forward to the many different get-togethers that Charlotte liked to organise. She'd never had such a busy social life before and she wondered when the other girls managed to get their homework done.

Just before the first party, she'd told her mum about the Queen Bees and the two of them had enjoyed a rare moment of mother-daughter bonding. Together they'd chosen an outfit for Claire to wear to the party while her mum had sat on her bed and for once, she didn't criticise or complain; in fact her mother had even told her about the club she used to be in when she was a teenager and for just a brief moment, Claire saw her as the girl she once was and not as a nagging, annoying mother.

But later, when she snuck a bottle of wine into her bag from her parents' cupboard, the good feelings evaporated. At the party, she'd managed to work out that most of the girls used Helen's older brother to get the alcohol and Claire placed her order for the next party, relieved she didn't have to go sneaking around her parents' wine cabinet any more. Why Anne hadn't just mentioned that option in the first place, she would never know.

'I hadn't forgotten,' replied her mum, slowly navigating the roads. 'What are you planning to wear?' Like a tried and tested recipe, her mum had found a fail-safe topic on which to communicate with her daughter. Clothes. For a moment, Claire thought about telling her about Paul and how, over the weeks, that trip to the cinema had developed into a relationship. She knew Paul thought of her as his girlfriend and she knew he was confused and hurt about her insistence on keeping their relationship a secret. But somehow, she'd convinced him that it was more fun and exciting that way.

But it wasn't. Not really. It was stressful, and it made her edgy, constantly having to look over her shoulder. But she didn't have a choice. The Queen Bees had made their feelings on Paul clear – he was the school nerd, the lowest of the low, and not even worth a moment's consideration unless it was for their own amusement. If any of them found out about her and Paul, she would be out of the club for sure. Instead, Charlotte and the girls had already picked out someone who they thought would be perfect for Claire.

'What?' exclaimed Claire when the Queen Bees had gathered together one break time.

'Chris Carmichael would be perfect for you! Oh my God, can you imagine the two of you? The babies you'd make!' squealed Nicola.

'He'd be perfect,' echoed Anne after Claire had instinctively turned towards her friend. Since then, the Queen Bees had come up with a multitude of ways to get Claire and Chris together including inviting Chris to the Queen Bee parties. So far, he'd never turned up and Claire was half relieved, half disappointed. She had to admit she was curious. But then she thought about Paul. She wondered what her mum's advice would be and decided not to risk it – she would have no clue. No, Claire thought, perhaps instead she could test out the topic of Paul tonight at the party. If she told them how much she liked him, how nice he was, how intelligent he was, then they might see him differently as well?

It was worth a shot.

'Have fun!' called her mum as she dropped her off outside Charlotte's house.

'Thanks. Anne's mum will drop me back home tomorrow,' confirmed Claire.

'Okay, have a good night and I'll see you in the morning.'

While Claire was thankful her parents were early sleepers, it was better to stay over at Charlotte's. While she never drank too much at the parties, she was aware that she probably smelled like a brewery when she came in. But for now, the night was just getting started, and Claire walked quickly up the pathway and rang the doorbell.

'Password!' cried a voice from behind the glass.

'Bros!' giggled Claire, naming Charlotte's favourite band. She was obsessed with Matt Goss. The door opened and Vivian, clad in tight jeans and pink crop top, let her inside. U2 boomed through the house. Down the hallway into the kitchen, Claire could already see a group of people mixing drinks and she dropped her sleeping bag in the hallway and walked towards them.

'Claire!' cried Charlotte. 'Hi!'

Charlotte hugged her, and Claire could smell Eternity by Calvin Klein. As she leant in to her, she heard her whisper, 'Guess who finally came?'

Claire looked up and saw a group of lads holding bottles of beer and laughing. She recognised them of course as they were known as the best-looking, most popular lads in their year. Taking Claire by the arm, Charlotte led her over to the group, which parted immediately as they approached.

'Guys, this is one of our newest members, Claire Sharpe. Claire this is George, Matt, and Leo.'

A low chorus of hellos met Claire's casual 'hi'.

'And this,' exclaimed Charlotte dramatically swivelling Claire around to a guy who was getting a beer out of the fridge, 'is Chris Carmichael.'

Chris nodded at Claire with a smile.

'Right, guys, let's leave these two to it – I have jelly shots in the living room,' announced Charlotte and just like that, Claire and Chris were alone.

Several hours later, Claire and the girls were in their sleeping bags on the living room floor, the others around her like caterpillars except for Charlotte, who had brought down her duvet from her bedroom and was on the sofa, the height making her look like she was holding court.

'I think he really likes you, Claire,' said Anne.

'Come on, Claire – share the gossip – what happened?' prodded Vivian.

'He's nice,' said Claire noncommittally before trying to change the subject. The girls screamed in protest and Claire knew she wasn't going to get away with being coy.

'He asked me out,' admitted Claire, unable to hide her smile, and the girls whooped and hollered as if she'd won the Nobel Peace Prize.

'And what did you say?' prompted Vivian.

'I said, I'd think about it,' replied Claire. More claps and whistles.

'I like your style, Claire,' replied Vivian. 'There aren't many girls who would keep a guy like Chris Carmichael hanging!'

The topic moved on and Claire snuggled down into her sleeping bag, listening to the girls recall the highlights of the evening. She hadn't had a chance to bring up Paul and decided she would do it another time. But then she heard one of the girls mention something that made her sit up.

'Got the shit kicked out of him. Poor guy, but he really doesn't help himself.'

'Who did?' asked Claire, hoping she'd misheard.

'Paul Jones,' came the reply. 'Oh yes, of course, he was your challenge! Well, apparently, the new boy from Manchester, Danny Lewis, has got his eye on him.'

Claire's stomach fell. She knew the lads gave each other a hard time but the arrival of Danny Lewis had definitely given everyone a lot to talk about. Even from the way he walked around school, you could tell he was trouble.

'Paul's not that bad, you know,' attempted Claire. 'He's actually a really nice guy – he just comes across a bit, you know…'

The girls looked at her in surprise and she quickly backtracked. 'Of course, compared to Chris…' She didn't need to go any further as the whistles resounded around the room.

'So, when are you going to say yes to Chris?' asked Charlotte. Claire looked up towards the sofa and she felt a ripple of energy emanate from her. It was a simple question, but Claire sensed the challenge in her tone. The message was clear.

'He said he'd call me tomorrow,' replied Claire and as she saw Charlotte's slight nod, she knew that she and Paul would have to remain a secret.

23

No one had been more surprised than Paul when Claire agreed to come over to his house. They'd been sneaking around for weeks and for Paul, the school library was no longer enough. He needed to be with Claire alone. He'd already taken her to the bike track where he and Brian regularly met, but he was still on edge in case they came across Gavin, or – even worse – Mohican, and he felt she was too. Claire seemed distracted. He'd taken her hand then and they'd walked through the woods without speaking.

Gradually, as the minutes passed, he felt the woods work their magic. It was a place he'd always felt happy, surrounded by nature, the trees camouflaging his movements as he walked, ran, or biked his way through the undergrowth. Here and there, the occasional strobe of sunlight managed to make its way through the thickness of the leaves and branches, casting flickers of sunlight. He rarely saw any movement with the exception of birds who preferred to remain in the branches or the odd squirrel who would quickly dart up the nearest tree upon sensing his presence. When they were deep into the woods, Claire stopped, closed her eyes and breathed in the air. When she opened them, she smiled.

'I can't believe I've never been here before and it's been right on my doorstep the whole time,' she said. 'It's so peaceful – unlike my house!' she joked and Paul sensed a hidden meaning behind her words.

'Really?' asked Paul, trying to keep his tone casual.

'Yeah,' replied Claire tentatively. 'You know, just my parents...'

Paul waited.

'They argue a lot.' Claire shrugged.

He looked at her and she looked so sad that in that moment, Paul knew he would do anything to make her happy.

'Yeah, mine too,' confided Paul. 'It's a bit crap to be honest. Especially my dad – once he loses it, he loses it. And my mum just never stops fussing.'

'Really?'

'Yep. I don't know if all parents are like that, but mine definitely are. My mum's all right though. She would like you, I'm sure.'

Claire looked up at him with a smile. 'Are you inviting me to meet your parents?'

Paul looked horrified and Claire couldn't help but laugh.

'I'm just kidding,' she said and Paul grinned. Spontaneously, he put his arms around her, breaking their stride. Putting his hand under her chin, he looked into her eyes. He was half a head taller than her and he leant down to kiss her. She responded to him, wrapping her arms around his neck, and Paul thought he was going to explode. He pulled his mouth away and buried his embarrassed face in her neck.

Suddenly, voices startled them both and they repelled apart like opposing magnets. Paul's body was taut and he tried to control his breathing. His first thought had been that it was Gavin. But it was just a pair of elderly walkers coming towards them up the path.

'Afternoon,' said the man politely while the woman behind him smiled indulgently at them. Claire returned the greeting, but Paul dropped his hands and his head and scuffed his trainers against a nearby rock. After they passed, he looked up to see Claire watching him curiously.

'You okay?' she asked.

'Yeah.' He kicked the rock once more before taking her hand in his. 'You know maybe it wouldn't be so bad for to you meet my mum,' he said. 'We could do our homework together there rather than hiding in the school library.'

At first, he thought Claire was going to say no, but then she smiled.

'Sure, how about tomorrow?' she suggested, and Paul was so overjoyed, he didn't see the shadow of relief cross Claire's face.

Paul watched Claire's gaze take in the gate hanging off its hinges, the overgrown front lawn, and the peeling paint on the front door. His mum had been nagging him to mow the front lawn for weeks but now it was almost winter and it was hard to find a day where it wasn't raining or bitterly cold.

As he took in Claire's first impression of his house, he wished he'd done as he was told. But shouldn't his dad be doing those jobs? Paul bristled silently. His dad never did anything around the house and both he and his mum knew that was never going to change. As Paul slid his key in the lock, he led Claire down the hallway. It smelled of baking. His mum hurried out to meet them.

'Hello! You must be Claire! Are you cold? Come through, I made a crumble. What would you like to drink?' Maureen chattered on and Paul knew she was nervous.

'That's okay, Mum, we're just going to go up to my room to study,' said Paul. But Claire interrupted him.

'Hello, Mrs Jones. Nice to meet you. Some crumble would be lovely, thank you.'

Paul groaned inwardly, but he watched his mother scurry about the kitchen and he knew she was impressed with Claire's manners. Good breeding, he could imagine her saying to him later after she'd left. He'd made the mistake of telling his mum that Claire lived on Cherry Drive in Castlefield.

'What, the posh part?' she'd said earlier.

'Mum, for God's sake don't say that to her,' replied Paul tersely.

'Don't worry, I won't. Fancy, my son bringing home a posh girl.' She smiled at him then and he could see she was happy for him.

Now, as the three of them sat round the kitchen table, Claire chatted easily with his mother and by the end of the twenty-minute conversation, even Paul felt at ease.

'Right, Mum, we're off to do our homework,' he said as he finished his last mouthful. 'Come on.'

Claire got up and began gathering the dishes and taking them to the sink.

'Oh, that's all right, pet, I'll do that – you go and get started on your homework.'

'Thank you, Mrs Jones – that was delicious,' said Claire and Paul could see his mum instantly fall in love with her just like he had. Claire had walked ahead of him into the hallway and as he left the kitchen, his mother gave him a pointed look. He knew what it meant – a reminder to keep his bedroom door open, but he pretended he didn't understand.

Climbing the stairs, Claire in front of him, he wished he'd tidied his room up a bit. But as he walked in, he saw that his mother had already been in, and even changed his bedding. He sent a silent prayer of thanks to her that she'd saved him from having his childish superhero duvet on display and shut the door behind him. They both sat on the bed, Claire already pulling her books out. Paul tried to concentrate but Claire's proximity, the fact that she was sitting on his bed, was like a dream. Maybe it was a dream, thought Paul, but when he felt her toes playfully touch his, he wanted to pinch himself.

A firm knock on the door made Paul leap up.

'Paul, your father's going to be home in twenty minutes,' came his mother's voice. It was a warning.

'Okay,' he replied. He stood up and tucked his shirt into his trousers. Claire ran her fingers though her hair self-consciously.

'I'd better go,' said Claire and Paul felt a rush of disappointment. He'd wanted to do more with her, more than kissing and holding hands but instead, despite the privacy, she'd gently moved his hand away when he tried to undo the top buttons of her school shirt.

'Soon,' she whispered, and Paul had had to supress his irritation.

Claire gathered up her books and Paul helped her with her bag. It was probably better she was gone before his dad came home from work anyway. As they clambered down the stairs, Claire sought out his mother.

'Nice to meet you and hope to see you again soon,' said Claire as she made to leave.

'Nice to meet you too, pet. Will you be okay getting home?' she asked as she followed them through the hallway.

'Yes, it won't take me long to walk and it's dry,' replied Claire opening the front door.

As Claire stood on the doorstep, Paul didn't know what to do. His mother was still hovering. *Why didn't she go away?*

'Bye then,' Paul said eventually and gave her a clumsy kiss on the cheek.

'Bye,' said Claire, hoisting her bag on her shoulder. Paul felt like an idiot but as he turned to look at her one last time, she turned and waved and he grinned back. Closing the door, he heaved a sigh of relief. He hadn't been sure about bringing Claire back to meet his mum but if it was between her and the prospect of meeting Mohican and Gavin, he knew he didn't have much of a choice.

He hoped that soon Claire would feel comfortable telling everyone they were together. He tried not to let it bother him that she wanted to keep it a secret. She'd mentioned something about her parents not being keen on her having a boyfriend. He didn't really believe her. But for now, nothing else mattered except her, and together they would build an incredible life, one far away from Mohican, Gavin and his stupid mates, and even his dad. He'd show them all.

NOVEMBER 1989

24

Claire closed her diary with a snap, lifted up the mattress and placed it on top of the wooden slats, letting the mattress spring back into place. She usually hid her diary under a few books in her bedside table drawer; however, she was pretty sure her mother had read her diary once before and, as she'd written several pages about Paul, she didn't want to take any chances on her mother finding it. Claire knew it was a bit of risk writing about him, but it felt like the only way she could unravel her confusion. Compared to Chris with his rugby-player physique and blonde classic good looks, Chris was definitely more attractive; so why did Paul, the school nerd, have such an effect on her, like an invisible power?

As her pen scrawled across the page, word by word her feelings became clearer. Simply put, Paul was unlike anyone she'd ever met before. She'd fancied boys in the past, her and Anne giggling about how gorgeous they were, but this was the first time Claire had been attracted to a boy not just physically but mentally as well. His intellect fascinated her, and their conversations ignited her imagination to such an extent that afterwards she would go and read up on subjects that she would never have even thought about before. *The cure for AIDS. How seahorses procreate. Buddhist practices. The state of Burma.* It didn't matter what the subject; her desire to learn was almost as intense as her desire for him.

She recalled sitting on Paul's bed, their limbs touching, their maths books open in front of them. His presence was so powerful, she couldn't even think straight let alone solve complicated calculus. It was only the thought of Paul's mother downstairs that had made her push his hand away when he wanted to go one step further.

Since then, they'd seen each other every day even if it was just for a few minutes in the school library during break time. But Claire's favourite times with him were when he took her down to the woods, him leading her through the maze of paths as they talked. He could be moody and uncommunicative, but Claire had learnt how to draw him out and little by little, he opened up. He told her about Gavin and his pranks, his dreams of being a doctor, and a little about his friend Brian. He talked about his dad and his ferocious temper and how he and his mum had to assess his mood each day. How he and his mum had a secret code to signal warnings to each other.

Claire's whole body had trembled as she listened to his stories of violence and how he and his mother did everything they could to avoid it. Paul told her that she, Claire, was his lighthouse in the storm and whenever his home or school life got really bad, he would think of her and it would make him feel better. She'd fallen silent then, determined that she would show him how he deserved to be loved, and as they continued sharing their dreams and talking about a future, she knew she could see him in it.

Claire lifted the gate and walked up the pathway to Paul's. She'd been thinking about her birthday party, which the Queen Bees had held the previous weekend. It had been incredible – the best party she'd ever been to. The only person missing though was Paul and she was eager to see him. It was four o'clock on a Monday afternoon and she'd come straight from school. He'd skipped the last class of the day and told her to meet him at his house.

She rang the bell and heard someone coming down the stairs and within seconds Paul had opened the door and let her in. She wondered if Mrs Jones was home and her question was answered when she came, apron-clad, into the hallway.

'Claire, how nice to see you again. How are you? How are your parents?'

'They're good, thank you, Mrs Jones. How are you?'

'Please, call me Maureen.'

'Okay... Maureen,' she replied with a smile. Claire knew she was good with parents – she always had been. She didn't really know why – maybe because she had good manners. Her own mother had drilled them into her from what felt like the minute she was born, but she would only become aware later in life that it was her wholesome image that made all parents secretly wish they had a child like Claire.

'Come through. I've been baking,' invited Maureen, walking through to the kitchen. 'I hear someone celebrated a special birthday at the weekend.'

Claire smiled. 'Yes, it was on Saturday.'

Just then she heard Paul thunder down the stairs to come and meet her, his face lit up in anticipation until he saw his mum had beaten him to it.

'There you are. I was just about to offer Claire some birthday cake. Would you like some?'

Paul was clearly embarrassed. 'No thanks, Mum, we've got lots of homework to do,' responded Paul. Claire watched as his mother tried to hide her disappointment.

'Paul, I'm sure we can spare a few minutes,' interjected Claire, gently leading him by the arm. 'Besides, I love cake.'

Claire quickly buttoned up her shirt, trying to bring her breathing back to normal. It had been a mistake to come to Paul's room. There was a part of her that was desperate to be alone with him but a part of her that was also very much aware that her relationship with Paul was racing ahead and leaving parts of her behind. So far, she'd managed to keep it a secret from the Queen Bees but for how long would she be able to manage that? She could tell even Paul was starting to doubt her story about her parents not liking her having a boyfriend.

The truth was Claire really, *really* liked him. Could she work it out with the girls and still stay in the club? She didn't think so. She thought about what would happen if the Queen Bees found out – how she would be publicly ousted. No one would want to be her friend after that – Charlotte's influence stretched far and wide. She wondered what Anne would do. She had a horrible feeling Anne would choose the club over their years of friendship. And in a way, she could understand because if she chose Paul over the Queen Bees, she knew she would have a very lonely existence.

'I'm just going to the bathroom,' she said to Paul, before hurrying out of his bedroom. Everything felt like it was getting too intense and she needed a few minutes alone. Locking the bathroom door behind her, she splashed her face with cold water. Taking a few deep breaths, she felt better. She would sort it all out once she got home and was alone; it was just when she was with Paul, she found she couldn't think straight – her body seemed to take over. But then her eye caught the beautiful bangle on her arm. It was a thick gold and cream bangle with ornate butterflies etched on to it. Paul had given it to her as soon as they'd got into his bedroom.

'Happy birthday!' he'd whispered, handing over the gift in its small black box with silver foiling.

She'd opened it slowly savouring the moment and when she'd seen it, she'd gasped. It was way more than she'd expected.

'Thank you,' Claire had whispered back, slipping it on and kissing him and then one thing had led to another.

After drying her face, she unlocked the door and walked straight into Maureen who was carrying a huge pile of bedding

'Hello, pet, you okay?'

'Yes, thank you Mrs— Maureen,' Claire corrected herself. 'Can I help you with that?'

'Oh, thank you, that would be very kind. If you could just help me fold them... these sheets, ever so tricky with just one person.'

Claire listened as Maureen chatted away and she wondered if Paul's mum was lonely all day in the house. She was clearly proud of Paul and his intelligence though, telling her all the things he could do when he was a baby.

'Reading by the age of three!' exclaimed Maureen. 'I couldn't get enough books from the library to keep up with him!'

'He's still the same now – always in the school library with all the books,' confided Claire and she saw Maureen cling on to the little piece of knowledge that usually would be forbidden to her.

And that's where Paul found them on the stair landing, chatting and laughing and folding laundry.

'Mum,' said Paul and Claire thought his voice sounded strange. 'What are you doing?'

'Just folding laundry – Claire kindly offered to help me.'

'I can help you with that later,' replied Paul. His voice was terse and his mother paused to look at him mid-fold.

'It's no problem, we're almost done,' said Claire but before she could finish the sentence, Paul had stormed off, his back rigid.

Claire looked at Maureen, wondering if she'd noticed anything strange. Maureen's face was closed but as she took the last of the folded laundry from Claire's arms, she said, 'Don't mind him, he's always been very moody – even when he was a young child,' clearly trying to keep the same upbeat tone they had both just been enjoying. But it fell flat, and Claire didn't know what to say. For a second, Claire thought his mum was about to say something else but then the moment passed, and Maureen turned away, her arms full of laundry, her lips pressed firmly together.

25

Stupid fucking cow!

What the hell was his mum thinking asking Claire to help her with the washing? Was she trying to make him look even more pathetic than he already was? Paul paced his bedroom floor, the dimensions of the room too small to diffuse his energy. Claire had left soon after and he didn't blame her. What had his mum said to her? His anger intensified, and Paul felt his room was like a prison rather than a sanctuary.

Gavin and his mates had driven him into hiding and he couldn't bear it any longer. He turned and ran out of the room, down the stairs, stopping only to put on his trainers, and out into the darkness. He didn't tell his parents where he was going, and he knew he would pay for it later, but for now he just needed to get out, to be anywhere but home. He jumped on his bike and pedalled.

The cold night air bit into him without his coat but he didn't care. He didn't even put on his bike lights. He cycled for twenty minutes, feeling the wind on his chest and face, cleansing his thoughts and when he finally stopped, he found himself outside Claire's house, a figure hidden amongst the darkness. He looked up at it in awe – it was far grander than he had imagined.

Through the elaborate bars of the wrought-iron gates, Paul saw a three-storey detached home where the golden lights from some of the windows allowed him a peek into Claire's world. Downstairs, he could see what he guessed to be the living room and her parents and Claire sat watching television. Paul slipped through the gates and crept up the driveway to get a closer look. Hiding behind a bush, he could see her mum was sat in a chair while her dad and Claire were stretched out on the sofa.

The sheer normality of it made him ache. His family were rarely in the same room together, even at mealtimes. Paul and his mum ate their evening meal together around five o'clock while his dad ate when he came home from work around half past six and, for as long as Paul could remember, his father didn't like to be disturbed during that time. His mum hovered around her husband, eager to anticipate anything he might need, before she, too, was banished to go and do *something useful*.

It was only when his dad sat down in his chair with his cigarette and the remote control that the whole house seemed to heave a sigh of relief. This was the least dangerous time when his dad was unlikely to erupt, and Paul and his mum could quietly go about their business. His mum often sat at the kitchen table reading her magazines, old copies that she quietly slipped into her handbag when in the doctors' waiting room or from the hair salon where she got her ends trimmed every two months. Paul would sometimes sit at the table with her doing his homework but usually he would go up to his room and splay himself and his books across the bed, lost in a world of calculations and revisions.

He couldn't ever remember being sat together as a family, not even when he was little. In fact, he didn't really remember much of his dad at all from when he was younger, only his mum. When he mentioned this to his mother, she told him it was because his dad used to work away a lot. Paul never questioned it but the older he got, the more he wondered about it. He knew his relationship with his father was different to other boys. It was Gavin's dad who'd taught him to ride a bike one Saturday afternoon and it had been Gavin's dad who'd driven them to various outings such as the sports field, the summer camp with YMCA, and the trips to the park. Paul's mother was ever present in his life but mainly from her usual spot in the doorway to wave him off or welcome him back.

Now as he watched Claire's dad get up from the sofa and ruffle her hair, the small gesture emphasised the void even further, repelling Paul from his crouched watching position to scrabble back down the driveway, through the gate and back to his bike. He held the handlebars tightly, pedalling his way back home, knowing all the while that once he arrived at his own house, the drabness would be even more apparent.

Now he knew what he must do; he had to work even harder to make sure he succeeded in his dream of becoming a doctor. Then he could provide for her, buy her a big house like the one she lived in and together they would create their own family.

★

Paul slipped through the back door quietly, hoping no one had noticed his absence. The house was silent and he was just about to leg it up the stairs when he heard the clattering of broken crockery as it smashed against the wall. Paul jumped and quickly ran upstairs to his bedroom. His heart pounded as he heard his dad shouting.

What had happened? What slight had his mother made? For God's sake, all she had to do was sit and read her magazines, keep quiet and not set him off. But deep down, he knew it was an almost impossible challenge. His father was sensitive even to someone breathing. The anger rose in Paul sharp and fast, and he felt the bite of pain as he slammed his fist into the wall. It was the only way to release everything inside of him.

He couldn't help his mum – he'd tried it before and it had made everything worse. Afterwards, when his dad had slammed out of the house, his mum had begged him never to intervene again on the basis that it just made him angrier. As Paul had sat hunched over on the kitchen floor surrounded by the shards of glass from the picture frame his father had thrown, his impotence had been as glaring as the purple bruising across his ribs, and he had reluctantly agreed. But now as he held his fist in one hand and flung himself on the bed, he wished to God he had never made such a promise.

Paul kept his eyes straight ahead, his only focus being to get to his classroom without incident.

'Knobhead!'

The insult ricocheted down the school corridor arousing the other students' curiosity. Paul hadn't needed to look up to know it was directed at him and as Gavin gathered pace in his verbal outpouring, Paul was relieved to see his maths teacher, Mr Addington, barrel down the corridor towards the classroom, his arms full of exercise books. With one last step, Paul reached the sanctity of the classroom, Mr Addington a few steps behind him, closing the classroom door with a satisfying thud.

Immediately, the noise from the corridor was gone and Paul felt himself breathe. He sat down at his desk pulling out his books while discreetly trying to look for Claire. She was usually towards the back of the room with some of the girls and Paul pretended to drop his pencil, so he could look behind and check. When he saw her, she caught his eye, and she gave him her secret smile that she reserved just for him. Paul could barely contain his joy. He might be a knobhead but he was going out with the prettiest, smartest girl he had ever met.

'So, what did he say?' quizzed Paul, impatiently.

'Nice to see you too, mate!' joked Brian.

They were sat down in their usual spot in the woods, having biked over. Usually, they would be doing a few ramps and tricks, but Paul was eager to hear what Brian had to say. Brian had promised that he would ask his brother his advice on getting a girl to base three and hopefully base four. Paul had turned sixteen at the beginning of September and with Claire's recent birthday, he was hoping they could both cement their relationship.

'Come on, tell me!' pleaded Paul, ignoring Brian's sarcasm.

'Whoa… easy,' replied Brian, putting his hands up in mock protest.

'Oh shit. You didn't ask him, did you? What happened?'

'I did, sort of,' protested Brian. 'Well, no not really.'

'Why not?'

'He was being a twat, that's why. I tried to ask him but then he started taking the piss, and then he got me in a headlock, and then he went off out with his mates.'

Paul felt his shoulders sag in disappointment. 'What am I going to do?'

'Who says you need to do anything? Just go with the flow,' encouraged Brian.

Paul paused for a minute, thinking about Claire. The last time he'd tried to take things further she'd gently removed his hand. He'd been too nervous to try again but he knew soon he wasn't going to be able to stop himself.

He looked up at Brian. 'Can you ask him again tonight?'

'I dunno, Paul, he just takes the piss… I can't get an answer out of him.'

'Please?'

Brian looked at him for a few seconds longer than was comfortable.

'You really like this girl, eh?' said Brian, quietly.

'Yep. She's the one.'

'Okay, I'll try again but no promises,' relented Brian.

Paul's relief was instant, and he looked at his friend gratefully before adding, 'You? In a headlock? Really?'

'Really,' replied Brian, grimly. 'Bastard.'

'Thanks, Brian – I owe you,' said Paul, knowing his friend would most likely end up tussling again with his brother on his behalf. But once he and Claire had reached fourth base, he knew nothing would keep them apart and Gavin and his mates could go and jump.

DECEMBER 1989

26

The school had been deserted, staff and students leaving as quickly as they could to avoid the torrential downpour. Sports practices had been cancelled and Charlotte had postponed the Queen Bee meeting to the weekend. Drama room three had seemed such a good idea at the time. Afterwards, Claire wondered how she could have been so stupid, so reckless. She'd thought it would be safe, where nothing bad would happen.

As Paul lay on top of her, she wasn't thinking straight. It was like when she was in the pool, the water filling her ears, blocking out everything and anything. But then a shriek had pierced the film of water that was Paul, his body covering every inch of hers, and then suddenly she was weightless, her skirt shoved up and her knickers around her ankles like the elastic game she used to play at primary school. *England, Ireland, Scotland, Wales, Inside, Outside, Puppy Dog Tails.*

Everything had happened so quickly; the hands that grabbed Paul and pulled him off her, her speechless shock, his pleading cries. Her shame lay open for everyone to see, raw and exposed. The singular voice that had interrupted them had grown into several and amongst them, Claire could hear Mrs Harrington, her usual confident baritone laced with panic as she instructed one of the girls to go and get the head teacher.

Claire felt like she was drowning. Her voice was submerged amongst the ever-growing noise in drama room three. She could hear the whispers amongst the girls. *Poor Claire. Attack. Got here just in time.* And then more adults arrived, and Paul was led away, still calling out her name beseechingly. It was only when she felt a blanket being put tenderly around her shoulders, that she started to sob but not even her tears could soften the cold hard accusation of attempted rape.

OCTOBER 2017

27

Claire closed her office door gratefully, drawn to her desk as if the huge solid slab of wood could act as a barrier against the memories. The desk was meticulously organised, with files and documents all neatly laid out in order of priority. A single photo sat on it, a close-up landscape shot taken the year before of her, Chris and the boys on a skiing holiday. Claire was the only one in the photo wearing her skiing goggles. Joshua and Jamie stood next to each other laughing, delighted to be out in the snow. Chris looked happy as well. He'd always loved skiing and she'd only got into it after she met him.

Outside in the corridor, she could hear the hum of the office and was glad of the privacy. She'd just spent a gruelling few hours in the meeting room working on the Rose Aiker case. Rose had come into the office for the last hour and Claire was only supposed to spend a few minutes with her, making sure Rose was confident with her representation, but of course, Claire had ended up staying for the whole meeting. And not just that; she had got involved.

Claire had seen the look pass between Greg and Chloe as she took charge of the case. She'd even heard Greg's not-so-subtle suggestion that perhaps Claire had other cases to be working on and Claire had wanted to excuse herself then. As a partner, Claire was the most senior counsel in the room so of course she was allowed to oversee the meeting, she justified to herself. But that wasn't the agreement and she knew it. So, what had compelled her to stay?

It was Rose. Each time, Claire had tried to excuse herself from the proceedings Rose had chosen those very moments to ask a question or seek reassurance and Claire's professional courtesy wouldn't let her leave the room. And who could blame Rose? She was still a child, just shy of twenty years old. What was Claire supposed to do? This was exactly why she didn't want to be involved in the case in the first place – it was impossible to do the half measures that Julia was suggesting.

Claire sighed and sat back in her chair, tilting her head side to side to release the knots in her neck. It didn't help that Rose was estranged from her parents and she always came alone to the meetings.

'It might help to have someone here to support you,' suggested Claire, gently, when she'd discovered that Rose hadn't even told her family about what she was going through. It also led Claire to wonder how Rose was paying her legal bills but she'd checked with accounts and all the billing was up to date.

Sitting up straight, she noticed it was getting dark outside and Claire switched on her desk lamp. Checking her watch, she saw she only had a couple more hours before she needed to leave for home. It was Friday and they usually had a family night, although Joshua had been doing his own thing more and more over the last few years. She tried never to push him to stay at home if he wanted to be out with his friends. He worked hard during the week and he deserved a night out.

Still, she loved it when he chose staying home over going out. The four of them together snuggled on the couch was one of the highlights of Claire's week and she knew Chris enjoyed it too, so she quickly sent Joshua a message asking what his plans were for the evening. Her phone pinged a response almost immediately.

Sorry, Mum, off out tonight with the lads!

She was disappointed, but she quickly texted him back telling him she would save him some pizza and then got back to work. She made notes on her legal pad, the rhythmic strokes of the pen organising her thoughts, the black ink a pleasing contrast to the yellow paper. While she used her laptop for official documents, all her notes were made the old-fashioned way. It helped her think. She had cupboards full of legal pads, all boxed, labelled and filed, and could retrieve them when she needed to. Julia often joked that they would have to move to a larger office just to accommodate them.

She was so focused on writing that she didn't see the door handle move, a figure slip in the room and walk towards her.

'Thanks for taking this on,' a voice suddenly said.

Claire jumped. Rose was standing in front of her desk, stock still, her heavily made-up blue eyes watching her.

'Rose! Goodness, you startled me!' Claire put down her pen. 'What are you still doing here?' she added.

'Sorry,' replied Rose. 'I just wanted to come and say thanks for representing me.'

'You're welcome but I'm not really representing you. I'm just here to support your team.'

'But you will be in court with me, won't you?' asked Rose, her fingers clasping each other anxiously.

'Yes, I'll be there.'

'Good, 'cos I'm not sure I can do it without you,' replied Rose.

Claire saw large tears slide slowly down Rose's face.

Claire got up from behind her desk. 'Shhhh, shhh, come on now, it's okay.'

Putting her arm around the young girl, she led her over to the sofa and the two of them sat down, Rose clinging to Claire like they were in a three-legged race. As Claire held Rose, she wondered what the young girl had heard about her. It was all such a long time ago, surely no one would even remember? But somehow Rose had and had sought her out. Perhaps, like Julia had said, this was an opportunity for some good to come out of the whole horrible experience she'd had with Paul. Unlike Rose, there had been no police involved, no charges pressed, no arrests.

Claire thought back to the aftermath of it. Charlotte's screams as she found Paul on top of her, Claire's own shame as she lay there half dressed, and finally Paul's aggression as he was taken away.

Even now, years later, she couldn't think of that afternoon without feeling sick. Humiliation filled her to the core when she thought of him, both as the young teenager he once was and the man he must now be. She wondered where he was, what he was doing. The last she'd heard was that he'd been expelled and had had to move schools. Afterwards, she'd tried to put him out of her mind and whenever he intruded on her thoughts, as he so often did, especially in the years immediately afterwards, she'd fought hard to supress the panic.

But sometimes fear coiled its way around her, so tightly that she couldn't breathe and that's when she'd increased her swimming sessions. At one point, she was going twice a day just to block out the images that filled her mind. For the most part, it had worked, although she'd lost a lot of weight. She remembered her mum worrying about it and trying to cook filling foods for her. Swimming had been the only way she'd been able to move on. With every stroke, she affirmed that the incident with Paul was over. She had nothing to feel guilty about.

She also had to hand it to Charlotte – it was then that the club had really come into their own. Charlotte and her swarm of bees had surrounded her, never leaving her side during school and then college hours. Charlotte had organised a rota so she never had to walk to or from school by herself and Claire was christened a survivor, a victim who had overcome the odds. Such was the girls' intensity that Claire almost started to believe it herself.

But then she would remember: Paul's breath against her ear, his hands on her, his scent. She remembered how he used to talk about his dream of becoming a doctor, the way his hair fell over his face, their first kiss in the cinema. And then she wondered how everything could have gone so horribly wrong. She was just grateful that it hadn't got reported to the police. They'd asked her of course, but she'd protested adamantly.

As Rose gradually quietened down, Claire could feel the slim frame of the girl in her arms. Even though Rose was tall at five foot seven, she would have had no chance against men intent on violating her, but here she was, brave enough to speak up about her experience, to take those who had hurt her to task through the British courts. Suddenly Claire knew what she had to do. She would fight for Rose to be heard, to have her say. Claire would fight, not from the side lines, but from the ring itself, front and centre, and leading the charge.

Still holding Rose, the girl's face hidden behind her hair, she leant down, bringing her lips close to the young girl's ear.

'I'm here for you, Rose, and we're going to do our utmost to fight this,' whispered Claire, and hoped her actions would go some way to alleviate her own pain and guilt.

28

Paul looked at his printed name and signature on the sign-in sheet at Manchester Royal Infirmary hospital where he worked as one of the caretakers: Paul Jacobs. He avoided writing his name down as much as possible, but the hospital employee registration system was down, and everyone had to fill in the timesheets. He'd been Jacobs for so long now but seeing it in print always reminded him of the events leading up to his name change, triggered by that fateful afternoon with Claire.

Things had quickly spiralled out of control. Thanks to that squawking parrot bitch Charlotte, who had burst in on them, the incident had spread throughout the school and then around Castlefield and he, and his parents, had become social pariahs. He'd railed and protested but expulsion had been swift and immediate, and he'd felt the familiar rage within. But this time he couldn't control himself and he'd flown at the head teacher, fists clenched. Afterwards, when all his pent-up frustration had been released, he'd cried in the privacy of his bedroom, tears of anger and shock.

But not even he could imagine how much worse the situation would become.

Despite not being reported or charged, the harassment would start that very evening and he'd woken up the next morning to the word *rapist* spray-painted on the garage door. His mother had been terrified, his father terrifying, but the abuse intensified over the months and eventually, his family had been driven out, forced to move to the other side of Manchester.

Still, the persecution persisted, the gossip having followed them like a stalker. In desperation, with their next move, they eventually changed their surname. Perhaps that would have been the end of it or at least something the Joneses could put behind them, but as the years rolled by, it was clear that a domino effect had been put in motion. His father lost his job, finding solace in the pub rather than at the job centre and there would be weeks when he and his mum wouldn't see him. What little money his father had often went on drink so his mum got a job as a cashier in a local supermarket.

Paul was supposed to be in yet another new school, but the students were rough, the teachers disinterested, and the textbooks he had once loved became a hideous visual reminder of his past. Gradually, he stopped attending and despite his mother's protests, he found work in the local pub.

Receiving his first wage was, if not life-changing, then certainly memorable for Paul. The little brown envelope bulged slightly from the wad of notes and the coins added a pleasing weight. It was then that he realised he could buy a little bit of happiness. He deserved it after everything he'd been through and as he discreetly exchanged his own little packet for a clear plastic one on the corner of Jamison and Ridge Streets, he felt slightly better at the thought of a little pill coursing through his body altering his shitty reality, even if it was only for a few hours.

He wasn't a drug addict, he told himself because he didn't do it every day, just on the odd Friday night when he needed a boost to get him through the weekend. Sometimes he bought more than he needed and sold it on to a neighbour or the odd punter in the pub where he worked to make a little extra money.

Paul never knew whether his father would be home or not and even though it upset his mum, he always hoped he was out somewhere on one of his benders. Paul preferred a sad house to a violent one. Eventually, Paul had moved out and rented a dingy studio on a council estate called Fairfield. There was nothing fair about it – it was every man for himself and it was the one time he was grateful to his father for giving him the experience in being able to dodge a fist. He would later go on to secure another flat from the council, but he never forgot Fairfield Estate. It was grim but after years of living with his parents, Fairfield was a haven of freedom and anonymity.

His various neighbours were mainly petty thieves, druggies, and, from the noises he'd heard through the walls, fighters. He'd seen a kid, who couldn't have been more than eight years old, pull out a knife on an elderly man as he'd come home with his shopping. And for what? Some bread, milk, and eggs. But it was how things got done around there and Paul knew, amongst all the violence and crime, no one would give a toss about his own past.

The estate also provided him with a more regular customer base for dealing. Paul had been in his early twenties then and his father had been on at him for a while to get out. Paul didn't disagree with him. Paul was big enough to take on his father, or at least stand between him and his mother when Bill got so enraged he wanted to take his frustration out on his wife. Paul had tried to get Maureen to move in with him, but she'd refused and he was bewildered by her response. He'd always assumed that she never left Bill because she had nowhere else to go, yet here she was turning down the opportunity to escape.

It was then that his belief in his mother as a coward solidified. There was nothing more he could do for her and there was nothing more she could do for him. As he packed his bags, his mother had begged him not to leave, her pleading tone so irritating, Paul was tempted to wallop her one himself, but he'd been dragged down by a female before and he was damned if he was going to let that happen again.

As he shut the door firmly behind him, immune to Maureen's tearful begging, he'd closed that part of his life forever. He didn't even give her his new address, as Paul knew she would only give it to his dad. Instead, he kissed her on the cheek, told her he would call her, and left his parents' house without even a backward glance. It was only when he went back a few months later, the first time he'd paid a visit since leaving, that he learned his mother was in hospital.

A stroke.

Found her last week. Nothing to be done.
Didn't even know until it was too late.

His father's slurred words from his armchair reached Paul's ears in a vacuum. What the hell was he talking about? When he saw the tears roll down his father's cheeks he knew it wasn't just a drunken ramble but a reality that Paul had in no way prepared for. Paul had started to shake, the disgust of his own actions staining his soul. He'd left his mother in her final months with nothing more to look forward to than the odd two-minute phone call. He felt his own tears spill and a silent but hopeful part of him wondered if his father would reach out to him. Just for a moment, amongst all the brutality, he would feel the comfort of his own flesh and blood. And if Bill had, perhaps it would have been enough to prevent what happened next.

But then again, perhaps nothing could have prevented the inevitable confrontation between father and son. With Maureen's illness, the precarious family triad had finally buckled, releasing an avalanche of testosterone as Paul and Bill dealt with the news in the only way they knew how.

With every punch, Paul learnt how his father had never wanted marriage and children so soon in his life; in fact, Bill had had his own plans but Maureen had got knocked up and Bill had done the right thing. And as Paul lay back on the couch, nursing a burst lip, he realised his mother wasn't a coward, just someone who was paying for a mistake. As his father continued his verbal stream of resentment and fury, Paul heard the words that he himself had been thinking since he'd heard of his mum's stroke.

'She did everything for you and how did you repay her?' snarled his father, leaning in so close Paul could smell his sour breath. 'By shaming her with that fucking fiasco with that girl. You know people would call your mother names in the street? She couldn't take it. It's your fault she's ill – years of harassment because of your actions – it's almost killed her.'

At the truth of it, Paul vomited, the grey sludge spraying his father's shoes.

'What was her name?' spat Bill. His father was so incandescent, he barely noticed the mess on the carpet.

Staggering, Paul managed to get up from the couch and wiped his mouth before uttering the name that would haunt him forever. 'Claire.'

'Well, I hope she was worth it, you fucking rapist,' finished Bill, before he'd turned away and collapsed back into his armchair, the blame for his wife's illness firmly placed on his son.

Paul, mind and body spent, knew it was pointless to even bother arguing with him.

Afterwards, he'd gone to the hospital and sat with his mother, her listless body held together with machines. He didn't leave her side until she died three days later.

Now, as Paul walked towards the hospital cleaning staff room, his rucksack slung over one shoulder, his hat pulled down low over his forehead, he tried not to think about his last interaction with Bill. Bill was right but it didn't make him any less than a dickhead and he couldn't care less about his dad.

But Claire.

Claire had always haunted him. Over the years and despite the distance, he had followed her life. It hadn't been difficult to keep track of her movements – Castlefield was a small town and she hadn't gone far. And then Facebook had arrived, and her life was all there laid out in front of him, without him even needing to leave the squalor of his bedsit. The photos of her only increased his desire for her. Tracking her was so easy, he almost missed the old-fashioned methods. His footsteps trailing her, his simple disguise of a hat, scarf and big coat in winter, baseball cap and sunglasses in summer, making him blend into the busy crowds of the city centre. He rarely went to Castlefield – that would be too risky, but he knew where her office was, what time she took her lunch, and where she liked to eat.

Over the years, he'd got lucky a few times like when he'd risked getting close enough to overhear her making some plans for the weekend as she chatted with colleagues in the queue in the café during a break. One time, he'd trailed her to a bus stop and at the last second he had followed her on, squeezing between the crowd of passengers.

Once mobile phones became the norm, information was available to him instantly. He watched her at weekends then with her family, her husband and children, but the jealousy was almost unbearable. It was like watching the life he could have had, and he preferred to watch Claire when she was alone. During that time, he could pretend that she was his, that their love had not gone so horribly wrong. He wanted her so badly and while she may have ruined their last encounter, he would make sure their next one would be one she would never forget.

'All right, Paul mate,' greeted Dereck, his supervisor, as Paul walked into the large staffroom. 'Just about to put the kettle on – you want one?'

'Cheers, mate,' said Paul, dumping his bag in his locker and double-checking the lock was secure. He had a few deliveries in his bag for a couple of the cleaning ladies, who had a nice little habit, which he would hand over once Dereck was out of the way. At this hour of the morning, there was only the two of them; the cleaning teams wouldn't arrive for another thirty minutes and Paul had come to appreciate Dereck's company as they sipped strong tea and reviewed the jobs for the week. It was one of the rare times Dereck wasn't talking about his various health issues. Between them, they did the gardens, the many odd jobs around the hospital and oversaw most of the cleaning rotas.

When Gladys at the Jobcentre Plus had told him about the hospital vacancy four years ago, he'd laughed bitterly at the irony, the unexpected sound from her surliest jobseeker causing Gladys to spill hot tea on her blue flowery top. He was glad. He'd never liked her. She was always looking down on him even though she could barely use the computer. It always took her ages to bring up his profile on the system.

He'd been in and out of the jobcentre over the years, and Gladys was always there, her large rolls of stomach fat resting on the tops of her thighs. Her mouth was always moving, either taking large gulps of tea or sucking on her boiled sweets, but rarely talking. That was one thing he was grateful for. Gladys was not a talker, unlike Dereck whose frequent chatter occasionally irked Paul. But Paul hadn't had the luxury of choice when it came to work. His last contract had finished, and he needed the job. Plus, if he was honest with himself, Dereck's yakking could sometimes be a welcome distraction especially on Paul's worst days when he struggled to believe that he'd ended up working in a hospital in the maintenance department and not striding around in a white coat followed around by adoring female nurses.

Dereck handed him his tea and the two of them sat down at the well-worn table, poring over the various printouts. Twenty minutes later, the staffroom door opened again, and the cleaning ladies came in, disgruntled before they'd even begun, their tired blue tabards little defence against the endless hours of cleaning up other people's shit. He watched them, his eyes falling on Susie. They'd shagged a few times, outside behind the bins after their shift. He'd tried to invite her back to his place the last time, but she'd pulled up her jeans, lit a cigarette and walked quickly away, the smoke puffing out behind her in the cold air. *Probably for the best.*

Paul gulped down the rest of his tea, stood up and opened the cupboard to get his toolbox. The cleaners were chuckling now, something about one of their husbands unable to get it up, their laughter cruel and mocking to his ears. As if sensing his stare, Susie looked at him then, her face still smirking. In his mind, they were laughing at him and he felt the fury rise in his chest before he turned and walked away, gripping the handle of the toolbox too tightly.

29

Rose sat in front of Claire, moody and unresponsive, and Claire had a flash of insight of what her life might have been like if she'd given birth to a girl instead of boys. The second time Claire had fallen pregnant, she'd secretly hoped for a girl. Not that she ever said that out loud. When anyone ever asked, which they did frequently, she'd trotted out the clichéd line about being happy with whatever the gender, but when the midwife announced a little boy, she couldn't deny she'd felt a flicker of disappointment.

However, ever since she'd started working on Rose's case, she'd gained an insight into the mind of a teenage girl and it made her wonder if she would have been able to handle a daughter. One thing was for sure, if Rose *had* been her daughter, Claire knew she would've struggled as a parent.

Rose came into the office several times over the weeks and it was always Claire's best guess as to what mood she would be in. Sometimes, she would be communicative and helpful, her manner almost friendly but then other times, she would withdraw, refusing to speak, the effort of going over every detail clearly difficult. Still, between Claire, Chloe and Greg, they'd managed to build up a profile. A rough childhood on one of Manchester's toughest housing estates. Absent father. Drug-using mother. A chaotic household of siblings. Too many mouths to feed and not enough money.

Although she'd left school early, at least Rose had a job and a roof over her head. But Rose had another weapon and that was her beauty. Or perhaps in this case, it had been her downfall. It was clear from her social media profiles and by her own admission that Rose spent much of her time partying. She never bought her own drinks, she had announced, almost proudly, and anyone could see Rose was used to being the centre of attention.

Claire needed to find something to counter the party-girl image Rose was portraying.

'Are you doing any form of study or training?' asked Claire.

'No,' replied Rose. 'What does that have to do with anything anyway? Rape is rape.'

Good point.

'Well,' said Claire cautiously. 'The defence will try their best to discredit you. They will alter the narrative so that the focus shifts to you and your lifestyle rather than what happened.' She paused. 'They may try and imply that you are lying. That it didn't really happen, or if it did, then there were other factors—'

'But it did happen!' protested Rose. Claire wasn't surprised she hadn't been able to finish her sentence. It was the ultimate insult to those brave enough to come forward. But it didn't change the reality. And it was Claire's job to make sure Rose was properly prepared for that reality. She couldn't afford for Rose to crumble.

'Of course, it did,' replied Claire soothingly. 'We just have to make sure there's no room for doubt in the jury's mind.'

Rose sighed and stared off into the distance and Claire watched her. What was she thinking? How her life could have been different? *Should* have been different? Rose was nineteen and at her age Claire had been in the first year of her degree. She'd had plans. She'd had a boyfriend. She'd had parents who were always there if she needed them.

What had led Claire and Rose to lead such different lives? Claire thought back to her own school years. Despite the gossip and the rumours, she'd gone on to the complete her exams. Her shock and horror at the *incident* with Paul had been channelled into her studies. She didn't want to go to parties, she didn't want to socialise, so each day after school, she locked herself in her room with her books and worked, her mind refusing entry to anything else that tried to get in.

During the day, the girls treated her like a wounded animal and while she was still part of the Queen Bees, she was on the fringes. The Queen Bees had never met in drama room three again. Charlotte had made the announcement while looking meaningfully in Claire's direction. Claire had pretended not to notice. Instead, the Queen Bees met in different classrooms during breaks or lunchtimes when they were empty. And just like her mother had promised, time helped.

After her GCSE exams, she went on to sixth form and she started to socialise a little bit more. When Claire asked her mother if she would take her shopping for an outfit for a party, Claire could feel the relief practically emanating from her mother at the typical teenage request. They'd spent the day shopping and by the end of it, Claire didn't just have a new outfit but a brand-new wardrobe. She remembered hanging up all the clothes, feeling like she was a normal girl after all and, eventually, she had learnt that the longer you pretended, the easier it was to convince yourself.

So, when Chris had approached her at a party, she didn't think twice. She went for a drink with him and ended up spending the summer with him. They collected their A-level results together, went to Manchester university, and for the most part she was happy. Paul had moved away, and that chapter of her life had been replaced with a law degree, a man who told her he loved her, and the prospect of an exciting career. Nothing could hurt or threaten her now and it was a relief; a relief to know that despite the *incident*, she was living what her mother often told her was a dream life.

So, now as Claire looked across her desk at Rose, it was understandable for Claire to feel uneasy – the case was a stark reminder of her own past, which she had worked hard to put behind her. But there was something else that had troubled Claire. It was the phone call that had done it. Her home phone had rung just after Chris had left with Joshua and Jamie that morning. Her initial thought was that it was Lucy telling her she was ill and couldn't come in that day. Who else would call so early in the morning?

So, picking up the receiver, she was already half planning a contingency plan to leave work early and pick up Jamie. But as she placed the phone to her ear, she could hear slow and steady breathing. It had happened before, not frequently enough to cause major concern though and Claire had just put it down to prank calls. They happened to everyone. What did people expect when the council shut down the youth club? You were left with a group of kids with nothing better to do. But over the years, Claire wondered if she'd had more than her fair share.

Pushing that morning's call to one side, she reasoned with herself that she had taken this case on against her better judgement and it was making her jumpy. Knowing she wasn't going to get much further with Rose, she decided to call it a day.

'I was thinking about us today,' said Claire to Chris as they sat at home eating their evening meal. 'About when you first asked me out.'

It was almost eight o'clock and the house was quiet. Jamie was in bed and Joshua had wolfed down his meal before heading to his room with his laptop. Chris looked up from his plate, the pasta poised on the fork.

'Really? What made you think of that?'

'Nothing in particular,' said Claire, not wanting to share details of Rose. 'Do you remember? You asked me out for a drink at the sixth form social. Later you told me you were worried I was going to say no.'

Chris laughed. 'Yeah, I wasn't a hundred per cent sure you would be up for it, but I got you in the end.'

'That was a great summer, wasn't it?' reminisced Claire, ignoring her husband's possessive language. Their first summer together, they hadn't done anything special like go on holiday. Well, Chris's parents had asked him to go on holiday with them to America, but he'd refused, wanting to spend every minute with her. At that point, they didn't know if they would both get into the same university. Claire remembered thinking it was the most romantic thing in the world, for him to give up a trip to the US for her.

Claire's parents usually took her abroad most years but that summer they hadn't planned anything in case she'd preferred to go away with her friends after finishing her exams. Instead, she spent it with Chris. They took romantic day trips to the Lake District, went for drives, enjoyed long walks and pub lunches. And they talked a lot.

After a few weeks, Chris had broached the subject of Paul; said that he'd heard what had happened, told her he would never hurt her, that she was always safe with him. He didn't press her for any details and she was glad. She couldn't talk about any of it. She just wanted to forget it. So instead, when he put his arms around her, she held him close, closed her eyes, and breathed in his scent, pushing away the memories of Paul. It was over and her new life was about to begin with Chris.

'It was a great summer,' agreed her husband, finishing his mouthful of pasta. 'Although it was a long time ago now. Do you remember going to collect our exam results? God, we got so drunk afterwards.'

Claire remembered. She'd got straight As and her parents had been so proud. They had both come to the school with her, her dad taking a rare day off work, and they were thrilled when she'd shown them the results paper. To his credit, her dad had barely flinched when she'd told him she was planning to go to Manchester university with Chris instead of her first choice, Edinburgh. He didn't try and persuade her to go further afield and for that Claire was grateful. Her dad had simply said it was her choice and she had to do what made her happy. Surprisingly, her mother hadn't said anything either and she suspected she was relieved she would have her daughter closer to home.

Now, as she sat at the dining table opposite Chris, she wondered how her life would have turned out if she'd gone to Edinburgh instead. Would she have met someone else? Would she be living somewhere else? It was a pointless hypothesis, but one Claire couldn't help occasionally wondering about.

But then she reminded herself how lucky she was to have met someone like Chris. He was good-looking, came from a wealthy family, and he loved her. Her parents had been thrilled when they announced their engagement and they'd had a great life so far. They argued, but what couple didn't? Chris was often tired and irritable but that was life when you had two kids and the pressures of work. Yes, she told herself, as she smiled across at him, everything had worked out for the best.

30

Paul peered through the window of the youth club, his hat pulled down low over his face, his scarf protecting him from the harsh November wind. Paul was pretty much bald now and had started shaving his head as soon as he noticed his hair thinning. His dad had had a comb-over for years and when he got really enraged, the carefully placed strands would fly around like ribbons on a maypole. It would have been funny if the circumstances had been different.

The first time Paul had shaved his head he'd watched the strands of strawberry blonde fall to the floor and they'd reminded him of a conversation he'd had with Claire years ago. She'd commented how nice his hair was and at the time, he'd ignored what he'd thought of as a girlie comment, his attention far more focused on her body than his own.

Paul scratched his beard and looked at the scene inside the youth club where he volunteered. He could just make out the young woman's outline, her long coltish legs clad in tight-fitting jeans and long blonde hair tied up in a ponytail.

Her name was Simone and she'd been coming to the youth club most Friday nights for the last few weeks. Paul had been coming for the last five years. Initially, it hadn't been through choice but as penance sentenced by the Honourable Judge Greenwood for getting caught in possession of weed. What started out as a six-month obligation had turned in to an easy supply of girls and Paul often thought the pompous, patronising Judge Greenwood would have been left speechless if he knew what he'd started.

This particular youth club was in one of the worst areas, not just of the city, but of the country – unemployment and crime were rife and the effect on the children of such families was everywhere to be seen. Paul had learnt this from Gloria, who had set up the youth club, and was almost as old as the church hall in which the club was held. On his first evening, Gloria had taken him into her office, a tiny box room piled high with papers. The majority of those visiting the youth club lived or had grown up in poverty, had little or no education, and didn't have much of a future to look forward to.

Paul had immediately felt right at home. He remembered Gloria telling him that the youth club received about five hundred kids a week between six and nineteen years old. Paul supervised the sixteen- to nineteen-year-olds and many of them were boys and young men. But there were girls too thought Paul now, his eyes following Simone as she chatted with her friends. He knew that in a few minutes, she would remove her coat and sit down at one of the tables where all the materials were spread out ready for the craft and textiles session. Simone loved designing and making clothes. She'd told him if she had the money, she would have gone on to do a proper design course. But Paul knew so much more about Simone than just her career aspirations.

He knew that like many of her peers at the youth club, she'd had a hard time living at home. She was just four years old when her father left. Her mother didn't work and they struggled to keep a roof over their heads. Simone moved around a lot with her mum who crashed on various friends' couches, and inevitably turned to drink and drugs to deal with the disappointment that her life had become.

He knew that Simone had watched as her mother became more and more dependent on drugs, to the point where she needed them just to get up in the morning. Simone was used to preparing her own breakfast and making her own way to school, desperate to escape whichever house or flat they were staying in at the time.

He knew that she'd dreamt of her father returning and rescuing her and that she imagined he'd gone off in search of a better life and that he'd always planned to come back for his daughter.

He knew that at five years old, Simone was worried her father wouldn't be able to find them because they moved around so much. At six, she went back to their old house on her birthday just in case he came by with a birthday present. At eight, she wrote him a letter and saved it in her special box for his homecoming and at nine years old she made of list of things that a *better life* might look like and thought maybe it would take a little bit of time for her father to do all those things. By ten, she asked her mother if she thought he was ever coming back, and at eleven, she screamed at her mother that it was all her fault.

After that, she tried not to think about him.

It was clear her mother's behaviour had made him leave because all she did was lie on the couch, half sleeping, half watching television. At night, she drank and smoked and talked with whoever was in the house where they were staying at the time. When Simone found her one morning passed out on the floor, her arm draped over another body, the smell of booze, vomit, and urine almost making her gag, Simone could understand exactly why her father had left. The only part she couldn't understand was why he hadn't taken her with him.

All this, Paul had learnt from his conversations with Simone and his reading of her case file. Now at sixteen, Simone reminded him of a young Claire – the blonde hair, the slim frame, the blue eyes.

Lovely. Perfect.

Paul left the window and went into the youth centre and as he stood there, relishing the warmth of being indoors, he caught Simone's eye and winked.

'How do you know all this stuff!' exclaimed Simone and Paul savoured the rare admiration. They'd been talking about artificial intelligence, a first for Paul with one of the youth club members. Usually, it was football or the next night out.

'I used to be pretty good in school,' he replied, noncommittally.

'How old are you?' asked Simone, intrigued. For a minute, Paul thought about lying, then decided against it.

'Forty-three,' he replied.

'Yeah, that is old,' replied Simone with all the nonchalance of a teenager.

'Thanks!' replied Paul sarcastically, but he was grinning.

Simone appraised him thoughtfully. 'You don't look forty-three if that makes you feel any better.'

'I don't?' said Paul. 'How old do I look then?'

'Still old, but maybe thirty-five or something like that.'

'Thanks, I'll take it.'

They were sat at the table where Simone was busy sewing two pieces of fabric together. A skirt, apparently.

'So, what was your favourite subject?' asked Simone, surprising Paul by returning to their previous conversation.

'Science,' replied Paul, trying to ignore the strange longing that shot through him.

'Urgh! I hate science, especially biology. I hate Mrs Jenkins – she made us dissect a frog. I thought I was going to be sick. And we have our mock exam soon – I'm dreading it.'

Paul felt the flutter of opportunity. But he had to go carefully. 'Why?'

'Because I don't understand any of it – Jenkins makes it all so bloody complicated! And if I skive any more classes, they'll end up suspending me,' announced Simone, grabbing her sewing scissors and furiously cutting the fabric. Paul watched as the material sliced in two, her blonde head bent over in concentration.

'When's your exam?'

'In a few weeks,' murmured Simone as she finished and put the scissors down and looked back up at him. 'Anyway, I don't care. I just want to work in textiles. My friend's mum works in a clothes shop and said she might be able to get me a job after I leave school.'

'But don't you want to study design?' asked Paul.

'Yeah, but I don't see how I'm going to do that without any money. Besides, a shop is a good place to start, understand what customers are looking for… you know…'

Simone tailed off and Paul heard her uncertainty.

'Well, you just need a handful of exam passes to go to sixth-form college and that doesn't cost anything. And I can help you if you like…'

Simone looked at him and Paul feigned disinterest by examining a hangnail.

'Help me? What do you mean?' replied Simone, curiously.

'Well, help you with your biology and other classes. You don't have to get A stars – you just need to pass.'

Simone didn't reply, and Paul panicked that he'd been too quick to propose his solution.

'I'll think about it,' she replied, but Paul could tell from her smile that it was as good as done.

31

Claire was relieved to see Joshua smile at her as she entered his bedroom. He was reading on his bed. She *had* knocked on his door before entering, she just hadn't waited for him to say 'come in.' As she placed the freshly ironed laundry on a chair, Claire made a show of straightening the room and aligning the curtains.

'I'm just reading, Mum,' said Joshua with a grin, knowing full well she was checking on him. Claire smiled back at him, grateful he was so understanding.

'I know – I'm just tidying up your room a little,' replied Claire, determined to keep up the pretence. 'Are you ready to put up the Christmas tree decorations this afternoon?'

'Are you going to make hot chocolate?' bartered Joshua.

'Of course!' said Claire.

'With marshmallows?'

'Yep.'

'And cream?'

'Absolutely.' It was a family tradition they'd had since Joshua was small. 'Just give me five minutes to finish up in here.'

Joshua went back to reading his book, not planning on moving until he could smell the hot chocolate. Claire adjusted the chair and picked up a fallen book from his desk. Joshua's room was always fairly presentable, just another example of the dream-child status that she'd attributed to him all those years ago when he'd first slept through the night at six months. From then onwards, Joshua had slept twelve hours pretty much every night.

At the mother and baby clinic, when other mothers complained about lack of sleep, Claire refrained from sharing her good fortune and instead, she listened to stories of sleep deprivation, feeding every three hours and babies screaming when placed in the cot. She couldn't imagine it, but having got to know the other mothers so well, she realised how lucky she was to have a baby like Joshua. And since then, he'd rarely given them any trouble. He'd been an open book.

Until last year.

He'd just moved into sixth-form college and Claire had been stunned by the sudden mood swings, backchat, arguments and excessive use of his mobile phone. Those things had been difficult enough but what followed had been horrendous and Claire tried not to think about it. Since starting back at sixth-form college for his second year, things had much improved, but Claire still worried.

At the time, she had suspected it was something to do with a girlfriend. She hadn't been sure, but she remembered one night, almost twelve months ago, as they were all sat around watching television, he'd received a message on his phone. He'd suddenly announced he was going out and he left the house in a cloud of aftershave and a fresh T-shirt. Claire didn't know who the girl was; she could only hope that she was nice and didn't mess him around.

But when he came back less than an hour later, it was clear that the evening had gone wrong. When she'd gently asked him about it, he'd muttered something about not even messaging to let him know she was no longer coming and Claire knew he'd been stood up. Her heart broke for him. But she knew there was nothing she could do and as he'd stormed off to his bedroom, Claire had hoped it would all blow over. Instead, it seemed to get worse, judging by Joshua's absolute refusal to speak some days. Chris had warned her not to pressurise him but after a couple of weeks of this, Claire had gone into his bedroom, sat on the edge of his bed and gently removed his phone from his hands. His closed laptop lay next to him on the bed.

'You okay, love?' she'd asked simply.

Joshua had nodded, looking out of the window, refusing to meet her eye.

'Anything on your mind?' she'd tried.

'All good. Just homework.' He'd continued to stare out of the window, his chin defiant.

'You know, if there's anything you want to talk about, I'm—'

'I know, Mum, thanks.'

Claire had nodded. It was clear Joshua hadn't been in the mood for sharing and she hadn't wanted to push him.

'Okay, well, I'll leave you to it,' she had said, reluctantly getting up from his bed. She had looked down at him, the top of his head reminding her of those early baby days when she would spend hours just holding him and smelling his hair. She had leant down then and given him a kiss and left the room.

After closing the door behind her, she didn't hear Joshua reopen his laptop. Or watch him as he stared at the topless photo he'd received in his inbox, the girl's name at the top of the email making his stomach flip in desire.

Chris had looked up at her questioningly as Claire sat down next to him on the sofa. She'd shrugged. 'Nothing. Maybe you'll have better luck.'

'Okay. I'll see if I can drop him off in the car somewhere this week, but honestly, Claire, you're overreacting. It's just normal teenage stuff.'

'I know, I know. I'm just not used to him being like this, that's all.'

'Well, it had to happen sooner or later – we've had it good with him so far. And to be honest, it could be far worse. At least this way, it's just girl problems.'

Claire recalled this conversation with Chris knowing now that he'd been right but at the time, she hadn't been able to shake the feeling that there was something more to it. But then she'd always been more sensitive about Joshua. When Joshua was little, Chris was always saying she spoilt him too much, hugged him too much, was too cautious with him. She used to watch in horror as Chris threw him up in the air and caught him again, her precious boy screaming with laughter. When the two of them would roll around on the floor play-wrestling, Claire's heart would be in her mouth that Chris would squash him or break one of his bones.

As Joshua had got older, she'd become used to it, but she still struggled with just how much physicality boys seemed to exert towards one another. Always moving, pushing, shoving, running, kicking, wrestling, jumping. Once, Joshua had run towards her, his head down, and she'd held the tears back as his forehead had connected with her pelvis, his boyish desire to hug her resulting in a painful head-butt.

But now seeing Joshua on his bed, relaxed and happy, she leant over to kiss him on his forehead, and he swatted her away playfully before grabbing her in a big bear hug, Claire leant in to him, thankful that her son had returned to his usual self.

'Come on,' she said, happily. 'Let's go and make hot chocolate and put up the Christmas decorations.'

'Did you see about the reunion?' asked Chris, as he took the empty boxes of Christmas decorations from her to put back into the loft.

'Reunion?' replied Claire.

'Yep – it was on Facebook.'

'A school reunion?' she asked, trying to not let the panic creep into her voice.

'No – university.'

'Oh right, any particular reason?' The panic subsided and Claire was curious.

'Well, they were supposed to have it two years ago to celebrate twenty years since we graduated but no one got their arse in gear.'

'When is it?'

'Next month – shall we go?'

'Yep, why not? Could be fun,' replied Claire distractedly, picking up her phone to check her Facebook notifications for the reunion date. She knew it was more likely that they wouldn't end up going.

'God, can you believe it's been over twenty years? Makes me feel ancient,' said Chris.

Claire looked up in surprise. It was rare for him to bemoan his age. 'You're still gorgeous though,' she complimented.

'Your mother thought so too,' he added with a wink, giving her a peck on the cheek.

Claire laughed. He wasn't wrong. When her mother had found out she was going out with Chris, she'd been absolutely delighted.

'Just the type of boy every mother wants for their daughter!' Claire remembered her announcing. Claire wondered how her mother knew about Chris and questioned her.

'Everyone knows the Carmichaels, love. Even your *father* knows the Carmichaels.' And Claire had understood then. It was about status. About appearances. About connections. In fact, her mother had done everything possible to encourage their relationship, but she needn't have worried – Chris was smitten. Everyone had told her how lucky she was to have a boyfriend like Chris.

So committed!

So thoughtful!

And for the most part she agreed but, occasionally, she wondered why no one said *he* was the lucky one.

'After everything that happened with Paul and *the incident*,' her mother had commented one night when she was back home for the Easter holidays in her last year of university, 'well, it's a relief he's so understanding. Didn't I tell you everything would work out?'

Claire had been surprised; Paul's name was rarely mentioned since she'd told her mother everything that fateful afternoon. But that holiday, between endless hours preparing for her final university exams, Claire had sensed something was going on. Her mother seemed almost euphoric. A couple of times, she'd heard her mother speaking in a low voice on the phone. It was only when she found a bridal magazine hidden between the sofa cushions that she started to suspect. Was Chris planning to ask her to marry him?

Chris himself was acting perfectly normal although they hadn't seen much of each other as they were both revising so hard. Later she learnt her suspicions had been correct and after they had both finished their final year exams, Chris took her on holiday to Santorini and presented her with an engagement ring.

When she came back from that holiday, her tanned skin showing off the diamond, she didn't think she'd ever seen her mother so happy. Claire had looked at the ring and she had to agree that its impressive size, cut and clarity were a stunning symbol of everything she had to look forward to in a future with Chris.

32

The first thing Paul did when he got back to his bedsit from work or the youth centre each evening was turn on his computer. He felt the hum of anticipation as he logged on to his social media accounts. He found Facebook the most useful and had hacked into several profiles as well as created different accounts for himself. He connected with Claire as Dr Bradley, a law professor at the University of London, who rarely posted on Facebook. Claire, however, had always been surprisingly active on her account and he'd found it easy to trace a lot of her movements and keep up to date with her life. It was certainly easier than trailing her. He hated going back to Castlefield and rarely ventured into the town.

Although he doubted anyone would recognise him when he walked the streets, he still remembered the fear of being jumped on by Gavin and his mates. While he'd watched Claire's house many times, he'd never been back to his own childhood home. Let someone else have it – it was a shithole anyway, haunted with violence and secrets.

Paul clicked on Claire's profile and quickly scanned to see if there was a new update since the day before. There wasn't and, disappointed, he searched through her other social media accounts, knowing it was unlikely he would be rewarded today. Claire was active on Twitter but only to communicate legal updates, and she rarely used Instagram. He didn't believe she had any other profiles, apart from a fairly static LinkedIn page, although he checked regularly.

His task finished, he sat back in the chair, thinking what to do next. He knew he shouldn't stay on his computer, typing, clicking, and scrolling through other profiles of people from his past, but it was like a scab that wouldn't stop itching. As he leaned in to the monitor, his eyes held hostage by the screen, he burned with resentment as he frantically browsed, their successful lives a stark contrast to his own.

It was past eleven at night when he finally shut down. The hours hadn't been for nothing though. During that time, a notification had popped up on Facebook saying Claire had posted an update and as he clicked on to her profile, he'd been rewarded with a photo of Chris, Joshua and Jamie, although he was disappointed Claire wasn't in it.

My boys x

They were in a park, all wrapped up in hats and coats, looking like something out of a fucking Ralph Lauren advert and he guessed she'd taken it earlier that day, cheerfully directing them to put their arms around each other, choreographing the perfect shot. He made a note of the location, Alexandra Park, in case it came in useful.

Paul was hungry, but he couldn't be bothered to make a meal, so instead grabbed a bread roll from the kitchen, slathered it with butter and lay down on his bed. He was tired. After work, he'd had to supply a couple of customers. As a dealer, he had about twenty regulars. He'd kept it deliberately small, as he didn't need the hassle.

Over the years, he'd accumulated and saved a fair amount of money, mainly because he never spent it on anything. He had a feeling that he should keep it safe knowing he might need it for something important one day. He'd always been careful not to get involved with any of the drug gangs or impose on anyone else's turf. Most of his customers were his old neighbours from Fairfield but he also supplied a professional footballer, a TV executive, and a couple of D-list celebrities. Not that he'd ever met them in person of course, and he knew all his clients appreciated his discretion.

As he ate, he thought back to a post he'd seen during his earlier social media search. One of his old classmates, Phil Newsom, had recently won some bullshit award at his boring job. He couldn't remember what the job was, or the award, but he remembered reading a comment underneath.

So proud of you, Love Dad.

He didn't *ever* remember his dad saying he was proud of him and though Phil clearly had nothing better to do if he was posting such things on Facebook, he'd certainly got lucky in the parent stakes. He remembered how Maureen had looked at him when he'd come home from school after being expelled. It was clear from her expression the headmaster had already called her and explained what had happened. He'd seen it in her eyes; the horror and dismay. She hadn't even bothered to ask him. Just assumed. He'd stormed upstairs to his bedroom, slamming the door, gulping down hot tears of rage.

It had all been Claire's fault. If she'd just...

But she hadn't. He would get her though. If it took a lifetime, he would get her and this time he would be in control. He would watch the fear flourish in her eyes and relish every moment.

JANUARY 2018

33

It was just a few days into 2018 and her third day back in the office after the Christmas and New Year holidays. Claire hung up the phone with relief and turned back to the document she'd been working on. It was just Natalie, the school secretary at Joshua's school, requesting a change of appointment for the parent-teacher meeting, which was happening the following month. Still, she struggled to concentrate on the paperwork in front of her. Whenever she saw the number of the school flash up on the screen, she always had a moment's anxiety, which turned into impatience as the speaker on the other end went through the verification process.

Yes, this is Mrs Carmichael; yes, I am Joshua's mother.

The anxiety had become worse since one particular phone call Claire had received from the school last year. It was during Joshua's *off the rails* phase and even now, she felt sick to her stomach whenever she thought about it. The phone had rung one Thursday afternoon when Claire had been playing on the floor with Jamie. The ring of her mobile had been a welcome distraction from the fifteenth round of car chases.

'Hello?'

'Is this Mrs Carmichael?'

'Yes.'

'Mrs Carmichael, this is Margaret Chillton, Joshua's headmistress. There has been an incident this afternoon at the school – Joshua is fine – but we think it's best if you or your husband could come in please.' The headmistress's tone had been firm and Claire had felt her chest tighten in response.

'What's happened?'

'It's a little delicate to discuss over the phone. What time could you or your husband be here?'

'I'm leaving home now,' replied Claire, already reaching for her handbag and Jamie. 'I'll be there in thirty minutes.'

'Thank you – see you shortly.'

Claire had hung up and quickly called Joshua on his mobile but it went straight to voicemail. She wasn't surprised. There were strict rules about phone usage in the school and it was probably in his locker. She left home, shooing Jamie ahead of her, and hurried to her car and strapped Jamie in the back seat. She would call Chris en route.

The traffic was heavy and as she weaved through the lanes impatiently, she'd tried to imagine what had happened. A fight seemed the most plausible. If there had been a serious accident, Mrs Chillton would have told her to go to the hospital. Bullying? Joshua didn't seem the type, but Claire knew it took all sorts. And Joshua had been acting strange lately, but she'd put it down to a girl. What if it had nothing to do with a girl? Or worse what it if it had?

She'd tried Chris's mobile again, but it went straight to voicemail and she left another message, trying to keep the panic out of her voice. Claire focused on slowing down her thoughts. In her mind, she envisaged talking to Chris and what he would say.

The school is probably overreacting.

Whatever it is we will sort it.

It can't be that bad.

No one has died.

Chris had developed all sorts of platitudes over the years to calm her down when she got overanxious.

Finally, Claire had arrived at the school, just before the official school day ended and as she raced up the steps and into the foyer holding tightly on to Jamie's hand, they got caught in a maelstrom of uniform-clad teenagers all heading in the opposite direction. While the sixth-form college had its own building on campus, she was sure the headmistress's office was in the senior school. Extracting herself from the crowds, she double-checked with reception where the headmistress's office was and was directed to the third floor, fourth door on the left. When she'd finally arrived, she was dismayed to be told by the secretary to take a seat for a few minutes.

Where was Joshua?

Jamie was getting fidgety and she'd been grateful that she'd remembered to grab the iPad on her way out to keep him occupied. Claire kept herself distracted by typing out another message to Chris to let him know she was at the school. After that, there was nothing to do but wait and

Claire reverted to a childhood habit where she would imagine the worst-case scenario in order to prepare for it.

Within five minutes, the door to the headmistress's office had opened and Claire instinctively stood up. She'd watched as a set of parents walked out of the office and tried to place them. Were those parents involved somehow? She didn't have a chance to pursue the thought as Margaret Chillton stepped into the doorway. Claire didn't meet her very often and the last time had been at the welcome event for parents whose children were transitioning from senior school to sixth-form college.

'Mrs Carmichael,' greeted the headmistress, smoothly. 'Thank you for coming in at such short notice. Come through.'

Claire turned to her son, checking he was still engrossed in the iPad before turning to Natalie, the school secretary. Without needing to say anything, Natalie had nodded at Claire, confirming that she would watch Jamie while Claire went to talk with her boss.

Claire entered the inner sanctum of academia and the first thing she saw was Joshua's laptop on the desk. She recognised it from the Manchester United sticker in the top right-hand corner.

'As you're probably aware,' started Margaret Chillton, sitting behind her large imposing desk and indicating for Claire to be seated opposite her, 'this is Joshua's laptop. Unfortunately, we've found some extremely sensitive material on it. In cases such as these, we're duty bound to inform the parents. I'm sure you understand.'

Porn?

Claire had felt her shoulders soften a fraction.

Porn she could deal with. It wasn't ideal, but didn't every teenage boy have some? Yes, he was an idiot for doing it on a school laptop but at least no one was hurt, and the incident hadn't involved anybody else. She imagined Chris's laugh when she told him, and no doubt Chris would regale her with his own teenage porn stash. Chris would have a man-to-man chat with Joshua and then the matter would be forgotten.

The headmistress had turned on the laptop and Claire had braced herself to see photos of stereotypical big-breasted random women in tantalising positions. But when Margaret Chillton had turned the screen towards her Claire had instinctively flinched. Gazing brazenly out at the camera was what looked to be a teenager wearing nothing but the bottom half of her school uniform.

Please God, let her be over sixteen years old. What the hell was Joshua thinking?

Claire felt sick. Porn was one thing but this was something else entirely.

'As you've probably guessed, this girl is a student,' said Margaret Chillton.

Claire felt the walls recede.

'We have learnt that she's in her second year at Trimour Sixth-Form College, seventeen years old, and she sent this to Joshua after a series of intimate email exchanges.'

Claire turned away from the image, trying to block out the photograph as the headmistress paused to let the information sink in.

'I can see you feel exactly as we do here at the school, Mrs Carmichael. Joshua has rarely been in any trouble before. In fact, he's been a model student. However, we take such things extremely seriously and our first step is to talk with the parents involved...'

Claire let the rest of the words float over her. She couldn't do this on her own. Where the fuck was Chris?

'What will happen next?' asked Claire, finally finding her voice.

'As far as we know, Joshua has only received this image and he's told us he hasn't distributed it or shared it.'

'You've talked to Joshua? What else did he say?' appealed Claire. 'Who is this girl and why would she send things like this to him?'

'I have talked to Joshua, Mrs Carmichael, and he was very upset to have the image discovered as you can imagine. He should have reported it immediately.'

Claire closed her eyes and tried to breathe.

'I know it's distressing, Mrs Carmichael, and I don't want to lessen the severity of the incident, but please bear in mind Joshua hasn't taken the photo or distributed it and this will be taken into consideration along with his previous excellent track record.'

Claire nodded.

'We also have to consider,' continued the headmistress, 'that this incident seems to be more experimental in nature rather than any aggressive form of sexting. Do you know if your son was romantically involved with a girl?'

Claire thought back over the last few weeks.

'We thought he could be, yes,' admitted Claire.

'Is she his first girlfriend?'

'I believe so – certainly the first one to have affected his mood so dramatically.'

'So, he's been acting different at home?' asked the headmistress, eyeballing her.

'For the last few weeks, yes. Slightly closed off.' Claire was trying not to feel interrogated.

'We have noticed,' continued the headmistress, 'that Joshua has got to know some different boys in his year, aside from his usual friends who he came up from senior school with.'

'Different boys?' asked Claire, puzzled.

'Yes. This year, we received an intake from Colston Senior Boys School. There are four of them and while they're academically strong of course, I do wonder if their… ahhh… interests might have influenced Joshua somewhat,' explained the headmistress delicately. 'Has Joshua ever mentioned any new friends over the last couple of months?'

'No,' replied Claire, bewildered. 'He's only ever mentioned Mark and the lads… the usual…'

Claire realised her stupidity immediately. The lads could refer to anyone and she'd simply assumed it was the same group of boys he'd hung around with all through senior school.

'I'll ask him about them,' promised Claire. She felt spent and was eager to leave the heavy atmosphere of the office.

'Yes, that might be worth doing,' confirmed the headmistress, standing up. Claire tried not to feel chastised.

'Let me update the school board of our conversation,' she continued, 'and I'll come back to you with our recommendations. He's with Mr Robbins now. Would you like someone to take you up to him?'

'Yes please.'

It was clear the meeting was over, and Claire rose from her seat with what little self-assuredness she could muster. Margaret Chillton opened the office door and let Claire pass.

'Natalie, can you take Mrs Carmichael up to Mr Robbins please – classroom four,' instructed the headmistress before holding out her hand and shaking Claire's firmly. 'I'll be in touch.'

'Thank you,' replied Claire. She went to Jamie, took his hand and obediently followed Natalie, her mind still trying to make sense of the conversation as they walked through the school corridors.

'Just through here, Mrs Carmichael.'

'Thank you.' From the doorway of the classroom, Claire could see Joshua sat at one of the desks, his head bowed as if he was doing his homework, but Claire could see his pen wasn't moving and she wondered what was going through his mind. A teacher, who she presumed was Mr Robbins, was sat working but rose from his seat when Claire and Jamie walked into the room. Yet, Claire's eyes were only on her son and as he looked up at her, she saw the fear in his eyes and all she wanted to do was take him in her arms and hold him.

When had it all become so complicated?

At the moment, she would have done anything to go back in time to when he was just a baby, all innocence and talcum powder. But it was an impossible wish and Claire knew with absolute certainty that how she handled *this* situation would have many implications. The enormity of responsibility, of successfully raising a boy into a good man, almost winded her.

It was Jamie who lightened the atmosphere though and his sheer delight at the unexpected meeting with his older brother broke the tension.

'Come on, let's go home,' she'd said to Joshua who was now holding Jamie in one arm and having his cheeks squeezed by his brother's pudgy hands.

With his free arm, Joshua grabbed his rucksack. Claire turned to Mr Robbins and nodded her thanks. She was surprised when the teacher spoke.

'I'm Mr Robbins, Mrs Carmichael,' he'd announced, holding out his hand.

'Pleased to meet you,' she'd said distractedly. All she'd wanted to do was get Joshua in the car and get home.

'I teach Joshua PE,' he continued.

'Oh right – how's he doing?' replied Claire, politeness overtaking impatience.

'Really well.'

'That's good to hear.' It was then that she looked at Mr Robbins a little more closely. He looked familiar. His tall frame, broad chest, and large ears.

'Have we met before?' asked Claire.

'No, I don't think so, why?'

'No reason.' Claire dismissed it, keen to get home. 'You ready, Joshua?'

'Yep,' replied Joshua already walking to the door. 'Bye, Mr Robbins.'

'Bye, Joshua.'

Claire had followed and gone to shut the classroom door behind her. It was then that she saw Mr Robbins sit down and pick up the small stress ball from his desk, squeeze it and start passing it from hand to hand.

It was that motion that had brought back another buried memory. It had been after school and most students had left for the day. Paul and Claire had been studying in the empty library. Anyone wandering in would have simply seen two students doing their homework, but underneath the table, their knees touched. Paul would occasionally take a break and reach his hand for hers, the caress concealed by the graffiti-covered desk.

After their study session, the school deserted, Paul had walked Claire home via the school field where the football team were wrapping up their practice, and it was there that she'd seen Paul wave to one of the players. She'd followed his line of sight and seen one of the boys wave back before picking up the football and passing it back and forth between his hands.

'I didn't know you and Brian were friends?' Claire had asked, trying to keep the surprise out of her voice.

'Yeah, we bike together,' replied Paul.

'Oh,' replied Claire. She didn't know him personally, but everyone knew of popular Brian Robbins.

'He's a good friend too,' Paul had added, and Claire had heard the pleasure in his voice.

But that had been the end of it and Brian's name had rarely come up again.

34

Paul lay down on the sofa bed and tried to get comfortable. He rarely opened it up into a bed, mainly because he couldn't be bothered; most nights he slept on it as it was. He pulled the duvet around him. He was already wearing a jumper over his pyjamas, but it was still freezing. It was one of the coldest months of the year, but he was reluctant to switch the central heating back on once he was in bed. He didn't want to waste his money on bills.

Lifting his head up to lean against the armrest, he debated whether to get up and put his hat on. He decided against it and instead reached down for the biology textbook Simone had given him earlier. He leafed through it, his eyes quickly scanning the contents. Not much had changed since his own school days.

He let the book drop on his chest, feeling the weight of it, and closed his eyes, going through the list of girls in his mind like an old-fashioned Rolodex. He never wrote any of their names down. He didn't need to – he easily kept track of them. He had eight now, all stunningly beautiful, and he felt himself grow hard at the thought of them. He would work on Simone next – he couldn't let such an opportunity pass by.

The youth centre had welcomed his volunteer services as tutor and he'd taught quite a few of the members over the last couple of years. It wasn't always easy; most of them didn't come to the youth centre to study, but gradually, little by little, he'd built up a reputation, mainly by making his study sessions different from school. The days of textbooks were long gone and instead he would use different techniques that would resonate with each student.

One of his students, Carl, had been passionate about boxing so he'd taught the periodic table along the same lines as a boxing sequence. Carl had brought in his gloves and before long all he had to do was imagine he was in the ring, punching out the elements. It was this technique, and others, that had got Carl an acceptable C in his chemistry exam instead of his predicted F.

Now all he had to do was find a way to help Simone prepare for her biology exam in a way that represented her love of textiles and then she would be putty in his hands. Paul mulled over his approach and eventually fell into a restless sleep.

Paul and Simone sat back in their chairs at the youth centre, grinning at each other in satisfaction. Comparing cell biology to fashion design had been a new one for him but somehow, he'd managed it. The proof was in Simone's blue eyes – the fog had lifted and they'd widened in comprehension as she started to sketch and label the cell structure. To most people, it was a scientific drawing. To Simone, it represented – and Paul was still trying to get his head around this one – a handbag – and every part of the cell – from the nucleus to the mitochondria – was a design element of the bag.

As he watched her sketch and correctly label the cell parts, Paul knew he'd succeeded in capturing her interest. She was so engrossed that she hadn't even looked up when the TV in the youth centre had been turned up high, the theme tune of *The X Factor* blasting out. Nor when Shelley, her mate, had shouted her name across the hall to come and watch. But the real test was when her phone had emitted a ping, signalling a message. Paul watched for her reaction, waiting for her fingers to drop the pencil and reach for her phone. It never happened, and Paul knew then he'd found a way to ensure she continued her extra study sessions with him.

'At this rate, Simone, you're going to pass biology with flying colours!' said Paul, after she'd packed up her notes and they sat chatting at the table.

'God, I wish Jenkins taught biology like you did! I'd have no problems then,' replied Simone. 'What will we work on next week?'

Paul saw his opportunity. 'The mock exam's in a few weeks, is that right?'

'Yeah end March – just before we break up for the Easter holidays,' groaned Simone.

'Well,' said Paul, 'I reckon we can review the majority of the syllabus if we meet two or three times a week – what do you say?'

'But I only come to the youth club once a week,' said Simone. Paul waited, holding his breath, knowing how critical it was to exercise patience. Move too fast and she might bolt. He watched her carefully out of the corner of his eye as he pretended to fiddle with his rucksack. He saw Simone frown before looking up at him.

Come on. Say it!

'Unless we meet somewhere else?' Simone suggested tentatively, and Paul allowed himself a split second of triumph.

'Sure, can do,' replied Paul, shrugging. 'How about the twenty-four-hour coffee shop on Steeple Street around eight-ish? I could do Mondays, if that works, and Wednesdays at a pinch.'

There was a pause as Simone went through her phone and his earlier elation was replaced with a sliver of anxiety. Even to his own ears, he'd sounded too keen offering specific days. He should have told her he would check his availability.

'Okay,' replied Simone eventually putting her phone in her bag. 'Thanks – I'll see you then.' And then she was walking away, her bag over her shoulder, a throwaway smile and a wave the only thing to remind Paul about the agreement. He waved back, the relief instantaneous, his own smile hidden as he turned away and began to pack up his things.

Paul walked home, his mind buzzing with possibility. He knew it was against the rules for volunteers at the youth club to meet up with the kids outside of the facility, which is why he had chosen Steeple Street. He'd met other girls there before and he knew it was unlikely he would bump into someone from the youth club, especially at that time of night. Anyway, he only had a few weeks to work on her.

He unlocked his front door, his mind still going over the various possibilities. It excited him. Made him feel that she was within his grasp. And Simone had the look he liked as well, part naivety, part gullibility. It was the hand-made friendship bracelet around her wrist, the Hello Kitty case covering her battered mobile phone and the ladybird earring studs she sometimes wore.

But more than that, it was the way she cocked her head to one side when listening to him, the concentration in her eyes as she focused on the test exam questions, and the eager way she looked at him to check if she had got it right. Yes, Simone was most definitely being added to his list.

Paul removed his coat, hat and scarf and dropped them on the chair in the hallway. He turned on the computer and while it loaded, he filled the kettle with water and switched it on, warming his hands close to the sides as it began to boil. First, he would do his usual checks on Claire, but he also wanted to track Simone's movements. It shouldn't be too difficult – she was on social media *constantly* – but he needed to create another different profile, so he could follow her anonymously.

Paul grabbed a dirty cup from the sink and quickly rinsed it out. He was about to put a teabag in when he remembered an old packet of hot chocolate. It wasn't Cadbury's, like his mum's, just some cheap crap from Aldi, but still, he was in the mood to celebrate.

FEBRUARY 2018

35

Claire woke up and immediately felt the ache in her right shoulder. She'd been dreaming about Rose, her long dark hair streaming behind her as she ran. Claire was following her down a series of dark, damp alleyways, but Rose was getting further and further away until she eventually disappeared, and Claire was left alone. In the dream, Claire had stopped running, realising she was lost.

As she looked around, all she could see were rows of closed garages, each with a rectangular window and although she couldn't see anyone, she knew there were eyes watching her, peering through the small windows as she tried to get her bearings. And then it had started to rain and she'd woken up, disorientated, sleep making the real and imaginary cross over. As she came to, she realised it was actually raining, February signalling its arrival with its tap-tap on her bedroom window. Never had she felt less like getting out of bed.

Wednesday. Just two more days until the weekend.

She lay for a minute, trying to muster the energy to get up. Eventually, she sat up and switched on the lamp. The other side of the bed was empty and she hoped Chris was downstairs making some coffee. She tentatively flexed her neck trying to loosen the muscles and prevent the inevitable headache that would follow.

Christ, she could feel it in her teeth.

Swinging her legs round, she opened the drawer in her bedside table, scrambled around until she found a packet of paracetamol and popped two into her mouth with a slug of water. Reaching around to the back of her neck, she massaged the knots, the pressure giving some temporary relief.

'Hey.' Chris had come into the bedroom holding out a cup of coffee for her. 'You okay?'

'Thanks,' she replied gratefully, taking the cup from him.

Swinging her legs back into bed, she pulled the covers over her. 'Yes, just a bit of a shoulder ache.'

Just five more minutes.

'Did you take something for it?' asked Chris.

She nodded and took a sip of coffee.

'It's stress,' announced Chris. 'With everything going on at work.'

Claire felt her shoulders climb a fraction higher. She knew where Chris was heading. That she'd gone back to work too soon especially after everything going on with Joshua during his off-the-rails phase. She wasn't ready to get into that conversation. Claire watched her husband. He was already showered and dressed, mobile phone in hand, pacing up and down the bedroom. It was exhausting just watching him. She didn't reply, not ready to get into the conversation, and instead held her coffee in her lap and lay back against the headboard.

'What do you fancy for dinner tonight?' she asked instead.

Just a few minutes more and then she would get up and get going.

'Claire, I already told you I'm going to be late tonight. It's the conference call with the US office.' She looked at him blankly. 'I told you about it last week,' he insisted.

'Did you?'

'Yes!'

'Chris, you've been late every night this week. I thought you were supposed to be making some effort to be back home in the evenings.'

'For God's sake, Claire, what do you want me to say? I need to work. I can't just turn around and tell the client "sorry, can't make the call tonight as my wife needs me to be home with the kids—"'

'All right, Chris, I get the point,' interrupted Claire resignedly. 'I'll leave on time tonight.'

Chris muttered a sarcastic thanks before leaving the bedroom. Claire didn't have the energy to make a retort.

It was only when the coffee had lifted the sleep fog that she remembered she had the Bar Association cocktails that evening.

Shit.

What time was it? Wasn't it at five thirty p.m.? Maybe it would be all right although she knew the traffic would be hell afterwards. Claire unplugged her phone, which was charging on the bedside table next to her, and began scrolling through her calendar. She really needed to start getting up earlier, but after she'd put Jamie to bed, and had a chat with Joshua, she'd worked late into the evening. No wonder she had aches and pains, leaning over her laptop for so many hours. She also hadn't been running for weeks now.

Still, Chris was right about one thing – thank God, she hadn't been working full-time when everything with Joshua had been going on. She recalled the conversation she'd had to have with her eldest son, or rather the few words she'd managed to get out of him after she'd picked him up from school following the meeting with the headmistress about the photo. Joshua had been angry; angry with the school for checking his laptop, angry about being caught with the picture, and angry with everyone thinking it was his fault. *He* hadn't sent the picture. *He* hadn't even requested it. Why was he in trouble?

And when Claire had tried to ask him about the boys from Colston Senior Boys School, he'd gone to his room, slamming the door, and Claire had heard the thump of music as he went to a place she couldn't reach. She'd put her head in her hands for a few minutes before going to the kitchen and pouring herself a large glass of wine. She'd downed it in several gulps and that's how Chris had found her, already halfway through the bottle. He'd barely acknowledged her when he'd come in and Claire lost it.

'Where the hell have you been?' shouted Claire. 'I've been calling you for the last three hours.'

'I messaged you,' replied Chris, looking puzzled. 'I've been in meetings all afternoon. Why? What's the matter?'

Claire had felt herself crumble under his gaze. She didn't remember getting any message but all she wanted to do now was unburden herself from the responsibility of parenthood, or at least share it with someone. As the story had tumbled out of her, the meeting with the headmistress, the sexting, her abrupt conversation with Joshua, she felt Chris take the load. When she'd finished, tears starting to form, he'd come over to her and wrapped her in his arms. She'd sobbed then, whether it was from sheer tiredness or the shock, she had no idea, but when she looked up into her husband's face, she soaked up his reassurances like a sponge.

'It's all going to be okay,' Chris had said. 'Besides, Joshua's right you know. He hasn't technically done anything. All he's done is exchange some messages with a girl. Did he ask her to send such a photo?'

'No,' replied Claire.

'Well, then. It's just some silly girl playing games with him. We'll sort it. And,' he added seeing the worry come back across her face, 'he won't get expelled.'

'How do you know?' asked Claire. It was her biggest fear.

'Because I just do – we pay a shed-load of money for him to go there and, like we've just said, he hasn't done anything wrong. I'll call the headmistress tomorrow, okay?' Claire didn't reply.

'Okay?' he asked again, lifting her chin to meet his eyes. 'It will be fine – I promise.'

'Okay,' replied Claire. She felt the relief that Chris would deal with it and hugged him hard. 'I love you.'

'I love you too,' he said. 'Now, is there any of that wine left for me?' he asked, with a smile.

She'd smiled back then, feeling better than she had all afternoon and poured him a glass. Chris had gone in to talk to Joshua and her husband had come back out all smiles and reassurances. And just as Chris had promised, it had been sorted and Joshua didn't get expelled. But later that evening, when Chris had gone to bed, she'd checked her phone, hoping that she'd missed his message, but there'd been nothing there.

Later that morning, still struggling with pain in her neck and shoulders, Claire dropped off the boys at their respective schools before driving into central Manchester to work. When she arrived in her office, she was surprised to see Rose already waiting for her. She was peering at the photo on Claire's desk and didn't hear Claire come in. It was only when Claire dropped her bag and coat on the chair with a thump that Rose turned in surprise.

'Rose – what are you doing in here?'

'Are those your kids?' asked Rose, peering at the photo, ignoring the question.

'Yes,' replied Claire, not volunteering any more information.

'What's this one called?' asked Rose, pointing to Claire's eldest son.

'Joshua,' replied Claire.

'Handsome,' remarked Rose but the compliment clanged clumsily.

'Rose – again – why are you in my office?' asked Claire.

'You told me to come in early, so we could run through the questions again and your new receptionist told me to wait in here.' Rose's thin coat was soaked through.

New receptionist?

Rose was right that Claire had told her to come in early, but she was pretty sure she'd said a few minutes early and not a whole hour. The meeting wasn't until ten. Still, even if that was the case, Rose should be waiting in reception.

'Follow me,' instructed Claire. She led Rose through to a vacant meeting room, told her to take off her coat, and make herself comfortable. Then she instructed one of the interns to make Rose a hot drink while Claire went to the reception desk. It had been unmanned when Claire had first arrived but now she saw that there was indeed an unfamiliar face.

'Good morning,' greeted Claire. 'My name's—'

The phone rang and the new receptionist held up one hand to Claire while picking up the phone with the other.

Claire raised an eyebrow but waited until the call had finished. Finally, the receptionist put down the phone and looked at Claire enquiringly. 'Yes?'

Claire didn't bother with any more platitudes. 'Where's Elaine today?'

'Off sick. The agency sent me.'

'What's your name?'

'Stephanie.'

'Okay, Stephanie, my name is Claire Carmichael,' said Claire briskly.

You might recognise my name from the big sign above the door.

'Let me know if you need anything. Just a quick one – we don't let clients into our private offices – they wait in reception.'

Stephanie looked at her blankly.

'Rose Aiker?' prompted Claire. 'She was in my office when I arrived just now.'

'Oh right,' replied Stephanie. 'With what the client said, I assumed—'

'Best not to make assumptions on your first day,' Claire interrupted.

'Sorry, I didn't know…' replied Stephanie, clearly taken aback.

'It's okay – any other questions talk to Barry – he knows everything,' replied Claire. 'Has someone showed you where the coffee is? The toilets?'

'Yes, thank you,' replied Stephanie, keen to make up for her mistake, now she realised exactly who she was talking to.

'Good,' concluded Claire. Walking back to her office, she closed the door firmly and sat down at her desk, rubbing her temples, the pain having made its way up to a full-blown headache. What the hell was wrong with people? It wasn't even half past nine in the morning and already she'd felt like she'd done a day's work. Why did she feel so overwhelmed? She thought back to a few months ago when she'd been so excited to start full-time again. But with the long hours, Chris's selfishness, and at the back of her mind, the worry about Joshua and whether he would stay back on track long enough to pass his A levels, she felt the mental load crush down on her.

And there was something else that bothered her about Chris. Yes, he always worked hard but he *always* picked up the phone. He'd never been unreachable and while it had happened only a few times over the last year or so, there was a silent call of instinct nudging her to question him further.

Out of the corner of her eye, she saw the Rose Aiker file and her heart beat rapidly in response. Despite all Claire's good intentions, she knew that the case had triggered a whole heap of supressed memories, but she was damned if she was going to allow herself to be dragged back to the past. It was over. This was work. Fighting the rising panic, Claire took a deep breath and went to interview Rose in the meeting room. She reassured herself that the case wouldn't last forever.

36

He'd never seen her before but as soon as Paul clapped his eyes on the girl, he felt attracted to her. She was perfect. He paused. Too perfect? He took in her long slim legs and curvaceous behind and smiled inwardly. There was no such thing as too perfect. She wasn't his usual type with her short, bobbed hair but those cheekbones! They could cut glass. He guessed she had Slavic roots somewhere. Despite her cheap clothing, she had an air of superiority about her that was magnified even further by the crummy backdrop of her surroundings.

Amongst the chaos that was the youth centre on a Friday night in one of the roughest areas of Manchester, Slavic Girl stood out. It wasn't just her beauty. Paul sieved through his mind looking for the right word; he liked to be precise about these things. Composed? Graceful? Proud? No. None of those were quite right. Elegant. That was it. She had an elegance about her and he supressed a sneer of lust as he quickly turned away and walked to the office to dump his bag.

'Hey, Paul.'

Gloria barely looked up from behind the desk, a slash of pink lipstick across her mouth, which had smudged onto her teeth. She refused to use a computer, so the small office was always filled with boxes and piles of paperwork. She couldn't navigate the internet, but she had a unique ability to find any document in seconds. An impressive feat when you considered just how many boxes there were.

Gloria had run the centre as long as Paul had been there and it was Gloria who had founded and got the funding for it years ago. Gloria, in her own words, was a scrubber who had married well. She'd grown up on a council estate that was so rocked with drugs even the police had given up, but somehow she had managed to slip through the net.

She'd been working in a café as a waitress when the man, who would become her husband just months later, had seen her and apparently fallen in love at first sight. The fact that she'd refused to go out with him only fuelled his longing. Eventually, she'd agreed and once they were married Gloria used some of his money to set up youth centres around Manchester. It was a well-known story, probably embellished over the years, and Paul had heard that she'd counselled hundreds of kids off the streets and into her youth clubs.

Still, he was disappointed to see her there. Now over sixty, she didn't come in to see the kids as much, and Paul had been hoping to sneak a read of Slavic Girl's file. None of the volunteers were allowed access to the files. Relevant information was shared in weekly meetings on a need-to-know basis by Jeremy, the youth club manager, so Paul had to develop his own system of getting the information on the girls. This was usually through his own conversations with them, but he'd built up a good enough rapport with Jeremy to get an overview. It didn't hurt that he'd also had great success with his tutoring, and while the youth centre was primarily a place for kids to come to relax and enjoy activities rather than to study, there was talk of setting up a more official tutoring programme. In fact, Jeremy had shared the info just last week that Gloria was keen to look at something as soon as this year.

So why isn't she talking to me about it herself?

Despite all his efforts with Gloria, he'd never clicked with her as he thought he would. Oh, she was polite of course, never rude. But still, he sensed that she kept her distance from him. Who was he kidding? He knew that she just didn't like him. It was as simple as that.

'Hi, Gloria, looking lovely today. Pink suits you,' said Paul, turning on the charm, hoping to strike up a conversation about Slavic Girl.

'Thanks, Paul,' she replied without looking up.

Stuck up cow.

'Busy?' he tried again.

'I am rather – did you need the room?'

'Nope. Was just dropping my things.' Paul slowly placed his bag in the locker giving Gloria an opportunity to make conversation, but he knew it was a waste of time.

'Right then, I'll get started.'

'Thanks, Paul.'

'Nice to see you, Gloria.'

Cow.

'Likewise.'

Paul left the room knowing he would have to either sneak back into the office later to read the file when no one was around or pick Jeremy's brains. He didn't like his chances of the first option, mainly because it was impossible to find anything and there was always a high chance of being caught as volunteers were in and out of there all the time. Jeremy wasn't in until tomorrow. He never liked to go in blind with a girl – he liked to have the advantage of knowing something about her before approaching, but tonight he had no choice. He would just have to talk to her himself. It was too good an opportunity to miss.

'Oh man! What're ya' doing?'

Paul picked up the ping-pong ball that had whizzed past him with a grin. 'Sorry, mate, you're clearly on top form today!'

Kyle grinned back at him, pleased at the compliment. He was only eleven years old and already on the circuit as a drug courier. He'd been doing it since he was seven. Gangs had identified him and groomed him and when he wasn't at school, which was most of the time, he spent his days on runs. He drew the only income for his family of five. His dad left years ago when he was small, and his mum was a user herself with four kids all younger than Kyle.

He'd started coming to the centre a few months ago and Jeremy and the volunteer team had put a loose strategy together to encourage him to keep coming to the youth club. He was a smart kid, quick too, thought Paul, as another ball bounced past him – but he knew it was just a matter of time before Kyle started on drugs himself. He thought this privately – Jeremy, the optimist, was confident they could show him a different path – but for Paul, as he knew from his own experience, some things were just inevitable.

'I win!' crowed Kyle as he slammed his table-tennis bat down.

'Good job, mate!' replied Paul as he conceded defeat. 'Now, I'm off for a coffee to recover.'

'Haha, on you go, mate, with your tail between your legs!' Kyle laughed.

Paul had been distracted during the game. Slavic Girl had been lounging on the sofa with some other girls and he could see from the group of guys surrounding her that he wasn't her only admirer. He discreetly watched as she managed the group with ease, gently flirting and then retreating, until the guys were completely hypnotised. She could have asked them to jump off a cliff by the time the conversation was over, and they would have gladly done so.

In his mind, he was trying to plan the perfect opening to meet her. He wasn't some stupid teenager, he was a grown man and if he wanted her – which he did, oh did he ever – then he was going to have to play a smart game. He casually walked to the coffee machine, keeping her in his line of sight. He could still hear Kyle crowing over his win and a flash of pleasure went through him that for just a moment Kyle could experience what it was like to be a kid.

But then, Slavic Girl looked over at him, and all thoughts of Kyle flew out of his mind. It took her less than a second to dismiss him and Paul curled his fist, supressing the anger that had ignited at the dismissive tilt of her head.

Time for plan B.

★

Paul looked at himself in the cracked mirror above the sink. He didn't have a full-length mirror, so he'd had to drag a chair to the sink and stand on it and move his body to see himself. Perhaps Slavic Girl had a point. He knew his appearance was mediocre and quite frankly he didn't give a shit. To get girls before, he'd always used other means but instinctively, he knew with Slavic Girl, such approaches would backfire.

Getting down from the chair, he collapsed onto the sofa, his only view being the yellow stains on the ceiling and, with a certainty he couldn't explain, he knew he would need a new plan. He leapt up from the sofa immediately energised and turned on his computer, scouring the internet for Slavic Girl. He'd heard one of the kids call her Jess, so he started by searching Jess and Jessica on Facebook adding the location to the search function. It didn't take long.

He also found her on Instagram, where she had several thousand followers. And once Paul started scrolling, he could see why. Pose after pose, mainly semi-naked, assaulted Paul and he felt himself get hard again. This time, he didn't need to hide it and he quickly pulled down his jeans, his finger scrolling through the images faster and faster.

Paul woke with his trousers around his ankles and quickly shrugged them off and went to the toilet. Fully awake, he saw his computer was still on but in sleep mode, and putting on some underwear, he sat down and restarted it. It was three in the morning, but he felt wide awake.

He continued his search; it was easier now he knew Slavic Girl's second name and he carefully memorised all her details, and then he saw a Facebook post that made his heart stop. She'd taken a picture outside an office block in central Manchester, hands behind her head, head to one side, eyes closed, like she was at the fucking beach rather than in a grimy city.

My first photoshoot! the caption screamed.

God, she was absolutely stunning. But it wasn't the fact that she modelled that made his heart stop – he could have guessed that. It was the name of the office block – Trident Square. He continued browsing for another half an hour. Eventually, he gave up, tiredness pulling at the corners of his mind and finally, he turned off the machine and went back to sleep.

For once in his life Paul had got lucky. He'd gone into the youth centre a little earlier than usual the next day. Saturdays were busy and because he didn't have a shift at the hospital during the day, he'd been less rushed. He'd spent the afternoon at his computer tracking various social media accounts. The problem was he sometimes got too impatient and the girls were just cockteasers. Especially Slavic Girl – her social media was like a porn site. He cautioned himself to give it time – if he rushed it, she would bolt.

So, when he arrived at the centre, he was the only volunteer there and there were only a couple of kids hanging out watching TV. He'd gone into the office to put his bag away and that's when he caught her. Red-handed as well, her long fingers wrapped around the notes in the petty-cash box. She'd started when she saw him come in and as he stared at her, he couldn't believe his luck.

He wondered if she would run – it was what he would do – but his bulk blocked the doorway and there was no other exit. Besides, she would most likely trip over the boxes in her haste to get away. He could see her realise the same thing at the exact same time he did, and he watched as she smiled at him. It was a smile of secrecy and possibility and Paul felt the familiar pull of arousal.

But he wouldn't be that stupid again.

'Planning on going on a shopping trip?' he said watching her closely. She hadn't expected him to say that and he watched her plan her next move.

'Just looking for some change for the coffee machine,' she said, innocently.

Yeah, right.

'Really? Well, you'll only find notes in there.'

'So I see,' replied Slavic Girl smoothly, returning the cash and closing the box. She must have opened it with a hairgrip, thought Paul. Honestly, Jeremy was such an idiot sometimes. She stared at him, daring him to make the next move.

'How about this. How about I buy you a cup of coffee – with a pound coin,' he added for emphasis, 'and you put that box back where you found it and we'll say no more about it.'

Slavic Girl smiled at him then, believing she had him completely under her control.

You think you do.

'Sounds good to me,' she replied calmly as if he hadn't just caught her stealing.

He held out his hand to her and she took it without hesitation as Paul guided her out of the office and into the common area where the coffee machine was. As she let go of his hand, he put his hand on her lower back and gently pushed her towards the sofa to sit down while he got the coffee. As he handed her the steaming cup of liquid, theirs eyes met in mutual understanding and Paul gently rested his hand on her arm.

MARCH 2018

37

As soon as Claire stepped into the office, she sensed something was wrong. Elaine, back from her sick leave, was the first person she saw and instead of her usual good morning, she quickly picked up the phone and spoke into it, not meeting Claire's eye. As she walked through the open-plan office, she felt eyes upon her but when she met their gaze, heads quickly dropped.

What was going on?

She was about to go into her office, when she saw the blinds of the main meeting room were drawn. Dropping her bags and coat inside her office, she went to investigate. Peering through the crack in the blinds, she saw Julia and the senior leadership team gathered around the table. They were standing up, clearly having finished whatever business they had been discussing but still listening intently to what Julia was saying.

Claire quickly checked the calendar on her phone. Had she missed a management meeting? There was nothing in her calendar. She was just checking she was looking at today's date when the door opened and Julia appeared.

'Claire – do you have a minute?' Not waiting for a response, Julia headed back into the room and Claire waited as everybody else filed out. No one looked her in the eye.

'What's going on, Julia?' asked Claire coming into the room and shutting the door behind her. She looked at her partner, immaculate as always, but her face was troubled.

'Maybe you should sit down for this, Claire,' said Julia, walking towards the window, her arms crossed.

'I'm fine – what's going on?' she replied, joining Julia at the window.

Julia turned towards her and for a second, Claire was reminded of a nature programme she had watched, *Lions in the Wild*, or something like that. Two females had circled each other, one eyeballing the other, as they fought to see who would crack first.

'Julia!' cried Claire, her impatience finally rising to the surface.

'I'm so sorry, Claire – I really don't know how to tell you this.'

'What?'

'We have to take you off the Rose Aiker case.'

Claire sat down, half relieved, half puzzled. 'That's it? That's what you wanted to tell me? Fine. But why all the drama? Did she complain about me because I told her she couldn't just come into my office anytime she wanted? You know I never wanted that case any—'

'Claire!' Julia's voice cut sharply into her diatribe, the tone unlike any she had ever heard from her friend before. Amidst all the confusion, she had a premonition that after this conversation, her life would never be the same again.

'Claire – we have to take you off the case because Rose Aiker has named Joshua as one of her attackers.'

'Joshua? Joshua who?'

'Your Joshua, Claire, I'm so sorry.'

Afterwards, she would try to recall the rest of the conversation but the only memory she could summon was of a picture hung on the wall at the end of the meeting room. It was a cheap framed black and white poster of New York and she and Julia had chosen it together when they'd first moved into the office, both having high hopes of expansion into the glamorous city. They'd renovated since those early days, replacing cheap furniture and décor with something more appropriate for a successful law firm but somehow that picture had escaped the cull. As Julia's words about her son pierced her consciousness, her only thought was that they had not expanded to New York as they had hoped.

'Claire?' Julia's voice flew over her. She didn't want to hear what else she had to say. The idea of Joshua doing something like that was so preposterous that Claire had the urge to laugh.

'Claire!' She felt Julia's arm on hers, as she guided her to a chair to sit down. Julia took a seat next to her and turned so she could look at Claire directly.

Slowly, Claire turned her face to her oldest friend. 'It's a mistake,' she said simply.

'Of course, it is,' replied Julia softly. 'I know it's a shock, but we'll get it sorted.'

Claire nodded, her mind slowly giving Julia's words access and then she felt her body revolt at such a suggestion and her eyes blazed on Julia's.

'Why would Rose say such a thing? How does she even know his name?'

'She said something about seeing a photo on your desk that triggered a memory,' replied Julia. Claire felt something click.

'I need to talk to her – she's confused,' announced Claire suddenly standing up.

'No!' replied Julia, quickly. 'Claire, that's not a good idea. Let me handle it. I'll sort it,' she continued. But it was too late – Claire had heard the panic in Julia's voice.

'I know Rose,' countered Claire. 'And I need to get to the bottom of this.' The photo of the half-naked girl on Joshua's phone from last year popped into Claire's mind and she quickly pushed it away.

'I know, I know you do,' replied Julia, soothingly. 'But we need to handle it carefully. Without emotion,' Julia added pointedly.

Claire knew Julia was right but in that moment all she wanted to do was shake Rose until she admitted her mistake. Claire sat back down into the chair and put her head in her hands. She felt nauseous. What was happening? She felt Julia's arm come around her shoulders and it was then she started to cry.

Claire felt a warm drink pressed into her hands. She had no idea how long she'd sat with Julia, shock suspending the slow seconds of time. She sipped the sweetened tea and looked at her friend.

'What now?' she asked, releasing herself from Julia's arm, which had been around her.

Julia adjusted her position but still left a hand on Claire's forearm.

'Well, first we need to make sure you're okay and that's why I met with the partners first thing. We've agreed it would be best for you to take some official leave – be there for your family – just until this is all sorted out.'

'You mean not work at all?' asked Claire in surprise. 'I thought you said I'm just off the Aiker case.'

But even as she said the words, Claire knew it was fruitless. One of the founders of the firm involved in a case? It was a potential PR nightmare, not to mention conflict of interest and the legal ramifications.

'We think it's the right thing to do, Claire – not just for the company but for you and your family.'

Claire closed her eyes, trying to think but her thoughts were hazy, their usual sharpness dulled. She felt Julia's fingers squeeze her arm supportively, but it felt too firm and suddenly, she wanted to get out of the meeting room. She couldn't breathe. She stood up quickly, surprising Julia. 'I need some air.'

'Of course,' said Julia, walking to the window to open it.

Claire continued to stand, a part of her just wanting to escape but another part of her needing to know more.

'We'll work this out, Claire,' reassured Julia. 'We'll talk to Rose and find out what's going on. It seems strange she's only just remembered and there will be an explanation I'm sure. I will work on the case with Greg and Chloe and I'm positive it will all be resolved, and you'll be back at work in no time.'

Claire took a deep breath. She felt reassured by Julia's words – she was rarely wrong about a case and she trusted her friend implicitly.

'But for now, you need to call Chris and go home and be with your family and leave this to me. Okay?'

'Okay,' agreed Claire, suddenly desperately tired.

'Are you okay to drive or do you want me to call you a taxi?'

'I'll be fine. The drive might help me clear my head a little.'

The two women left the room and Julia waited while she went to get her bag. Claire went to reach for her laptop and some files to pack but Julia gently removed them.

'You won't be needing those. Take a break, Claire – we'll handle everything,' said Julia softly.

As Julia walked her to reception and called the lift, Claire felt the unease that she was being walked out. With a last hug, Claire watched the lift doors close on Julia's retreating form.

She'd called Chris as soon as he got into the car. He'd listened in disbelief.

'What will happen to Joshua?' Chris had asked.

'Hopefully nothing – it won't get that far,' replied Claire trying to sound more confident than she felt. 'At the moment, his name is just on a list, nothing more.'

'Should we not ask Joshua about this?' asked Chris.

'What good would that do?' replied Claire. 'It's simply a mistake – he doesn't even know who Rose is!'

Chris didn't respond, and Claire waited for him to agree.

'What?' she asked when Chris didn't say anything.

'Nothing,' replied Chris. 'Where are you now?'

'I'm in the car driving home. Shall I meet you there?'

'I'll be there in two hours.'

Two hours?

'Chris – I...'

She'd wanted to tell him about the partners voting for her to take a leave of absence from the firm. That she wouldn't be able to work until this was all over. How she had a really bad feeling about it all. How she didn't know how she would cope being at home for two hours alone. How she was frightened.

But he had already hung up.

Two hours later and Chris still hadn't turned up. She'd told Lucy to go home early and made arrangements for both boys to be collected by their grandparents after school and for them to stay the night. She'd put away the laundry, unloaded the dishwasher, and wiped down the bathrooms. She'd drunk endless cups of tea. She'd called Chris again to find out where he was, but he hadn't picked up.

Eventually, she decided to call Julia to see if she had any more news. She'd been on hold for almost fifteen minutes. She realised then it had been a mistake to leave the office. Her fingers itched for the Rose Aiker file. In the absence of Chris, all she wanted was to go back to her own office where she could review everything and just have a few minutes to think. She knew that if she was alone with the file, she would work it out. She would discover what the hell had happened that had Rose accusing her son of sexually attacking her.

A nauseating panic rose inside her and Claire pushed it down knowing that she would need every brain cell focused on the task at hand. Eventually Julia came on the line.

'I need the file, Julia,' said Claire.

'Claire,' replied Julia gently. 'I just told you that the board agreed for you to be off work.'

'Julia, I—'

'Claire – I know it's frustrating, but it's my top priority to find out what's happened here. Chloe and Greg are due in my office in ten minutes and we'll work out what's going on,' assured Julia.

I thought you were doing that two hours ago!

'And what about Rose? Is she coming in today?' demanded Claire.

'Well, no,' said Julia, 'she's not due in until next week.'

'Julia – I'm telling you, the only way to find out what's happened is to ask Rose directly. She's a liar!' Claire was struggling to control her temper.

'Claire, I can't just accuse one of our clients of lying. You also have to remember she's a victim. Besides, she's already asked about the possibility of moving to a different law firm...'

Claire listened in disbelief. 'So that's what this is all about? Money? You're worried that we're going to lose her as a client?' Claire was shouting down the phone now.

'Claire, I know this is difficult, but you have to calm down—' stated Julia.

'Calm down?! This is my son we're talking about and all you're thinking about is money!'

'That's not true – all I'm saying is, we have to be careful about how we approach this.'

But Claire wasn't listening. 'Why is Rose suddenly mentioning Joshua now? She just suddenly remembered?' Claire was pacing around her living room, the adrenalin pumping.

'I don't know,' replied Julia, calmly. 'She says it was the photo and that's what we need to understand. And until we can find out, I've agreed with the other partners that—'

But Claire didn't want to hear it again. They were asking the impossible – for her to watch her son be accused of something he didn't even do. She hung up, trying not to give in to the sobs that threatened to overwhelm her, and hurried through to Joshua's room frantically searching for something, anything to prove his innocence.

When Chris finally arrived at dusk, she was sat stewing on the sofa, angry with him for being so late and not picking up his phone. Why hadn't he come home immediately? Where had he been? What was more important than this? She was worried sick about Joshua and her nervous energy needed to be unleashed at someone. Which is why she attacked Chris as soon he came in.

'Just for once, Chris, can you put your family before work? I've been waiting here for hours, worried to death. What is wrong with you?' She was so worked up she didn't see his tight jaw. She didn't see his fists clench or his hand pull back. She saw the release though – smashed glass halted her diatribe and she looked in shock, but not surprise, at the broken picture frame, the two of them on their wedding day now criss-crossed with fractures.

'What the fuck, Claire? Why do you never stop complaining?' roared Chris, his voice reverberating off the walls. He was like a caged tiger, prowling, hunting and Claire knew she had to calm him down quickly.

'I'm sorry – I was upset about Joshua and—'

'You're always upset! Has it ever occurred to you that maybe none of this would have happened if you hadn't started working such ridiculous hours? If you hadn't wanted change so much? If you couldn't just be happy with the way things were?'

Claire tried not to retaliate. Trying to reason with him would only make it worse. She had to let him burn himself out. It could have only been fifteen minutes but it felt like a lifetime as Chris shouted and stormed his way around the house before finally leaving and slamming the door behind him. During that time, she didn't move, she didn't speak; she just kept perfectly still, too frightened to move. Tears silently poured down her cheeks and she was glad the boys were going to their grandparents for the night. Sometimes he came close to her and she almost lost her nerve but then he moved away perhaps not even trusting himself. As the door slammed behind him, Claire finally collapsed into an armchair, wrapping her arms around herself, crying softly.

Chris hadn't always had an anger problem. It hadn't been a constant companion throughout their marriage, a silent threat that could make its presence known at any moment.

No, it had only started a few years ago when Claire had slid into depression, or what Chris and her mother referred to as her *breakdown*. Even then, his outbursts weren't frequent, not by any means, and in a way that made it harder, because then his explosions were so easy to dismiss as isolated incidents.

But how many did you count before it went from someone just having a bad temper to someone having anger issues? It wasn't a question Claire had liked to dwell on. The problem was that everyone had focused so much on Chris's positive attributes – of which there were plenty, she reasoned – that they disguised anything negative. And by everyone, she meant literally *everyone*. Her parents, her friends, people from Castlefield who had seen Chris in the park playing with his sons.

But now thinking back, had it started earlier? She remembered when Chris had been hauled into the university dean's office for fighting. At the time, she'd dismissed it as normal student behaviour until she'd found out that the other guy had ended up in hospital with a broken arm. Or the time they'd gone on holiday and there was no space left in the business class lounge and the poor guy manning the desk relaying this information had received such an earful security had had to step in.

So perhaps it had always been there but because he had never directed his anger at her, not until a couple of years ago anyway, and never at the boys, it hadn't registered as a problem. Although occasionally, she had felt a churn in her stomach – a tiny web of worry that had wound its way around her intestine. At those times, she simply upped her efforts to create the perfect home and family. It came easily to her

– she'd had years of practice dealing with her own parents, but she perhaps knew on some level she couldn't sustain it and her breakdown had certainly triggered something in her husband. It wasn't the major upheavals in life, such as when Joshua went off the rails, but more the smaller everyday stresses – the dishwasher hadn't been unloaded or his shirt wasn't ironed in the right way. Each time, the anger passed quickly, and she'd learnt to live with it.

Sometimes, he recognised it himself and he left the house immediately, walking it off. He returned, calmer, apologetic but as she sat now, her arms wrapped around herself trying to contain her own frustration and helplessness, wondering when he would come back, she knew that her return to work full-time had impacted him more than she'd realised. Now she could only hope that he wouldn't use it as leverage as a way to stop her working. But even if he did, once word got out that her son was involved in a criminal case, who would want to work with her or be associated with her organisation?

Claire swallowed hard and tried to think. This had to be a bad dream or at least a horrible mistake. If she could just talk to Rose... Without thinking, she got up, grabbed her keys and bag and put on her shoes and coat and left the house. If she'd remembered it correctly, Rose lived at 61A Sherbourne Road and she programmed the address into the satnav. She knew she shouldn't, knew it might damage the case, but she had to know. This was her son and whatever Rose was playing at, Claire was going to find out.

Claire drove the ten miles, thinking only of what she would say when she saw Rose. Every so often she checked her rear-view mirror, but it was dark and the only thing she could see were beams of headlights. As she pulled off the main road, and into a side street, she didn't notice the car behind. She turned left, then right, right again, and then a final right before stopping on a nondescript, quiet residential street.

Slowly driving along the road, she found number 61 and parked just before it, not wanting to draw attention to herself. The terraced houses looked small but each one rose at least three floors and most likely had a basement too. There were small gardens at the front and a quick glance through the windshield told Claire that number 61 was overgrown. A gravel path ran up to the front door, splitting the paved terrace in two, which housed a few shrubs and dead flowerbeds.

Now she was here, she hesitated. She caught herself in the mirror and stared back, shocked. Her earlier crying had caused her mascara to leave a trail of shadow under her eyes and her hair was wild around her face. She quickly got a tissue from her bag and wiped the residue away, and then pulled a comb through her hair. Taking a breath, she stepped out of the car and walked up the path, unaware of the eyes watching her from a car parked further down the street.

The house was divided into flats and Claire rang the buzzer for 61A, the noise sharp against the darkness of the house. She didn't see any lights come on, nor hear footsteps in the hallway. The house remained silent and closed off. Without thinking, she placed her hand on the door handle, and was about to move it when she heard a rustle behind her. She whirled around and saw on the pavement outside the house a man of about sixty with a Jack Russell who was scrabbling in the leaves.

She removed her hand guiltily, hoping he hadn't seen her. Claire watched him walk away before checking her surroundings again. She tried the handle, but it was locked. Disappointed, Claire turned back towards her car. There was nothing left to do except go home.

38

Paul cursed under his breath. Despite the month of March promising the early signs of spring, his feet were like ice. He had broken his golden rule of avoiding Castlefield unless absolutely necessary but the desire to see her had been overwhelming. She hadn't updated social media in days and he felt desperate.

Steady, he'd cautioned himself. *Don't blow it now*. He knew he needed to try and control his impulses but today was a significant day and after prowling around his tiny bedsit like a caged animal, he knew he wouldn't be able to control himself. The computer screen glared at him from the corner of the room, inflaming him even further with its lack of updates. Why couldn't she just post something? Anything?

His frustration with Claire rose like bile and he knew he had to do something. He would take a drive. Perhaps stop off for a pint. But as soon as he got into his car, he found himself heading in the direction of his hometown. He *needed* to see her. Which is why he found himself hidden in some bushes just metres from Claire's house, in a crouched position. It wasn't comfortable, but it gave him a decent vantage point of her home, the smart navy-blue front door with its gold knocker and sweeping driveway.

It was almost dark, whatever daylight there had been slowly ebbing away. A train of lampposts had come on, one of which had a fault, the constant flickering provoking Paul's peripheral vision. He scrabbled in his pocket and found an old piece of chewing gum, unwrapped it, and put it in his mouth wishing he'd brought more supplies.

Just minutes ago, he'd watched as Chris had left the house, his shoulders hunched against the cold, his face raging. Paul felt a moment's irritation. What did *he* have to be angry about? He had it all, if only the dumb fuck would realise it. Paul looked at their house – three floors of success right there.

Some of the windows were lit and he wondered which one was Claire's bedroom. He didn't let his imagination stretch to Chris. In his mind, it was just Claire and Paul – her long blonde hair splayed on the pillow, a novel in her hands. It would be literary fiction of course, and every so often she would look up at him and ask him a question. *What did he think the writer meant by this?* And then she would read the paragraph out to him, her voice low and honeyed, just like she used to all those years ago when she came to his house and lay on his bed, their textbooks spread out around them.

Claire had been fascinated with his mind: his ability to recall information, his quick understanding of subjects. He remembered one afternoon when she'd asked him about the encyclopaedias that lined his bookshelf.

'What do you mean, you've read them all from cover to cover?' she'd asked, disbelieving. Her fingers had been running along the spines of the blue faux leather books, but her head swivelled to look at him. 'No one reads encyclopaedias from beginning to end – you use them for reference!' She'd laughed. Paul had narrowed his eyes then, trying to work out if she was taking the piss, but she'd come over, one of the encyclopaedias in her hand, and kissed him on the forehead, and any anger he'd felt had immediately melted away.

Just like that.

She had the power to literally change him from the inside out.

'Okay, let's see, shall we?' Claire had giggled as she opened the book to a random page. 'We'll start with C for Claire,' she added, indicating the volume of the encyclopaedia. Flicking through the pages, Paul observed her as she scanned the book, drinking her in. 'Okay, Cambodia,' she continued. Paul barely heard her. Instead he took in her bowed head, the way her blonde hair fell across her face, her fingers as they trailed the pages. He imagined those fingers on his body. God, it was almost too much for him.

'What is the capital of Cambodia?'

It was an easy question and he reluctantly dragged his brain to focus on what she was saying. Hadn't Brian's brother, Simon, said that girls loved it when you listened to them? Christ, it was hard though. All he wanted was to kiss her, feel her lips pressed on his. He remembered shaking his head as if to clear the thoughts away, and Claire had laughed, thinking he was pretending not to know the answer to her question.

By some miracle he'd managed to control himself and he screwed up his face, joining in her game and giving fake answers. She'd seen straight through him of course and she'd playfully swatted him, giving him the opportunity to grab her and pull her body closer to him. He'd whispered the correct answer in her ear, and then they'd kissed. And after that, she didn't get the chance to ask him any more questions.

He was so lost in the memory; he almost didn't see Claire leave the house. The front door opened, and she slammed it behind her, the noise alerting Paul to her movement. The outdoor porch light lit her up and he watched as she walked quickly to her car. He was lost in her and he felt his whole body respond like a drug addict taking a long-awaited hit. Claire was wearing a long formal coat and a pair of trainers and Paul guessed she'd been in a hurry to leave. Even he knew, with his limited knowledge of fashion, that she was mismatched.

But he didn't get a chance to wonder why she was dressed so oddly. Her Mercedes came to life and he quickly emerged from the bushes, keeping close to the wall and away from the lampposts as he walked the few steps to his own car. He could already see the white reverse lights on Claire's car as she inched her way out of the driveway and he cursed as he fumbled for his car key, hoping she hadn't spotted him.

Just then, several cars passed on the road in front of her house forcing Claire to wait to let them pass and giving him some much-needed cover. Shoving the key in the lock, he swung open the door and sank low into the driver's seat as he put the key in the ignition. The Mercedes was now reversing out onto the road and Paul shoved the gearstick into first and followed behind her.

He trailed Claire for about thirty minutes, his old Renault often struggling to keep up with the speed of the Mercedes, but he managed to keep her within sight. It didn't matter where she was going. He'd seen her and that was enough. He was curious about the state of her marriage as he recalled the twisted look on Chris's face. It reminded him of the time he was watching the family, a few years ago now, at a summer carnival.

Jamie had been a baby and Joshua was still young enough to enjoy such a family event. The crowd was dense which is the only reason he'd felt safe enough to attend. He knew Claire was there because she'd checked in on Facebook. By sheer luck, he'd managed to find them, guessing correctly that with a baby, they would head for a quieter area where families were picnicking on the grass.

He'd observed them, his presence camouflaged by the crowd and the trees. To anyone passing by, they were the perfect family enjoying a picnic. Joshua was playing with his football a few metres away and the baby was gurgling happily in his mother's arms. So only Paul saw Claire's forehead crease in annoyance as Chris had abruptly got up from the grass and walked off without a word. He saw her eyes trail after him, and the baby, perhaps sensing his mother's tension, started to cry. Joshua looked up just at that moment and Claire was left to play a solo performance. *Daddy's just gone for a walk, he'll be back soon*, he imagined her saying in a sing-song voice. And she would jostle the baby and wave to Joshua and her smile would never leave her face.

But inside, she was pulled taut and Paul didn't need to be next to her to feel the tension emanating from her. But then Chris had returned ten minutes later, all smiles and ice cream and he watched as Claire looked up at him, her relief and desire naked for all to see, and Paul had retreated, jealousy and anger his only company.

39

Transcript – Witness Statement

'*I hadn't arranged to meet Rose at the opening night of Studio 65 but I was aware that she was going. It was all she'd talked about for a while. She was excited about the footballers. I had arrived early, about nine-thirty in the evening. I went inside and sat at the bar mainly. I talked to a few people I recognised and had a drink.*

'*About an hour later, it was getting busier. The bar area was crowded – they were giving away free shots – so I moved away to the end of the bar. There was no one really queuing there because that's where the dirty glasses were dumped. It was then that I saw Rose. She was with a crowd of people waiting for drinks. Someone in her group was getting the shots in and handing them back to the group including Rose.*

'At that point, she saw me and waved. After a few minutes, she came over to where I was sat and asked me if I had any spice. I said no and then she went back to her mates. There seemed to be a few of them, three guys and a girl. The guys looked like posh knobs – you know, floppy hair and boating shoes. They looked out of place if I'm honest with you.

'After that, they took a table in the VIP area. I don't know whose table it was – I doubt Rose would have the money for that. A few minutes later, Rose came up to me and invited me to the VIP section to sit at their table. I thought why not? Free booze and it beat sitting by the empties. Was Rose drunk? Perhaps a little. She was laughing a lot – perhaps she'd taken something, I don't know. She was having a good time, drinking and dancing like everyone else.'

40

Claire slumped back against the dining room chair, looking at her son as if he was a complete stranger. While Joshua had vehemently denied even touching Rose, the fact remained that he knew her. Not only that, but he was at the crime scene that night. Claire tried to focus on her son's obvious bewilderment and confusion at the news that Rose was accusing him of sexual assault.

Of course, she'd known all along that he would never do something so heinous, but to learn that he was there on the night in question was a shock. Claire had long ago developed the skill of identifying a liar – her client list was often full of them – and she'd had no doubt that Joshua was telling the truth about his role in the events of that night. He went to the opening of the nightclub, met Rose, went to an after-party with her, and then left in a taxi.

She watched Joshua now, her mind rapidly going over her phone conversation with Julia the day before. Rose had already identified her two attackers and they had denied all charges, hence the preparation for the trial. But now Rose had named a third person – Joshua – whom she'd confirmed with photo identification. Claire felt the vomit rise in her throat.

Chris was stood, leaning against the dining room wall, his expression unreadable. She'd been asking Joshua questions for almost half an hour, trying to work out any way Rose could have got confused, and they were both exhausted.

'Joshua, is there anything else you can tell me that might explain why Rose is linking you to this incident?'

When did it become an incident and not rape? When her son became involved.

'Mum! Bloody hell! I told you already! I did not *do* anything to her!'

Claire started at the unusual expletive coming from her son. She'd never heard him swear before.

'I'm sorry, love,' she replied trying to hide her frustration under a gentler tone, 'but I need to examine this from every angle, so I can clear your name.'

Joshua looked up at her, his eyes on hers. There was something in there, and for a moment Claire felt she might be able to reach out and grab it, but then it was gone.

'This Rose – she's crazy! She was high as a kite and drunk as well. Besides it's not like Lee would—'

Claire froze. 'What did you say?'

'Nothing.'

She watched Joshua realise his mistake. Claire had never mentioned the name Lee. She quickly thought back over the conversation. Had she? No, she was pretty sure she hadn't because she never disclosed names of a case, but Lee was one of the named defendants.

Mother and son looked at each other for a split second before Claire stood, the force pushing the dining room chair over. Out of the corner of her eye, she watched Chris turn and walk out of the room and she felt a part of her collapse inside. But she would have to deal with that later.

'How the hell do you know Lee?' she asked, the quiet steel of the words almost, but not quite, making Joshua cower.

'Mum! I didn't do this – I promise you!'

'How the hell do you know the name Lee?' she asked again. Her eyes bored into her son's and she remembered the picture of the naked girl on his phone, their exchanges.

'Mum! Please – you have to believe me – I didn't do anything to that girl.'

'Joshua, I'm asking you one more time – how do you know that name?' She wanted to shake him, make him understand how serious this was. He started crying then, and Claire felt her leg muscles contract to keep her upright. She scrabbled for the chair, righted it, and sat down.

'Mum, I promise you,' cried Joshua, 'I didn't do anything to Rose.'

'But you know Lee?'

Joshua wiped his eyes and nodded. 'Sort of. He's older than us but he was a friend of Jinty's and he just sort of... started hanging out with us.'

Jinty. She knew he was one of the Colston lads that Joshua and Mark had been hanging out with the year before.

'How long was he hanging out with you?' asked Claire.

'I dunno – maybe six months? Maybe longer?'

Claire forced herself to let the silence settle between them, waiting for Joshua to continue.

'He was a bit weird to be honest, but he was… useful,' he continued after a few moments. Claire looked at him quizzically. She thought he wasn't going to answer at first, but her patience won out.

'He could get served in the off-licence,' he explained, reluctantly. 'He would bring us booze and we'd drink and listen to music. I didn't really talk to him that much. And then he started talking about these girls he'd met and how he would introduce them to us.'

'And then what?' asked Claire, hardly able to breathe.

'And then, nothing.' Joshua shrugged. 'Lee occasionally came around to Jinty's and that was it.'

'And was one of these girls Rose?' asked Claire.

The silence was unbearable.

'Joshua?' But Claire already knew the answer.

Joshua sat, his shoulders hunched over in despair. He looked up at his mother, his eyes filled with tears; for the first time looking frightened as he answered.

'Yes. What will happen now?'

Claire looked at her son and knew that the only thing she could do now was what she did best. Her job.

'Well, I'm sure that Rose will realise that she got confused and made a mistake,' she reassured him. 'Julia is working on that now. Like you said, Rose was high and drunk and there were loads of people at that party.'

'And if she doesn't?' asked Joshua.

'Well, we'll deal with that if it happens, okay?' Claire pulled Joshua into her arms and although she wasn't religious, she said a swift prayer that it would all be sorted before Joshua got arrested.

41

'I remember that some of the guys from the group had disappeared during the night for a while or rather they seemed to be taking it in turns to leave the VIP area. I assumed they were snorting coke in the toilets. I don't remember the time exactly, but I remember Rose was dancing with the other girl. And then three other guys came along who Rose's friend seemed to know and they joined the table. Their names were Lee, Nick, and Armin. Rose's friend introduced me to them as well as to the floppy-hair guys Rose had first come in with. I didn't talk to any of them really but I did hear them talk about an after-party.

'By this time, it was almost one in the morning. Everyone was pretty drunk and high. The after-party was at a friend of Lee's house. One of the original guys in the group seemed put out because he kept trying to dance with Rose but she was all over the place, dancing *with one guy, then another, then having a drinking competition. Her friend was sat on Armin's lap and they were at it pretty heavily. I probably would have left then if the party hadn't been near my flat but it was in Crossway Avenue, so I thought I'd go for a free drink and then head home. An hour max. Except Rose and her friend had an argument because her friend didn't want to go to the after-party.'*

APRIL 2018

42

Claire, having somehow got out of bed and managing to get dressed, sat at her dresser and looked at herself in the mirror, tiredness making her look old. Since talking to Joshua, she'd barely slept, the crushing weight of worry snaking its way through her body, refusing to let her rest. As agreed, she hadn't been into the office although she'd talked to Julia several times on the phone. Julia kept referencing her time off as if she was on holiday.

Just to catch up with yourself while we sort this out. Those had been her exact words and Claire thought of them now. *Catch up with yourself.* What did that even mean? She couldn't sleep, she couldn't eat, or concentrate or sit and read a magazine. She felt trapped in a void, stuck in a no-man's land, helpless to help her son. And Chris. Where was he? The one person who should have been able to support her had gone on a business trip to America. How convenient. He'd not offered to cancel it or even to postpone it. He'd simply packed his bag and got ready to go. When she'd questioned him, he'd shrugged. *It's all a misunderstanding. It will all be sorted by the time I'm back.*

Claire had looked at him in disbelief. *Our lives are falling apart and that's all you can say?*

She'd asked him not to go but he'd gone anyway, and it suddenly struck her that over the last year or so, he'd had more business trips than ever before. He used to hate them, would do anything to avoid them, claiming he didn't want to be apart from her and the boys. *I don't want to miss bath and bedtime with Jamie. I made that mistake with Joshua.* Chris would race home from work, eager to play his role as a father. Afterwards, he and Claire would eat and snuggle on the sofa with a glass of wine.

Now it was almost like he couldn't wait to get away. Claire paused. Was that really true? She jostled with the question in her mind, but sheer exhaustion made her fumble for the answer. The truth was she didn't know and as her lined face stared back at her, she realised only one thing was certain: she didn't know anything any more.

Claire woke up and felt something stuck to her face. As she lifted her head, she heard the tearing of a page from a novel as it peeled from her cheek, the dried trail of salvia causing her to wipe her mouth. Reading was her latest attempt to help herself sleep. She'd exhausted her TED talks and besides she couldn't concentrate.

She looked around the room in confusion, trying to work out what time it was. The weak daylight through the curtains suggested it was well past noon and she put a hand out to check her phone on her bedside table. But it wasn't there. *Shit*. Where was her phone? She must have left it in the living room. What if someone had called?

She snatched the covers back and swung her legs out of bed to reach the floor. She was surprised to see herself fully dressed. As her sleep-induced fog lifted, she remembered being sat at her dresser earlier that morning before crawling back into bed. Exhaustion must have taken over and with no phone to disturb her, the unconscious hours had crept up.

She could hear Lucy in the kitchen downstairs. Seeing her wristwatch on the dresser, she stood up and checked the time. It was ten past two in the afternoon. She'd been asleep for almost six hours. Not caring how she looked, she left the bedroom and went in search of her phone. She saw it on the kitchen table, her anxiety so high she barely even heard Lucy's greeting.

Picking it up, she unlocked it before quickly scrolling the notifications. Seeing a missed call from her mother, she ignored it, and tapped the email icon, certain there would be some news regarding Joshua. But to her surprise, there were just two new emails – a reminder about the upcoming Easter bank holiday from Sylvie who did their HR and a request from Elaine to submit her expenses before the end of the month.

She looked at her phone in disbelief, wondering if her inbox was working properly. Quickly, she sent a test email to herself. It arrived, pinging into her line of vision immediately. She should have been relieved. No news was good news, she reassured herself. Of course, it was. So why then did she feel such an intense sense of foreboding?

Claire woke the next day to the trill of her phone. Instantly awake, she thought it would be Chris and quickly grabbed her phone from her bedside table and slid her finger across the screen.

'Chris!' she said, in relief.

'Claire?'

'Yes?' Claire was confused. This was a woman's voice and it took her a few seconds to work out that it was Julia.

'Sorry to call you so early,' said Julia.

'What time is it?'

'Just gone six.'

Claire felt her stomach clench in suspense. 'What is it?' she asked.

'I'm sorry, Claire, but Joshua is going to be arrested. Rose is sticking to her story.'

Claire felt herself crumple. She'd hoped that they would be able to get Rose to admit she'd made a mistake without it getting this far. Now he'd be in the system, interviewed, questioned, statements taken. It would all be on file. In court.

Oh God.

'Claire, you still there?'

Claire lifted her head. 'Yes, I'm still here. You believe her?'

'To remember someone so late in the game, well it's odd. But we've had her assessed for trauma and it's possible that she blocked some of it out. The photo just triggered the memories. There's also the matter that another witness has come forward,' said Julia.

You didn't answer my question.

'A new witness? Who?' asked Claire.

'I'm sorry, you know I can't tell you that. Even telling you this much… But once you get a lawyer everything will be disclosed then.'

Claire closed her eyes tightly. *This couldn't be happening.*

'I'm sorry, Claire,' said Julia eventually. 'You should also know that Rose will be getting new representation from another law firm, which is disappointing but no surprise really. We can't continue to represent her with the conflict of interest. She's hired Miller & Co.'

As Julia continued to talk, something about meeting the board again, getting a lawyer, Claire felt herself tune out. The only thing that mattered now was telling Chris.

'I'll call you in a day or two,' finished Julia.

'Yes,' replied Claire not having heard a word.

'Call me if you need anything, okay?'

'I have to go now.' Claire hung up abruptly and tried Chris's number. She wasn't surprised when he didn't answer. Opening a new message, she typed out the latest update.

Joshua about to be arrested. Call me now.

She didn't need to wait long. Less than a minute later and her phone rang, Chris's name flashing up on the screen. She picked it up.

'Claire – what the hell is going on? I thought Julia was on it?'

'Joshua is going to have to go in and give his side of the story. There's a new witness who has come forward.' Claire felt the steel in her tone, drawing upon every inch of self-control she had not to blast him. *Selfish shit.*

'What? No! I thought it was being sorted!'

Chris sounded scared. *He should be.*

Claire didn't respond and then the silence was broken with the words Claire had felt like she'd been waiting to hear forever.

'I'm coming home,' said Chris.

Claire hung up and went to her son's room to wake him up with the news that his life would never be the same again.

43

'It was freezing outside but once we left the club, Rose's friend left with Armin. Rose was pretty pissed off and was screaming at her down the street that she was a bitch. I thought her friend would come back and there would be a catfight, but she kept on walking. Good job too the state Rose was in. We all tried to calm Rose down, but it took a while, then we tried to get taxis to go the party but there weren't any, so we ended up walking. It took like fifteen minutes, maybe less. Personally, I thought it was a good thing – give Rose some fresh air and a chance to calm down and at that point, I was ready to just go home, but Rose was still pretty upset.

'When we arrived at the party, it was already well underway and although Rose was pretty hammered, she seemed to get a second wind. I don't know – maybe she took a booster or something. She immediately started *dancing in the living room and Lee went to get some drinks. One of the floppy-haired guys started dancing with Rose, but she seemed irritated by him. He kept trying to put his arms around her and she kept moving out of them. And then Lee came and handed them some drinks. Rose started dancing with Lee and that's when another argument started...'*

MAY 2018

44

Claire's feet pounded the pavement hard and fast. It was just after two in the morning. Apart from the light from the lampposts, it was pitch black, the rest of the neighbourhood asleep, unaware of how grateful they should be to have the ability to switch off for a night. Claire hadn't slept properly for several weeks now.

Chris had returned from America leaden with jet lag and irritability. She had been in bed watching the clock on her bedside table. It was just after midnight and she hoped he would come into their room and get into bed beside her. The loneliness had been stifling. There was no one she could talk to about everything that was going on. Even her conversations with Julia had been brief. There was no room in this scenario for business partner and best friend to exist side by side, and the role of partner had won, leaving Claire hollow and alone.

As she'd heard Chris go into the spare room, she'd felt a level of despair so deep she wondered how she would ever get out of this black hole that had encompassed her so ferociously. He'd been sleeping in the spare room ever since, their marriage on hold, each of them unable to cope with anything else. So, whenever her thoughts started tumbling over each other in the early hours of the morning, threatening to overwhelm, she got up, put on her running gear, and slipped quietly outside. It had become a habit and the only way she could collapse into a dreamless sleep for a few hours. She woke up exhausted, but adrenalin charged through her from the minute she woke up.

Chris and Claire had hired the best solicitor Claire knew, Gerald Livingstone. Watching Joshua being arrested had been the worst moment of her life. He'd been held in custody and she'd been waiting at the station the whole time, letting Livingstone do his job. Joshua, who had always been her perfect child, her golden boy, was being held in a stark grey room and being interviewed by the police. He had always looked older than he was but his immaturity was present for any fool to see. It was so blatant; Claire couldn't understand why the police had even bothered to interview him. Anybody could see that he hadn't raped anyone. He wouldn't even know how to!

Would he?

The first interview seemed to go on forever, and Claire knew the same questions would be asked over and over again. *How did you meet Rose? How did you know Rose? How long had you known her before you agreed to go back to the party with her? How did you get to the party? Did you travel together? What time did you leave the party? Did you take drugs? What drugs? How much did you take?*

Claire was taken aback when she found out Joshua had admitted to having taken drugs that night. Chris and Claire had always talked openly about drugs to Joshua – they both knew they were absolutely rife in Manchester and had agreed to get ahead of it rather than pretend they didn't exist. Joshua had always said he'd had no interest. They knew he drank a little at parties because he told them openly that he did. At that time, Claire remembered feeling proud that they had such an honest and communicative relationship with their son. Joshua had even told them of the night he'd gone too far and was so hungover the next day he vowed never to drink that much again.

So, what the hell had gone wrong that Joshua had gone to a party with a strange girl and taken coke? Joshua was all set to take his A levels and go on to one of the best universities in the country. Why was this happening? It just didn't make sense. She'd read every parenting book so how had she got it so wrong?

The night Joshua was kept in custody overnight, Claire couldn't sleep at all, wondering about him in the dank cell. She must have drifted off eventually because when she woke up, it took her a few minutes to realise her new reality: her son was in jail being prosecuted for rape.

They eventually released him on bail. Livingstone communicated everything. He called her or Chris regularly, keeping them updated – witnesses, people at the party, their testimonies. It all started to blur and Claire having previously known the case inside out only seemed to have enough mental energy to focus on her son. But Claire felt reassured by Livingstone – he was calm and capable, exactly what Claire needed. And there were some words of his that she hung on to the most: there was no forensic evidence, it was all circumstantial. But still, Claire knew, whatever the outcome, her son's life would never be the same again.

45

'One of the floppy-haired guys was pretty pissed off when he saw Rose dancing with Lee. He started shouting at Rose. The music in the party was loud that I couldn't really hear what he said. Give Lee credit, he didn't seem to take it personally and didn't retaliate. The other guy though was getting pretty heated until his mates pulled him away towards the kitchen. Posh knob.

'Rose seemed to like the attention though. She carried on dancing with Lee and then another random girl started dancing with Rose and that seemed to be the end of it. I stayed around for another twenty minutes and assumed posh knob and his mates had fucked off back to wherever they came from and decided to go home as well. I told Rose I was leaving and she gave me a hug and carried on dancing.

'My flat was only a two minute-walk away so I went home and went to bed. But I couldn't sleep because I was too wired and I felt like I should have made sure Rose got home safely. I knew she was with Lee and that, but still. So, I got up and went back to the party. This was about an hour later, maybe four in the morning.

'And that's when I saw him. He was coming down the stairs. I saw his boating shoes first and then I saw him tucking his shirt in as if he'd been for a piss, and laughing with two guys I didn't recognise. I went up to him and asked him where Rose was. He seemed surprised to see me. He told me Rose had gone home ages ago and I believed him. It's only when Rose told me what had really happened a few months later...'

JUNE 2018

46

Whether it was because she'd managed to get a few hours' sleep or because she could no longer tolerate being at home, Claire had got up, got dressed and gone into Manchester one morning in early June. It had been the right thing to do. She lost herself for a few hours in the streets of the city, window-shopping, stopping to look at the street performers, and occasionally people-watching.

She had messaged Julia to let her know she was in town if she wanted to meet for a coffee and surprisingly Julia had messaged back to meet at two o'clock. As soon as Julia saw Claire, Julia wrapped her in her arms as if she was a child. It briefly occurred to her that it should be Chris holding her, but Claire had stood silently, clinging to Julia, surrendering herself to the comfort. It was all Claire had needed to feel that everything would be all right, and she had to hold back the tears.

And she'd felt better then – better than she had in weeks, in fact. Just because Joshua knew the main perpetrator.

Just because he'd been caught with a picture of a naked girl on his phone. Just because he knew Rose. None of these things meant he was a rapist and despite all the connections, Claire knew it was all just a misunderstanding. And over cappuccinos and skinny lattes, Julia had smiled and reassured her. It was only towards the end of their conversation when they were both getting ready to leave, that Julia said what she did.

'You know, Claire,' she said, picking up her handbag and walking towards the door, 'with everything that's going on with your family, maybe it wouldn't be a bad idea to think about taking a more permanent break from work.'

'Permanent break? What do you mean?' replied Claire walking through the doorway as Julia held it open for her. The café was noisy and Claire wondered if she had misheard.

'Well, you know,' said Julia as they started walking together, 'it's been a difficult time for you and I suspect it's only going to get more difficult as the trial starts. Perhaps it's time to think about selling your share in the firm and taking some proper time off.'

Claire had slowed then and stared at Julia, trying to understand. And then it hit her – of course, Julia's meeting with the board members. Hadn't she said something about meeting them? But this?

'And who would I sell to?' asked Claire icily as they drew up outside the main entrance of Stephens & Carmichael.

'Well, I know a number of people who would be interested, and there's always me.' Julia smiled as if she was recommending a restaurant and not suggesting that Claire give up the one thing that would keep her from going completely insane.

'But I built this company,' protested Claire. 'I know I took a bit of a break with the kids but—'

'Of course, I know that,' placated Julia. 'That's why I'm suggesting you let me buy you out – because you would be irreplaceable. Just think about it, okay? Because once the trial starts, well... it's going to be tough on you, Claire...'

Claire looked up at the offices and tried to gather her thoughts.

'Listen,' said Julia. 'It's just a suggestion, okay? Just have a think about it.' Julia leaned in to give Claire a hug. 'It's been so nice seeing you – you're doing so well.'

Claire returned the embrace automatically, and as she watched Julia walk into their building, the only evidence of the conversation was her friend's perfume lingering in the air. And it was then Claire understood. Julia didn't want to be associated with the mother of an accused rapist.

'Where are you going?' Claire asked Chris as she saw him packing. He'd done a long day in the office only arriving home that evening at half past eight. She was looking forward to spending an evening with him and she hoped they could talk. But since everything with Joshua, he'd been elusive when he was at home, which was infrequently. He'd said the trip to the US would be the last for a while, yet here he was packing again.

'Germany – there's a problem with the developers and I need to get over there to sort it out.'

'You? Why?'

'Because otherwise they're not going to deliver on time and I've promised the US they can have it within a month.

Now the bloody developer is saying it's going to take two months.' He threw his toilet bag into the suitcase and snapped it shut. 'I need to get over there and find out what the hell they're doing.'

'Isn't there someone else who can go? I mean, someone with more knowledge of the technology?' It had been the wrong thing to say and she swiftly corrected herself. 'I mean, your strength is sales…'

'You don't get it do you, Claire? If I don't deliver this product on time, there will be no sale.'

'Okay,' replied Claire, slowly. 'What time is your flight tomorrow?'

'I'm leaving in the early hours. There's a six thirty a.m. to Frankfurt.'

'What?'

'The sooner I get there, the sooner, I can start work.'

'But surely there's a later flight that means you could get a good night's sleep first,' protested Claire.

'I can't sleep with all this developer crap going around in my head. And being here…'

'Being here what?' replied Claire, dangerously.

'Well, it's hardly a relaxing environment to come home to is it, with all this stuff with Joshua going on.'

'All this stuff? Chris – this is your son!' exclaimed Claire. 'We need to talk about it – not have you dash off again.'

'I'm sorry – I can't deal with this now. I've talked to Joshua. He's knows I'm there for him but now it's up to the lawyers.'

Claire watched in disbelief as he picked up his suitcase and walked out of the bedroom.

'Chris!' she shouted, not caring if she woke Jamie. 'Where are you going?'

He ignored her and carried on walking onto the landing. He was halfway down the stairs when she felt a murderous rage rise up in her and she ran after him.

'You can't just up and leave like this!' Her face was contorted but her eyes were dry. She was fed up of handling everything by herself and his selfishness scored through her like a deep paper cut.

He looked back at her then, his eyes blazing. 'Watch me,' he replied, and he turned away from her and continued down the stairs. He was on the penultimate step when Claire pushed him hard and she watched as he flew forward, headfirst. He'd let go of the holdall to put his hands out to break his fall, the bag coming to a stop at the foot of the stairs with a thud.

He sat up, stunned, his expression of disbelief mirroring hers, and she waited in fear for his reaction. But none came and as he got to his feet, picked up the bag, and left the house without a word, she let out a scream of frustration.

She'd called Chris's mobile phone for most of the night until the early hours when his phone had been switched off and she assumed he was in the air. She'd gone over the scene a thousand times and with every replay, it paused on Chris's final glance as he left the house. His eyes had told her then, more clearly than words ever could, and she'd felt the disgust and pity radiate from them, piercing their marriage. Eventually, she'd gone to bed, slipping into a troubled sleep.

She'd woken the next morning, dragging herself out of bed, grateful for the arrival of a new day. Yes, things had got out of control, but they couldn't let things get so bad between them, especially now, when they needed to present a united front for the sake of their son. Claire thought of Joshua. For the most part, he seemed to be doing okay and Claire was in two minds whether that was a good thing or not. On the one hand, it indicated that he was innocent and felt he had nothing to hide. On the other, it might mean that he simply didn't understand the seriousness of the situation.

The trial would start next month and Claire felt a quiver of fear run through her. Frankfurt was one hour ahead; she would keep trying Chris until he answered. He had to pick up at some point; last night he'd been angry and rightly so. Today, they would both be calmer and she would apologise and they would sort this out.

Claire had tried to keep busy, but she was struggling to concentrate. She called Chris's mobile every hour, on the hour, but it had simply rung out. Clearly, he still wasn't ready to talk. She willed herself to be patient. Eventually, she'd sent him a message telling him how sorry she was and to call her when he felt ready. She was satisfied that she'd done everything she could, but by lunchtime, she knew she needed to get out of the house.

She drove into Manchester, parked the car and wandered the city centre before stopping to get a coffee. As she waited for her order, she rubbed her eyes distractedly, the tiredness threatening to swallow her whole. When she opened them again, she was surprised to see Linda walking into the cafe.

She hadn't seen Linda since their night out; in fact Claire hadn't been out at all since then, although she knew that Lucy and Luke's nanny often arranged playdates, so the boys could get together. Linda stood in the queue for a few minutes before she noticed Claire and waved.

'Hi! What a coincidence! I was just thinking about you!' greeted Linda.

'Hi, how are you? You look fantastic!' Claire took in her slim figure and tailored suit. It fit perfectly, accentuating her slim waist and long legs.

'Thanks! Yes, I've been running a few times a week and it's been great! How's everything with you?'

Claire tried not to notice that Linda didn't return the compliment. She didn't blame her. She wondered if Linda would ask why she was in jeans and a T-shirt on a weekday.

'I'm good. You know, busy...' Claire trailed off and Linda threw her a look of sympathy.

'Full on with the boys and work?' guessed Linda.

If only you knew. 'Yep – it never stops!' lied Claire.

'Time for a chat?' asked Linda, indicating a free table.

'Why not?' agreed Claire.

'Great – give me a minute – I'll just get my coffee and join you.'

As Claire walked to the table, she saw Linda take out her phone and type a message before ordering. Claire sank down into the chair and closed her eyes, grateful for a minute to breathe. She opened them as soon as she heard the chair opposite her move and smiled at Linda as she sat down.

'So, how are things?' asked Linda, removing the lid from her coffee. As the two of them chatted, Claire felt herself slip into the role of the woman Linda knew before: a working mum whose only challenges ranged from getting home on time to what to put into a lunch box. Nowhere in the conversation did she mention her argument with Chris or the worry about her son being named as part of an investigation. And by the end of the twenty minutes, Claire almost believed it herself, but then Linda brought up Chris.

Linda had been talking about bumping into him outside his office. It wasn't a huge surprise, Chris worked in the Trident Square building, which was round the corner from Linda's office, a fact Linda had shared when she'd first gone round to her house for breakfast. It was one of those coincidences that pleased both women, keen to have something in common. As Linda talked, Claire assumed Linda was referring to bumping into him a few weeks ago. It was only when she discovered that it had been that morning that Claire queried her.

'This morning? You sure?' asked Claire.

'Yes, just as I was walking into the office. I waved but I don't think he saw me to be honest. He seemed busy on his phone.' Linda shrugged, the matter clearly of little interest to her.

'You must have been mistaken, Chris is in Germany – he flew last night.'

'Oh probably,' replied Linda a little too quickly. 'I was rushing – just like I usually am!' But her laughter was forced and after Linda had made her excuses to get back to the office and Claire had said her goodbyes, Claire continued to sit in the coffee shop watching Linda's retreating back until it could no longer be seen.

★

Claire didn't know how she'd made it through the rest of the afternoon. She'd eventually received a message from Chris saying he'd landed safely, and he'd been busy with work and they'd talk when he got back. Ordinarily she would have been relieved but now she didn't know what to think. Had it been a mistake on Linda's part? Claire tried to reassure herself that it was – there were thousands of people in central Manchester. So why then, did she feel so uneasy?

With extreme effort, she'd managed to lose herself in the city for another hour and it was almost five when Claire decided to simply give up and go home. She knew she needed to sleep because her eyes were starting to blur on the drive home. She would try Chris again tonight.

JULY 2018

47

Claire looked at the man she had known for over twenty years. The mere sight of him caused a reaction in her so physical she had to swallow down the bile. He'd eventually confessed to what she'd suspected for a while – he was having an affair. The trial had started a couple of days before and it was the evening before Joshua's appearance in court and although she didn't know it at the time, she would look back on this night as an omen. She was never meant to find out that night – Chris was going to tell her about it after the trial was over and everything with Joshua was sorted.

It was the irritating ping of Chris's mobile that had made her curious. Usually, he had it on silent and he *always* had it on him but that evening he'd left it on the kitchen counter. Months later, she would wonder if he'd wanted to be found out. She'd been making a cup of tea and his phone lit up and she saw the first line of the message. Seeing the words *I miss you* pierced a part of Claire's being she didn't even know existed. It could be from his mum, she thought, trying to open the message while dipping the tea bag again to make it stronger. But the number she typed in to unlock Chris's phone didn't work and then she started to laugh, a wild hysterical laugh that reminded her of a homeless woman she'd once seen in Manchester.

What was she doing? She didn't need to open the message to know it wasn't from his mum. And then she was crying and as Chris came rushing into the kitchen looking for his phone, Claire knew her marriage was over.

Claire wasn't sure how much more she could take. It was three in the morning and the house was empty. Both Jamie and Joshua were with their grandparents and Claire had arranged to pick up Joshua at eight a.m. the next day to take him to court. Chris had left; she'd no idea where he'd gone. Most probably to this other woman. He refused to tell Claire her name or how he had met her. He said he'd been seeing her for a few months, but Claire guessed it must have been for at least a year if not longer.

On a conscious level, she knew she would have to deal with her marriage at some point but for now it was impossible. Every fibre of her being was focused on her son. As she sat on the bathroom floor unable to get up, the cup of tea gone cold in her hands, she remembered the words of a friend from years ago. *You think you love your husband but wait until you have a child – it's love on a whole different level, a love you're willing to die for.* And as Claire sat there, completely alone, she realised it was true.

Claire woke up cold and wet, still on the floor of the bathroom. At first, she'd thought she'd wet herself and then she realised that the remnants of the tea had spilt over her as she'd fallen asleep. Stripping herself off, she grabbed a towel and wiped herself down before picking up the mug and going into the bedroom to check the time: 5:36 a.m. She wondered if Joshua was sleeping. She imagined him in the spare bedroom of her mother's house, tucked into a bunk bed, his younger brother beneath him. She then wondered if Chris was sleeping.

Was he having sex?

And it was then that she flung the mug she was holding as hard as she could at the wall, the pieces shattering in a single satisfying smash.

Somehow Claire had managed to get into bed. She was naked and cold when her alarm woke her at seven. She felt ill with tiredness but as she rose from the mattress, the other side of the bed still made up, she felt a tinge of relief that the day of Joshua's appearance in court had finally arrived. She would get through this and then her marriage could be dealt with.

Pulling on her dressing gown, she padded downstairs to the kitchen and made a strong coffee. She had half an hour to get ready before she left the house to go to her parents' house to pick up Joshua. Livingstone and herself had prepared him thoroughly – now it was just a case of letting Joshua do the rest and waiting for the verdict.

★

Claire and Joshua drove home in silence. He'd done well; he'd dressed exactly how she'd told him to and he'd responded to the questions exactly as they'd practised. Livingstone had been pleased too. Afterwards, Claire and Joshua had left quickly not wanting to be in court any longer than they needed to be. She was relieved not to have seen Rose in court.

Lying bitch.

Occasionally Claire thought about Julia and the firm. She thought about her job and her career and her time spent in court working on cases but it all seemed like a lifetime away, as remote as another planet in the solar system. She couldn't even remember the last time she'd been in the office. She wondered if she ever would be again now that Julia had emailed her the offer to buy Claire out.

Now, driving home, Joshua in the front seat beside her, she watched him as he leant his head back and closed his eyes. Despite his youth, he looked tired.

'Has Dad gone back to work?' asked Joshua suddenly and although she was staring straight ahead manoeuvring through traffic, she could feel her son's eyes on her.

'Yes,' replied Claire. No point lying about it. Claire and Chris had been in court together, but she could sense Chris couldn't wait to get back to the office afterwards. 'Why? Did you need something?'

'No, I was just wondering.' Joshua fell silent before adding, 'When can I go back to school?' he asked, changing the subject.

'In September when everyone else,' replied Claire. 'Do you want to go back?'

'Yes,' he said. 'I don't want to miss any more than I already have.'

Claire smiled in spite of the grim proceedings they found themselves in. This was the Joshua she knew.

'Okay, well let's have a chat with the head and see what she says. The trial will be over in a couple of weeks.'

Out of the corner of her eye, she saw Joshua nod. He seemed like he was about to say something else but then he leant his head back again and closed his eyes for the rest of the journey home.

48

Claire had been watching the trial in court most days. Each time she was there, she could almost believe that it was just another day on the job. She only saw Rose once, her long dark hair tied back primly, her posture ramrod straight. As soon as Claire left court, she would call Chris with an update, their conversations terse and brief. They had decided to keep the state of their marriage to themselves until the trial was over. She wondered whether Joshua had noticed that his father had been sleeping in the guest room. She knew her son was struggling to hold it together.

In just a few weeks, he had lost a lot of weight. Most of the time he was in his room. She had tried to talk to him, to support him, but he was closed off, his only escape the hours of video games. Chris had had a little more success and for that she was truly grateful. They'd both reassured him that the trial would come to nothing. Joshua himself had continually denied that he'd ever do anything like that to a woman.

And the witness?

Claire pushed the thought from her mind as she drove home that afternoon. It was almost five o'clock. Lucy had been a complete lifesaver especially as it was now the school holidays. Both Chris and Claire's parents had rallied and babysat in the mornings until Lucy arrived in the afternoons. Jamie, unaware, had adored seeing so much of his grandparents.

Claire parked the car in the driveway and turned the engine off and Joshua had already headed inside. But instead of grabbing her things and following him, she sat in the driver's seat, reluctant to leave the brief refuge of the car. She opened the window a few centimetres and breathed in the fresh air. She noticed now that it had been a beautiful summer's day. Above she could see an endless basin of cloudless sky and she imagined some ethereal higher power watching over her.

Suddenly, she realised that she didn't want to go into the house, not just yet. She needed just a few more moments of escapism where she didn't have to answer any questions or find the energy to deal with an exuberant Jamie. Stepping out of the car, she walked down her driveway, messaging Lucy from her phone as she went, telling her she'd be back in an hour. Claire didn't know where she was going; all she knew was that she would walk until she felt ready to go home.

Claire had ended up in one of the little coffee shops in Castlefield. It was almost closing time and fairly quiet. She had ordered a pot of tea and sat at a small table at the back of the coffee shop. There was only one other table occupied, a twenty-something girl wearing headphones and trying to look at her phone and computer screen simultaneously.

Claire was staring into her cup when she heard the little bell at the door go but didn't bother to look up. It was only when she heard a voice ordering four scones to take away that she realised it was Linda. Claire kept her head down hoping Linda wouldn't notice her but then she heard her call out her name.

'Claire, hi!' greeted Linda walking over to the table. 'How are you?'

Claire dutifully stood up and the two women embraced.

'I'm fine – you?' said Claire hoping to deflect attention on to Linda.

'Good thanks! I just stopped off to get some scones for after our meal tonight. Ian came back last night for a week.'

'That's great – you must be happy to have him back.'

'Yes, very much,' replied Linda. 'Listen…'

Claire waited and hoped that whatever would come next would just be something simple like a playdate request. Whenever someone started a conversation with *Listen*, it was never good.

'I wanted to say sorry for getting confused about seeing Chris when we last met. Thinking about it after, I realised it wasn't him at all. Sometimes, I just get so busy that my mind isn't thinking straight.'

Claire looked at her friend, realising what she was trying to do.

'It's okay Linda, honestly. It probably was Chris that you saw. We've— That is— He's been—' Claire struggled to finish and as she saw the look of concern on Linda's face, tears started streaming down Claire's face and she reached for a tissue, frantically wiping them. But they wouldn't stop and Linda slowly guided Claire to sit back down before pulling up her own chair opposite her, the bag of scones between them. Linda was quiet, only handing tissue after tissue as Claire let the tears fall, releasing some of the stress and worry from her body.

Claire realised she didn't need to explain anything to Linda and Claire felt the tears lessen.

'Is there anything I can do?' asked Linda quietly, one hand on Claire's back rubbing it gently.

'No, but thank you. I'm so sorry – I don't usually break down in the middle of coffee shops. And you were only here to get some scones!' said Claire, trying to cover up her embarrassment with a joke.

Linda smiled. 'Don't worry I've had my fair share of crying in public places,' she reassured.

'Really?' replied Claire, doubtfully.

'Yep! Mainly just after Luke was born. I would suddenly be out with him minding my own business and then the next thing, the waterworks!'

Claire smiled back. 'Yes, I remember those days too. Actually, it's not just problems with Chris – we have some stuff going on with Joshua at the moment as well, so it's been a bit of a stressful time.'

Linda nodded and waited to see if Claire would continue.

'Joshua has been accused of rape,' said Claire finally. The words felt strange on her tongue and as she saw Linda's face turn from sympathetic to confused to something else indefinable, she knew she'd made a mistake confiding in Linda.

'What do you mean? By who? How?' Linda's questions came out quickly, panic overtaking curiosity, and Claire watched Linda work through her confusion.

'But Claire, Joshua babysat my son, what are you saying? Are the police involved?'

'Yes, but he didn't do it,' replied Claire, trying to backtrack but it was too late – the damage was done. 'The trial will prove that.'

'Trial!' At this, Linda stood, her heels struggling against shock and the force of gravity as she inched away from the table. 'I'm sorry, Claire, I have to go,' said Linda. She fled leaving the café so quickly, the scones remained on the table, forgotten. It was only then that Claire realised the coffee shop was empty apart from the young barista who was discreetly scrolling on his phone but had no doubt heard everything. And just like that, Claire knew that her friend's reaction was nothing compared to what she would have to endure from the rest of Castlefield. Years ago, she'd been the subject of speculation, but this time she would be on the wrong side.

It was early afternoon the following day and Claire quietly slipped back into the public gallery. Court was already in session and she was late because a traffic accident had delayed her. She was anxious – this was Jacobs, the witness Livingstone was most nervous about. Silently cursing because she could only get a seat at the back, she sat down and put her bag beside her. The familiar wooden bench was uncomfortable, and she adjusted her position trying to get a better view.

As she moved, she could feel the waistband of her trousers gape at the back, the cut of her belt into bare skin. Miller was standing, examining the witness, and it took Claire a few minutes to recognise him.

He was talking about the night of the party, how he'd taken some photos on his phone.

How everyone was having a good time.

How Joshua was having a good time.

How Joshua was drunk and high.

How he'd seen Joshua come downstairs laughing and tucking his shirt in.

And after he'd finished, the witness looked directly at her and Claire had locked eyes with the man she knew was going to destroy her.

49

They stared at each other and in that glance, a thousand memories poured over her like hot lava. Her skin burned with it. Paul Jones. But the witness on the stand was Jacobs.

Oh God.

She half stood, clinging on to the chair in front of her, her body poised for action. She could see the back of Livingstone, his attention placed firmly on the witness. Why was he calling himself Jacobs? She wanted to shout at Paul to stop talking but the words wouldn't come, and she sat back down, impotent, oblivious to the irritated tutting behind her. She swivelled in her seat towards the exit, her limbs acting upon thousands of years of instinct to flee, but her mind was tethered to the court, trapped like one of the captive monkeys she'd seen on holiday.

She stood up again and a strange cry emerged from her vocal cords, the sudden noise causing the people around her to stare.

Why was he here?

But she knew why. She'd always known, hadn't she? That some day, it would all come back. But if she'd ever imagined that her son would be the one to...

Claire felt the room spin.

This couldn't be happening.

But it was. And there was nothing she could do to stop it.

Not her son. Please God, not her son.

Claire tried to swallow but couldn't and instead took a step forward. She wanted to run towards Paul and smash his head against the floor. She wanted to smash it over and over again until he was nothing more than a mush of brains and blood seeping across the courtroom floor. But she was stuck, paralysed by the sight of him, and after years of supressing the worst of the memories, the last of her resistance trickled away and she surrendered to the onslaught.

DECEMBER 1989

50

'Are you sure, Claire?' Paul asked.

Claire nodded, wishing he would stop talking, stop checking with her. His tenderness just made her want him even more. They'd been in the library after school on a Friday. It was raining outside, a torrential downpour that threatened to flood the school field. The place had seemed deserted and even the librarian had left early.

Claire couldn't explain it but she knew something spectacular was going to happen that day. As soon as she'd opened her eyes that morning, she'd felt a sense of anticipation. She'd dressed carefully, taking the time to put on a little make-up. Not too much as her mother would tell her to remove it but just enough to enhance her eyes and gloss her lips. She'd moved through her morning from class to class expectant and excited.

When her eyes met Paul's in the corridor, they shared a private smile. Perhaps he also knew that they were about to embark on something special together. The fact that their relationship was still a secret just made it even more exciting. She knew she'd have to tell the girls at some point, but not yet. For now, it was just her and Paul wrapped in their own world of possibility and Claire didn't want anything to tarnish it.

So, when Paul had touched her leg under the table in the library that Friday afternoon, she'd felt utterly in control when she took his other hand across the table. There was no one around, no one to see them. Still holding his hand, she stood up and led him to a quiet corner of the library behind some bookshelves. She kissed him, and he responded immediately, wrapping his arms around her. She leant in to him, her whole body pressed against his, and she could feel his hardness. She was excited and curious. She wanted more. She pulled away and he stared at her in confusion.

'Are you okay?' he asked concerned.

She smiled at him and saw him relax. 'Let's go and find a place,' she whispered. He knew exactly what she meant.

'There's nowhere private here,' he said.

Claire thought. 'I know one place,' she replied mysteriously. 'And it's got a lock.'

Drama room three would be empty. There was no meeting because of the rain, which threatened to flood everywhere, and the school was pretty much deserted. Instead they were meeting on Saturday morning at Charlotte's house.

Claire and Paul grabbed their bags and practically ran through the empty corridors, Claire leading the way until they came to the old classroom.

'Never been here before,' commented Paul.

'It's never used,' replied Claire not wanting to share any more details about the Queen Bees. She opened the door and led him inside.

Paul walked in and looked around while Claire shut the door behind them. She went to lock it, but strangely the key wasn't there. Claire wavered. It was too risky. But then she saw Paul waiting for her and she knew she didn't want to wait. No one knew about the room anyway except for the girls and they'd all gone home. She saw Paul pick up a T-shirt and hold it up, the words Queen Bee written across the front. Shit. She went up to him and playfully snatched the T-shirt away and he pulled her towards him.

Within seconds, they were kissing, their hands exploring each other's bodies and Claire forgot about the unlocked door. She'd never felt anything like it before. She assumed, like her, that this would be his first time and a thrill went through her. She'd kissed other boys of course and the odd fumble but this... this was like having fireworks going off inside her.

Between kisses, she indicated the old sofa and they moved awkwardly towards it eventually collapsing onto the cushions in a pile of nervous giggles. But then the laughter had subsided, replaced with an urgency to explore something new. They were moving together, sometimes out of sync, inexperienced, but it didn't matter. Nothing mattered. As he lay on top of her, his fingers about to unzip her skirt, he stopped and stared at her intently.

'You are so beautiful,' he whispered, and he kissed her on the forehead. 'Are you sure you want to do this?'

'Yes,' she replied.

England, Ireland, Scotland, Wales, Inside, Outside, Puppy Dog Tails.

Perhaps if it all hadn't happened so quickly, she would have said something. Defended Paul. *Told the truth!*

But she hadn't. Instead, she'd seen the look on Charlotte's face and panicked. And within seconds she and Paul were surrounded by a clutch of Queen Bees and Charlotte's boyfriend, and the explosion had drowned out anything that she had intended to say.

At the time, she'd convinced herself that she couldn't speak. The embarrassment of being caught had caused her to feel a sense of shame so intense, she'd wanted to run. And a part of her mind had run away. It had shut down, blocking out the unbearableness of the situation. And if truth be told, it had been easier to let everyone believe what they wanted to. Afterwards, of course, she'd *wanted* to do the right thing. She'd *wanted* to tell the teacher that Paul hadn't attempted to force himself on her. She would have told the school the truth as well if it hadn't been for her mother.

Her mum had come and collected her that afternoon from school after the head teacher had called her to explain what had happened. It was the worst car journey of Claire's life. Her mother had been silent, but as Claire stared straight ahead into a dark December afternoon, she could feel her mum's worried gaze. As they got into the house, her mum told her to go upstairs and she would bring her a hot drink.

Claire, numb, had done as she was told and lay down on the bed hugging her knees. It was only when her mother came into her bedroom, warm drink in hand, that Claire started crying and the truth had spilled out. For the first time ever, she remembered her mother actually listening. She didn't interrupt; she didn't shout or berate her daughter. Instead, she lay on the bed with her and held her like a baby, whispering.

'Poor baby, what a shock for you.' Over and over again, until Claire wondered if her mother had actually understood what she'd said, that she'd let everyone think Paul was about to sexually assault her when he wasn't.

She pulled away from her mother's embrace and looked her in the eye.

'Mum, I need to go to the school tomorrow and tell them what really happened,' she said urgently. 'They'll expel Paul; they'll call the police. If I know Charlotte, by tomorrow, the whole school will think he's done this. And he hasn't.' Claire broke down and it was then that her mother had gently pulled them both up to a seated position on the bed.

'Claire, listen to me and listen to me very carefully. Paul will recover from this. We won't get the police involved. Yes, he will probably get expelled. But he will go to a new school and everything will be fine and forgotten about.' Her mother stroked Claire's cheek and continued. 'But... if you tell the school now what really happened, it will be your reputation that is brought into question. And trust me, Claire, girls *never* recover from such situations. Do you understand me? You're sixteen years old – you have your whole life ahead of you.'

Claire searched out her mother's eyes, trying to comprehend what she was hearing. 'But you and Dad have always told me to do the right thing,' protested Claire.

'Claire, I'm not totally convinced that he's completely innocent in all this. You say it was all your idea but was it? Was it really?'

Claire thought back. Yes, it was.

Wasn't it?

When she'd visited Paul at his house and they'd lain on the bed together, she always knew he wanted more. But he'd never pushed her.

Had he?

There was the one time he'd put his hand up her shirt and when she'd gently pulled it away, he tried again. But didn't all boys do that? Try it on? Had she actually said no to him then? Claire pressed the heel of her hand to her forehead in frustration. It was all becoming such a confusing mess in her head. She'd spent the last few hours convinced that she needed to own up and now here her mother was telling her to leave things alone. If she *did* own up, she knew she would be a social pariah at school. But there would only be two more years and then she would be off to university. She could cope with being ostracised for two years... surely?

She thought of Jennifer O'Reilly, the ousted Queen Bee, walking the corridors by herself, her only companion the odd lobbed insult. Lunch by herself. Break time by herself. No one willing to partner with her in class. No one picking her for sports teams.

'I promise you, love, in this case, it's least said, soonest mended and I know your dad would agree.'

As Claire looked up at her mother, she started to believe her mother was right. Paul *would* move on. He had the brains to succeed whichever school he was in. Whereas she would always be known as the girl who had cried rape and it would follow her everywhere. Castlefield was a small town. She'd hugged her mother then, for the first time feeling relieved that someone had made the decision for her.

JULY 2018

51

Even from this distance, she could see his fingernails bitten down to the quick and her body tensed instinctively, resisting the urge to run towards her son. It would only make things worse. Instead, she caught his eye and reassured him with a confident smile.

This will soon all be over, and everything will go back to normal.

Those had been her mother's words as they had all left the house that morning. She'd noticed her son's light brown hair had grown and it desperately needed cutting, but he'd resisted a haircut and instead combed it down with some gel. It was coarse hair, like her own, but unlike hers, it hadn't been subjected to various treatments. Had it only been six months ago that she'd laughingly squirted her son's stubborn tufts with water, threatening to tame his hair herself if he didn't do something about it? He'd giggled then, rewarding her with a glimpse back into his childhood when she used to tickle him as he sat on her lap for story time.

The memory assaulted her and her right hand involuntarily went to grasp her husband's, despite the gulf between the two of them. She could feel the tension emanate from him and she gently squeezed his fingers before releasing them and placing both of her hands together in prayer on her lap, reverting to her own childhood habit. She focused on her crossed thumbs, right over left, the usually long, manicured nails bare and jagged, and began the silent chant.

Everything will be all right. Everything will be all right. Everything will be all—

'All rise!'

She quickly got to her feet, her eyes urgently seeking her son's once more as the judge swept into the room, but all she could see was his taut back and the nape of his long neck as he looked at the ground. *Head up*, she wanted to cry out. *You've done nothing wrong!*

The judge indicated for the court to sit before the clerk spoke.

'Would the foreman of the jury please stand,' instructed the clerk.

Claire noticed the foreman was wearing a wedding band. Most likely he had kids himself. Surely, he wouldn't let an innocent child be convicted for something he didn't do? She caught herself on the word *child*. He was almost eighteen. If found guilty, he would be sent to an adult prison along with the country's worst offenders.

'Have the jury reached verdicts upon which they are all agreed?' asked the clerk.

'Yes,' replied the foreman.

They couldn't take him away. Could they?

She felt her chest tighten.

Everything will be all right. Everything will be all right. Everything will be all right.

Her throat was closing, and she coughed frantically.

Everything will be all right. Everything will be all right. Everything will be all right.

She was struggling to breathe, and a silent primal scream rose in her throat.

Everything will be all right. Everything will be all right. Everything will be all right.

The clerk spoke again. 'In the matter of Aiker versus Carmichael, do you find the defendant guilty or not guilty?'

'Guilty,' replied the foreman.

The court erupted but she didn't hear the rest because just at that moment, Paul swivelled his head towards her, a glimmer of triumph playing on his lips, and the primal scream in her throat released itself in an explosion of agony.

52

'...by that time of course, Rose had already done everything she was supposed to do. Call the police, report the sexual assault, be examined, the full works. But her case was thrown out by the Crown Prosecution Service because there wasn't enough evidence. She'd looked into private prosecution by then too. I'd known Rose since I'd started volunteering at the youth club a few years ago. I knew how damaged some of these kids were – it's my job, isn't it – and then to be raped and told it wouldn't stand up in court? What kind of system is that?

'Anyway, she didn't say very much about the case after that and I didn't ask her about it. I knew it would be confidential and I didn't want to pry. It's only later when she asked me to give a statement... I didn't want to at first and I'm ashamed to say it took me a while to agree. I'm not one for the police especially as I'd *done community service for having a bit of weed on me. But Rose told me it would make a difference, so I eventually agreed and here I am.*

'I hadn't even remembered that I'd got some pictures on my phone from that night until Rose asked me. Photos of her and Joshua arguing. Joshua going for her, his mates holding him back. Well, it didn't look good did it? Thank God I took them...'

Epilogue

Paul

It was such a bittersweet moment watching Claire as they led her son away after the verdict. It's not easy seeing someone you have loved fall apart, but all these years I have lived under the shadow of a reputation that Claire gave me.

A rapist.

I was never arrested or charged but I might as well have been the way everyone looked at me. No one believed me, no matter how much I denied any wrongdoing. Charlotte's version of events was so powerful in its monstrosity that everyone thought it must be true. The teacher, the head teacher, even my own parents. And the only person who could've stopped it all was Claire.

But she chose not to.

She destroyed my life because she didn't speak up. And it never seemed to bother her. She seemed to carry on as if nothing had ever happened. I watched her live her perfect life.

Her marriage.

Her career.

Her family.

Her house.

Her friends.

And I wanted to destroy it all just as she had destroyed me. Justice needed to be served but as a woman, she had the upper hand. Don't they always? So I went for her son.

Do I feel bad that Joshua was an innocent party in all this?

Not really.

It *is* a shame though because he's a bright kid. To be honest, it was Chris I had initially targeted when I started grooming the girls at the youth centre. I just needed one looker to catch his eye and then accuse him of rape. And one certainly caught his eye, but the silly cow went and did exactly what I told her not to do – she fell for him. Or rather she fell for his lifestyle. She loved going with him on business trips, all the presents, the secret phone calls. And he loved having the attention of a twenty-year-old. It was the perfect match.

And even though I couldn't persuade her to implement the second part of my plan, which was to cry rape, at least she had destroyed their marriage. Still, it wasn't enough. I needed Claire to suffer as I had. I needed her reputation ruined.

The first time I saw Rose, I didn't approach her at the youth club. I'd seen her type before and knew if I did, she would have brushed me off in a second. Initially, like I'd done with all the girls, I needed to find out her weakness. Everyone had one – hers, amongst other things, was money. She had expensive tastes in clothes and drugs. She also had a thirst for danger and excitement. And a little bit of revenge against her father, although it took me a while to discover that.

For months, she was just Rose, a loud, sometimes irritating presence. Rose was always at the centre of the action. The loudest, the funniest, the one with the more interesting tale to tell from the night before. She liked to draw attention to herself – in fact, there was little she wouldn't do for attention. She was one of those girls you noticed immediately. I left her alone though because I had originally wanted girls who were vulnerable. Anyone too mouthy would be a turn-off for Chris, I knew that much.

Rose was many things but vulnerable wasn't the first thing that came to mind. She was what my mum would have called a looker. Nineteen years old, curvaceous like the old-fashioned pin-ups, and sexy as hell. She would have made a good actress too. It didn't take a psychologist to work out that she was severely messed up. Gloria had once mentioned Rose's childhood was one of the most violent cases she'd ever read. But Gloria didn't realise that some people just couldn't be saved. It was too late. The damage was done.

Rose was one of them.

So was I.

Rose didn't want to change. She liked living life on the edge. She liked using boyfriends for everything she could get out of them. Whatever she'd grown up with, it made her angry. She wasn't smashing things, screaming at people, or anything like that. No, it was subtler than that, and I saw it in her the first time I met her. She was ambitious. She also liked to party. And when Rose mentioned the name Joshua Carmichael a plan began to form.

'They were a bunch of arrogant tossers, anyway,' Rose had announced scrolling through her phone. 'Surrounded by security and they weren't having any fun at all. Just standing around drinking posh water.'

Rose was obsessed with footballers. She'd kept scrolling through her photos and one of her friends had seen a picture and asked who the good-looking guy was.

'Oh him – a guy called *Joshua Carmichael*,' replied Rose, putting on an accent similar to the Queen. Her friend giggled. 'So posh, but sooooo cute,' Rose had said. 'A real gent – and loaded too. Lives in Castlefield, don't you know.' Rose and her friend had laughed at her imitation.

What were the odds? Seriously, what were the fucking odds?

And what would a posh boy from Castlefield want to do with a girl like Rose? And then I looked at her slim figure, large breasts, and squeezable bum – the same thing every seventeen-year-old boy would want to do with her.

After that it wasn't difficult. I trailed Rose every night. I went to the clubs she went to. She was always surrounded by guys – she was that type of girl – Joshua was sometimes there but usually only on a Friday or Saturday night. He was obsessed by her – that much was clear. He was usually with his posh friends. I was surprised to learn they did drugs – Joshua didn't seem the type but maybe it was his friends or maybe it was Rose. I didn't care – it just made it easier. I sold to him a few times. I sold to Rose too.

I wasn't really sure what I was waiting for. I was biding my time, I suppose, to convince Rose to cry rape on Joshua.

I had the whole story worked out but when I saw Joshua coming down the stairs laughing, I knew that was the night. There was a party, there were drugs, Rose was there, Joshua was there, they'd argued, and it wasn't difficult to convince Rose that she didn't *need* to regret having sex the night before. Had she actually consented? She couldn't remember. Had she perhaps said no? She wasn't sure, she told me, she was drunk and high but perhaps she had tried to say no when the guy was on top off her and pulling her skirt off.

Actually, thinking about it now, she had said stop and not just because the guy had accidentally caught her earring and it had pulled painfully. And when I asked her about Joshua and suggested he had been there as well, she replied perhaps he was, especially when I told her that I'd heard Joshua had been accused of sexual assault but had got off because there wasn't enough evidence.

Completely untrue of course, but necessary.

Perhaps someone should pay and if Rose had the opportunity to punish someone who had escaped the system why not? When her case fell through with the CPS, it was easy to give her a recommendation to Stephens & Carmichael – a nice touch, even if I do say so myself.

And when I offered to pay for it, Rose didn't hesitate. I knew that the money I'd saved selling drugs would come in useful.

The fact that I also offered to introduce her to one of my clients who just happened to be a show biz agent helped sweeten the deal.

It was the perfect lie. But then you would know all about that, Claire. And now you have a choice to make: come forward and confess your own lie to clear Joshua's name or watch your son go to jail. And I know exactly which one you're going to choose because it's different when it's your own son, isn't it? Oh, I'm sure I'll suffer a few legal consequences too – abuse of process or perjury or whatever bullshit they come up with but that doesn't matter. Because finally, *finally* my name will be cleared.

Acknowledgements

As always, my gratitude goes to Luigi and Alison Bonomi for their support, encouragement and ideas and to my editors Sarah Ritherdon and Hannah Smith. Their feedback and direction were invaluable. The copyediting, sales, and marketing teams at Head of Zeus and Aria, including Helena Newton, Sue Lamprell, Victoria Joss, Nikky Ward, and Dan Groenewald, always do a fantastic job and I'm so grateful for their expertise.

During the writing of this book, there were many people who helped me with my research and answered my questions. Friends and family generously gave up their time without question and special thanks goes to Barbara Grzelczyk, Lisa Perelman, Margaret Bannister, and Chloe Fairley for reading the first draft of the manuscript and sharing their thoughts. Any liberties with the truth rest firmly on my shoulders. Thank you to Sandra and Chris Whittle for the endless conversations about plot and character as well as always helping out with daily life to ensure I have the time to write.

Special thanks also to Sam Armstrong, Reim El Houni, and Punam Verma who do a fantastic job making sure people know about my books.

My novel writing journey started at the Emirates Airline Festival of Literature (EAFOL) winning first place in the Montegrappa Novel Writing Award in 2016. Thank you to Isobel Abulhoul, Yvette Judge, Ahlam Bolooki and the whole team at EAFOL as well as Charles Nahhas of Montegrappa Middle East for creating such an opportunity for new authors.

I have a lovely group of author friends based in Dubai who have generously shared their time, encouragement and advice including Rachel Hamilton, Jessica Jarlvi, and Annabel Kantaria.

To my readers, thank you for your ongoing support and reviews. I'm very lucky to be able to say this is my third novel and without you, I wouldn't have got this far – thank you.

And finally, thank you to my husband, Fahad Osman, who supports everything I do.

About Karen Osman

KAREN OSMAN is a bestselling author. She won the Emirates Airline Festival of Literature Montegrappa Novel Writing Award in 2016 with her crime thriller debut novel, *The Good Mother*, and went on to secure a three-book deal with Head of Zeus. When she's not writing novels, Karen is busy bringing up her two young children and overseeing her communication business Travel Ink.

Hello from Aria

We hope you enjoyed this book! Let us know, we'd
love to hear from you.

We are Aria, a dynamic digital-first fiction imprint
from award-winning independent publishers Head
of Zeus. At heart, we're avid readers committed to
publishing exactly the kind of books we love to read
– from romance and sagas to crime, thrillers and
historical adventures. Visit us online and discover a
community of like-minded fiction fans!

We're also on the look out for tomorrow's superstar
authors. So, if you're a budding writer looking
for a publisher, we'd love to hear from you. You
can submit your book online at ariafiction.com/
we-want-read-your-book

You can find us at:
Email: aria@headofzeus.com
Website: www.ariafiction.com
Submissions: www.ariafiction.com/
we-want-read-your-book
Facebook: @ariafiction
Twitter: @Aria_Fiction
Instagram: @ariafiction